D0873937

"For whatsoever from one place doth fall,
Is with the tide unto an other brought:
For there is nothing lost, that may be found, if sought."

—Edmund Spenser, *The Faerie Queene*

Savannah Secrets

Savannah Secrets

Resurrecting Trouble

DeAnna Julie Dodson

Guideposts

Danbury, Connecticut

Savannah Secrets is a trademark of Guideposts.

Published by Guideposts Books & Inspirational Media
100 Reserve Road, Suite E200
Danbury, CT 06810
Guideposts.org

Cover and interior design by Müllerhaus
Cover illustration by Pierre Droal, represented by Illustration Online LLC.
Typeset by Aptara, Inc.

Printed and bound in the United States of America

10 9 8 7 6 5 4 3 2 1

Resurrecting Trouble

Chapter One

JULIA FOLEY PULLED UP BESIDE Forsyth Park and smiled to see it bursting with spring-colored streamers and banners welcoming Savannah's children to the Boys & Girls Club Easter Egg Hunt. It was a beautiful Saturday morning with a clear blue sky and a riot of newly blossomed flowers, a perfect example of why April was her favorite month. Even though the event didn't start for another twenty minutes or so, there was already a party atmosphere, and there were children everywhere. She was eager to get into the middle of it all.

She locked her car and walked onto the park grounds, hoping she wasn't going to regret adding a light linen jacket to her spring-green tank top and skinny jeans. She looked for Wyatt, her sister's son, and his daughters, Madison and Kennedy, who were practically Julia's granddaughters. Wyatt's wife, Anna Beth, was at her mother's for a week, and he had been glad to agree to bring the girls out to the park today, giving him a well-earned break.

She tried to see if she could spot Carmen and Harmony somewhere in the crowd too. Carmen served as assistant to Julia and her business partner, Meredith Bellefontaine, at their private investigation firm, Magnolia Investigations. She was also a mentor to eight-year-old Harmony through the Boys & Girls Club. Carmen had been encouraging everyone to come to the hunt and was probably more excited about it than Harmony was.

Julia had almost reached the park's enormous fountain when she heard someone call her name.

She turned and smiled. "Maggie Lu."

As always, Maggie Lu looked cool and elegant. Today, a broad-brimmed white hat with pink roses shaded her dark eyes and beaming smile.

She hurried over to Julia, pushing a green stroller that held a chubby little boy with coiled black hair who seemed determined to get out. "I was hoping I'd see you here."

Julia gave her a hug. "I'm supposed to meet Wyatt and his girls, but I haven't seen them yet. I'm sure Carmen's here too." She leaned down to the little boy in the stroller. "Look at you, Jake. You're getting so big."

Jake reached out both hands and gurgled at her, clearly demanding to be released from his seat.

"He's nearly sixteen months old," Maggie Lu said, drawing his attention to the brightly colored woven basket that was in the stroller next to him. "And all he wants to do is run."

"Well, he can do plenty of that here."

"Tell me about it." Maggie Lu pursed her lips. "And I'll be the one running after him."

Julia chuckled. "I'll help you keep an eye on him. And Wyatt will help too, I imagine. Once his girls start hunting Easter eggs, they won't need us."

They started walking along the pathways, under the shady arches of live oaks draped with Spanish moss. More and more people were coming along behind them, their children racing ahead toward the opposite side of the fountain. That must be where the sponsors' table was.

Maggie Lu looked around. "Where's Beau today?"

"You know my husband," Julia said. "If it's a nice Saturday, you can almost bet he'll be on the golf course."

"Well, it's definitely a nice Saturday."

"What about Clarissa?" Julia asked.

"Oh, I'm looking after the baby all day. She and Philip had a chance to go sailing with some friends, and they really didn't want to miss that."

"I can't blame them."

"And, of course, Saturdays are busy for Charlene at the diner." Maggie Lu's eyes warmed as she looked down at Jacob. "But I don't get to see him enough as it is, so there's no way I was going to say no when I had a chance to keep him all day. It reminds me of when I had Charlene and then when she had Clarissa. Keeps me young."

Julia remembered when her nephew was born and then when Kennedy and Madison came along. "They grow up fast. I suppose before I know it, Wyatt's girls will be having little ones of their own."

Maggie Lu chuckled. "That'll be a while yet."

Just then, Julia spotted the girls looking up at the sparkling water spraying from the fountain's white central pillar and arching out of the horns being blown by the four tritons surrounding it.

"There you are," she called.

The girls turned, their eyes alight.

"Nana!" they shrieked in unison as they ran to her.

Julia took them both into a big hug and then embraced her nephew, who was right behind them.

"Hi, Aunt Julia," he said, and then he held out his hand to Maggie Lu. "How are you, Mrs. King?"

Maggie Lu laughed and pulled him in for a hug. "I'm doing fine, honey. It's good to see all of you."

"Girls," he said, "you remember Miss Maggie Lu."

Maggie Lu smiled and leaned down. "Kennedy and Madison, right?"

Both girls nodded vigorously.

"Hello, Miss Maggie Lu," Kennedy said. "Are you going to hunt for Easter eggs too?"

"Oh no, honey. I'm going to let you get them all."

Madison looked at Jake, who was still struggling to climb out of the stroller. "Is that your baby, Miss Maggie Lu?"

"That's my great-grandson, Jacob. We call him Jake."

"Is he going to hunt for Easter eggs?" Kennedy asked, looking unconvinced.

"We're going to let him run around a little bit and see what he can find," Maggie Lu told her. "But you'd better watch out, or he'll find more than you."

"Not me," Madison said firmly, "but he can have some of mine if he can't find any."

"That's very thoughtful, Madison. Thank you."

"Is Harmony coming, Nana?" Kennedy asked.

"She's probably already here," Julia said. "We'd better catch up with everybody else and find her and Carmen. The hunt is about to start."

4

As Julia had expected, Carmen and Harmony were up near the sponsors' table. They wore matching pink pedal pushers and pink T-shirts that had bunnies on them, and they both had pink ribbons in their shiny dark hair. Harmony was small for her age and wore very thick glasses that didn't hide the excitement in her big brown eyes.

She and Carmen waved as soon as they saw Julia and the others, but they didn't have time for more than a hello before the man in charge—a short, broad man with a contagious smile—asked for everyone's attention. The crew from the local news station started filming.

"We're so glad you could all come to our Easter egg hunt. There's nothing more important to us than providing the boys and girls of Savannah with what they need. And sometimes what they need is a lot of fun and prizes, am I right?"

Everyone clapped and cheered at that. There were even a few approving whistles.

After some instructions for the event, the man added, "Please remember that this is Easter time. We're all here to enjoy ourselves and not squabble over what we find. If somebody gets the egg you were after, keep looking. There's plenty out there for everyone. Now who's ready to get started?"

Again there was clapping and cheering and whistling.

"Okay, ready? Set? And...go!"

Children scattered in every direction, and little Jake started to whimper.

"All right, baby," Maggie Lu said, unfastening the safety straps. "All right."

She lifted him out and set him on his feet, and he immediately started to toddle away.

She caught his right hand and put the little basket into his left. "You can lead, but I'm going with you."

"You two go on," Wyatt told her. "I'll look after the stroller."

Maggie Lu smiled at him. "Thank you. We'll be around somewhere."

Julia, Wyatt, and Carmen stood where they were, watching the chaos around them. The three girls had headed off together, and Maggie Lu held on as Jacob waddled right behind them.

"I told Harmony to leave the easy ones for the little bitty kids," Carmen said.

Wyatt nodded. "I told my girls the same thing. I'm sure they'll all find plenty of treats and toys."

"I don't know how many eggs are out there," Carmen said. "I helped fill some of them, but there were lots of us doing that. We had boxes of stuff coming in from all over Savannah. It was *loco*. Even the boss ladies chipped in."

"We gave some candy and some toys small enough to fit into plastic eggs," Julia said. "It wasn't much, but we were glad to help."

"I wish we'd heard about it ahead of time," Wyatt said. "Anna Beth and I would've liked to contribute. But isn't it a little early for Easter?"

"It was something the club decided," Carmen said. "They thought they'd get a better turnout if they weren't competing with church and family activities on Easter Sunday. It's only a week away, and who doesn't like an extra day of fun?"

Wyatt smiled. "True. Very true. And it's a good way to get people to notice the kind of work they do. I hope it gets them more donations and volunteers."

Julia watched as Maggie Lu stopped and pointed out the bright green egg that lay at Jake's feet. He picked it up and immediately stuck one end in his mouth. Maggie Lu tried to get him to put the egg in the basket, but he only waved it defiantly at her and then threw it back into the grass.

Julia chuckled. "I told her I'd help her. I think I'd better stay a little closer."

"We'll be right here," Wyatt said.

"As long as the girls stay in sight," Carmen added.

Julia went over to Maggie Lu, who was trying to keep Jake from pulling away from her.

"Why don't you let him run? We'll be right here."

"Okay," Maggie Lu said. "He's not very fast, but he's determined. And I don't think he's very interested in the eggs."

"That's all right. We can pick up a couple for him to have later on."

Julia and Maggie Lu followed Jake as he waved his arms and wobbled through the grass. Every once in a while, Maggie Lu would point out an Easter egg to him and try to get him to put it in the basket. She and Julia clapped and cheered when he did it the first time, and that seemed to be his favorite part of the game. After he had picked up a few eggs, though, he plopped himself down in the grass and didn't seem to want to move again.

"I think that's about as far as we're going today," Maggie Lu said, picking him up and holding him against her shoulder. "Are you tired, baby?"

Jake huffed and put his arms around her neck.

Julia picked up his forgotten basket, and they walked back to where Wyatt and Carmen were waiting.

"Somebody's tired," Wyatt said once they reached him.

"I know that's right," Maggie Lu said. "And I think it's me." She put the baby into the stroller and gave him a bottle of water from the bag in the back.

"He ought to have a good nap today," she said. "I might just join him."

"Just don't sleep through tonight's news," Julia said. "The two of you might be on it."

Maggie Lu chuckled. "Might be. I think they did get him on film a couple of times."

"It'll be good publicity for the club," Carmen said. "And I believe we had a good turnout too."

"Everybody will go home happy," Wyatt said. "We'll see what the early reviews have to say."

The three girls ran up to them, each with a basket full of brightly colored plastic eggs.

"I got the most," Madison said smugly, and then she bit her lip. "But I can give some to Jake if he didn't get enough, Miss Maggie Lu."

Maggie Lu touched her arm. "You're very sweet, honey, but I think he has plenty. Have you looked inside? Did you get some good prizes?"

The three girls started opening their eggs, squealing and chattering about what was inside, and a man from the camera crew came up to them and introduced himself to Maggie Lu.

"Excuse me, ma'am, I'm Stuart Dillard from *News Now*. It looks like you're all having a good time here. Would you mind if we did a quick interview?"

Maggie Lu glanced at Julia and Wyatt, her eyebrows raised.

Julia shrugged. "What do you think, Wyatt?"

"I don't see what it would hurt. Girls, would you like to be on TV?"

"Do we get money?" Kennedy asked.

Stuart chuckled. "No, no money. But you can tell your friends you were on TV. What do you think? We just want to ask you how you liked the hunt and see you open a couple of eggs. Sound good?"

"Okay with you?" Julia asked Carmen.

"If it's all right with the girls, then no problemo."

"What do you say, girls?" Stuart asked.

"I want to be on TV," Madison said.

"Me too," Kennedy chimed in.

Harmony looked at Carmen uncertainly.

"You don't have to," Carmen told her. "You can do whatever you feel like."

"It'll be fun," Madison assured her. "You don't have to talk if you don't want."

After a moment's hesitation, Harmony nodded. "But I don't want to talk."

"That's all right," Stuart said. "All you have to do is stay right where you are and open up some of your eggs and see what you have, okay? You don't even have to look at the camera."

Harmony nodded again, and Carmen gave her an encouraging smile.

Stuart turned to his cameraman. "Okay, Max, let's go on three."

"On three," Max said.

Stuart took the microphone, straightened his shoulders, and smiled into the camera. "One. Two. Three. This is Stuart Dillard with *News Now,* and we're at the Boys & Girls Club Easter Egg Hunt here in Forsyth Park. Thanks to donations from local businesses and Savannah citizens, the Boys & Girls Club was able to provide a little bit of springtime fun for hundreds of our city's children."

He stepped back to let the camera focus on the girls, and then he dropped to one knee beside them.

"What have you got there?" he asked Kennedy. "Anything good?"

Kennedy opened a pink egg and then looked up. "Um, chocolate is in this one. But the best one was in this blue egg." She opened the blue egg and then beamed at him. "It's a tiny baby bunny!"

"Wow, aren't you lucky! Is this your sister here?"

Kennedy nodded. "That's Madison."

"Hello, Madison," Stuart said. "What did you get?"

"I got chocolate and jelly beans and a little butterfly," Madison said as she twisted open a bright yellow egg. "And I got—" She frowned, clearly puzzled. "I got this. What's this, Nana?"

She handed it to Julia, and Julia caught her breath.

It was a small crystal egg on an ornate enameled pedestal set with luminous pearls. But inside the egg—

She held it lightly in her hand, almost afraid to touch the delicate creation. Inside the egg was a depiction of the risen Christ above His empty tomb as two kneeling angels looked on. The tiny figures were works of art in and of themselves, graceful and meticulously crafted. This was no plastic freebie.

"What is it?" Wyatt asked as he, Carmen, and Maggie Lu leaned closer.

"Hey, Max, zoom in here," Stuart said. "What do you think we've got?"

"I think we need to talk to the people in charge," Julia told him. "I doubt this was meant to be given away."

"What do you think it is?" Stuart asked again, clearly intrigued.

"I'd rather not say quite yet. Not until I've had a chance to investigate."

"Investigate? Wait a minute, aren't you one of the women with Magnolia Investigations? Julia Foley, right?"

Julia nodded. "And I'm going to find out what this is and who it really belongs to."

Chapter Two

JULIA WAS WAITING FOR BEAU when he got home from his golf game late that afternoon and immediately told him what had happened at the Easter egg hunt.

"So I took it up to the guy who was in charge of the event," she said, "and he agreed that it must have been put in Madison's egg by mistake and said he would make sure it was returned to the person who donated it. I wasn't too sure about letting him have it back, but the reporter got it all on film, so if it disappears or something, at least everyone will know I didn't keep it."

Beau ran one hand over the thick gray waves of his hair. "And you think it's really valuable?"

"I'm almost sure of it. I mean, when you first look at it, you might think it's just an Easter toy, but if you look closer it seems very ornate. And it just feels like it's made well."

Beau shook his head. "You know who's famous for fabulous Easter eggs, don't you?"

Julia bit her lip. "I know. And I know some of the famous Fabergé eggs are missing too. I'm not sure what to think about it."

He gave her a knowing grin. "I can guess exactly what you think about it. You want to track it down and make sure it goes back to its rightful owner."

"Yeah, I guess I do."

"But there's nothing much you can do until Monday. A little research or something but not a lot more. So why don't you relax till then?" He glanced at his watch. "It's almost time for the local news. I'm going to take a shower and get changed. I don't want to miss your big moment."

She rolled her eyes. "I'll be in here making dinner. Call me when it comes on. And save it too, okay? In case I need to review it later."

She'd made several chicken casseroles a few weeks ago and put them in the freezer. By the time the oven was hot and she put one of them in to bake, Beau called her.

"It's on."

"Okay, coming."

She went into the living room, and Beau waited for her to sit down before taking the TV off pause.

"This morning," Stuart's voice said over footage of the hunt, "children from Savannah had a chance to hunt for Easter eggs filled with toys and candy, thanks to the local Boys & Girls Club. But one child found something no one was expecting."

The picture cut to Madison finding the crystal egg and handing it to Julia. The scene ended with Julia saying, "And I'm going to find out what this is and who it really belongs to" and then cut to her handing the egg to the man who was in charge of the hunt.

"Baxter Jost with the Boys & Girls Club was as surprised as anyone at the find," Stuart said in voice-over.

"We got a lot of donations from our supporters," Jost said as a concerned-looking Stuart held the microphone. "But one of the volunteers who helped us pack the boxes is fairly sure she knows where the egg came from. We think it was a mix-up of some kind, and we'll make sure it gets back to its rightful owner."

"Do you have a guess as to how valuable this egg might be?" Stuart asked.

Jost held up one hand and shook his head, smiling faintly. "I really couldn't speculate on that. Though, if it was intended as a donation to our club, we'll certainly be grateful for it."

"For the moment," Stuart said to the camera, "the egg remains a mystery, but *News Now* will keep you updated as more information comes to light. This is Stuart Dillard."

"Thank you, Stuart," the anchorman said. "And here's Razor with sports and a late-breaking story on the Falcons' coaching staff."

Beau muted the sound and turned to Julia. "At least the agency got a little bit of free publicity."

"Meredith and I were talking about that earlier today."

"I figured you'd have to tell her right away," Beau said as their tabby cat, Bunny, jumped up into his lap and stretched out. "What did she think?"

"She thinks it might be Fabergé too."

"Maybe you can help the Boys & Girls Club track the owner."

"I will if they need me to," Julia said. "No charge. But they sound like they're pretty sure who gave it to them, so I guess there's no real mystery there."

"I hope Madison wasn't upset about having to give it up."

"She was really good about it. I told her it was in the egg by accident and someone was probably missing it. She told me it wouldn't be right for her to keep it if it belongs to someone else."

Beau's eyes warmed. "Wyatt and Anna Beth are doing a good job with the girls."

"Yes, they are. Plus we took everybody for burgers afterward, and that kept the girls happy. Fortunately, Jake slept the whole time."

"I'm glad you all had fun." He stroked one hand along the cat's side, and she kneaded his stomach in response. "And I beat Quin by three strokes. So I guess Bunny here is the only one who didn't get to go out today."

"Not because she didn't try." Julia reached over to pet the cat too. "I feel bad enough about hitting you with my car last year, Bunny. I sure don't want anything to happen to you now."

"That wasn't your fault," Beau told her. "It was an accident, and if it hadn't happened, we wouldn't have her now. And she'd still be homeless. So it all worked out for the best."

Julia smiled on both of them. "I think it did."

***

After dinner, Julia checked the office email account. There were several from clients and potential clients that could wait until Monday, but there was one that immediately drew her attention. The subject line was *I need your help about the egg.*

Julia opened it.

> *Ms. Foley,*
>
> *I realize this might not be seen until your office opens on Monday, but I saw you on the news tonight, and I hope you can help me. My name is Rayna Clarke, and my grandmother is the one who owns the jeweled egg that the little girl found in*

Forsyth Park today. I won't go into details now about how it ended up in the Easter egg hunt, but I would very much like to talk to you. Can I possibly meet with you first thing Monday morning? Please reply to this message or give me a call. Thank you for any help you can offer.

Rayna

There was a telephone number underneath the name. Julia considered contacting her but then decided she'd talk to Meredith about it first.

Once she had forwarded the email to her partner, she called her. Just as she thought her call was going to go to voice mail, Meredith answered.

"Julia. Hey."

She sounded a little breathless.

"Is this a bad time?" Julia asked.

Meredith chuckled. "I'm scrubbing out my refrigerator, so yeah, I guess you could say it was a bad time. I'm glad to have an excuse to stop for a few minutes. What's up?"

"I forwarded you an email about that egg we found today. It's from a woman who says the egg belongs to her grandmother. She wants to talk to me about it. I thought you'd like to be in on the meeting."

"Oh, definitely. Let me know when, and I'll be there."

"Do you have time Monday morning? Say nine?"

"That ought to work fine for me. After I finish with the fridge I'll check my schedule to be sure. If there's a problem, I'll let you know. Otherwise, count me in."

"Great. I'll tell her we can see her at nine on Monday. Now go finish up your refrigerator."

"Yeah," Meredith said glumly. "Thanks a lot. See you Monday."

Once she ended the call, Julia typed a reply to the email.

Thank you for contacting me, Rayna. My partner, Meredith Bellefontaine, and I would be happy to meet with you at our office at nine on Monday morning. We're located on Whitaker Street across from Forsyth Park. We would like to discuss your situation with you and the ways our agency might be of service.

Please let me know if you would like to meet with us.

Julia Foley

She hit send and received a reply only a few minutes later.

Yes, I would definitely like to meet with you at your office at 9 a.m. on Monday. Thank you!

Rayna

Julia immediately sent another email.

Carmen,

Just FYI, Meredith and I have an appointment at nine Monday a.m. about the egg that Madison found today.

After she sent that one, she decided to not even think about the case until the weekend was over.

***

Julia reached out to silence the piercing beep of the alarm clock on Monday morning.

Next to her, Beau groaned and buried his head under his pillow.

"It's too early to be morning," he muttered. "Come here, Bunny."

He grabbed the blinking cat that lay curled up between them and pulled her under the covers with just her head out. She gave a little bleat of protest but then immediately closed her eyes and purred herself back to sleep.

"Come on, you two," Julia said, forcing herself to get up. "Breakfast time."

Neither of them responded, so she went into the bathroom and turned on the shower. Half an hour later, her silver hair was neatly arranged, her makeup was done, and she was dressed for work. Beau and Bunny hadn't moved.

She stood at the side of the bed, hands on hips. "Are you getting up, or should I let you take care of your own breakfast?"

"I've done it before," Beau muttered, not opening his eyes.

"I was going to make waffles."

Usually that was enough to get him moving, but he only yawned. "What if I make the waffles, and we both get an hour or two more sleep?"

She laughed softly, shaking her head. "If you'd bother to look, you'd see I'm already dressed. New client, remember?"

"The Easter egg lady. I remember. Still, I'm retired. I don't have to get up."

"Suit yourself. I see Bunny's in no hurry to get up anytime soon either."

Bunny snuggled closer to Beau.

"She's a princess. Princesses don't have to get up." Beau rolled over onto his back, settled the cat on his chest, and smiled into her green eyes. "You're not hungry, are you, Jack?"

"You really shouldn't call such a dainty little girl cat Jack," Julia told him.

"She's my little jackrabbit." He stroked the black stripe down the cat's back. "Aren't you, baby?"

Bunny gave him an adoring slow blink.

"So you think she's not interested in food?" Julia let her mouth turn up at one corner. "Bunny," she said softly, "time to eat."

The cat launched herself out of the bed, through the bedroom door, and toward the kitchen.

"The little traitor," Beau grumbled. He closed his eyes and rolled back over.

Julia went into the kitchen to find Bunny pacing back and forth in front of the pantry, meowing nonstop.

"All right. All right. You're not going to starve in the next two minutes. Hang on."

She fed Bunny, decided to forgo the waffles, and grabbed a blueberry muffin.

She walked out of the kitchen and picked up her purse and car keys. Bunny burst out of wherever she had been hiding and bolted to the door.

"No," Julia said. "You're not going out. You're never going out. It's too dangerous for you."

Bunny had been a street cat until Julia and Beau adopted her, and she had obviously never forgotten her life on the outside. But it was too easy for a cat running loose to be hit by a car, as Julia well knew, or to be attacked by another animal or to bring home diseases and parasites. Neither Julia nor Beau wanted anything to happen to her.

"I'm sorry, Bunny baby," Julia said, softening.

She bent down to pet the cat, but Bunny skittered away, no doubt headed back to Beau.

"He's not going to let you out either," Julia called after her, and with a snicker, she went to her car.

As she headed toward the office, she had to force herself to drive at a reasonable speed. No use getting a ticket when the client wouldn't even be there until nine anyway. Still, she couldn't help the little frisson of excitement that ran down her spine when she thought about the egg.

Despite her resolve to forget about it over the weekend, she had done some reading about Fabergé eggs, and she had searched out any mentions of the egg being found at the Easter event. The tale of how it had gotten there was bound to be an interesting one, and she was finally going to hear it.

Chapter Three

JULIA GOT TO THE OFFICE at about a quarter till nine, but before she pulled around to park her car at the back of the gracious antebellum home that housed Magnolia Investigations, she stopped the car for a moment. Two years. It had been two years now since she and Meredith had taken the plunge and started their own agency. Despite the ups and downs, and despite the danger that was sometimes involved, she wouldn't trade it for anything.

She glanced over at Forsyth Park across the street. Every vestige of the Easter egg hunt had been cleared away. It wasn't very likely that anything left would apply to the case, but there was no way of knowing until they looked. She'd never before been hired to investigate an Easter egg, especially one that might prove to be priceless.

She parked the car and went inside. Carmen was watering the ferns in the conference room, looking stylish and springlike in a cream-colored dress and enameled rose earrings. She gave Julia a cheery good morning.

"You're in early."

"Just a little," Julia said. "I want to make sure I'm ready for our new client."

"The Easter egg lady." Carmen gave her a cheeky grin. "Too bad Madison couldn't keep it. I know I wouldn't mind finding one of those in a park somewhere."

"You and me both. Is the coffee ready?"

"I was just about to make it," Carmen said. "Let me get finished here, and I'll take care of it."

"*Gracias*," Julia said, and she went into her office. Meredith joined her there not very long afterward. She wore white linen slacks and a matching jacket, perfect for spring, and her intricately woven top was the same shade of aqua as her eyes.

"Anything I should be particularly aware of before our client gets here?"

Julia shook her head. "Only what I told you already. She ought to be in anytime now."

"Fine. I told Mr. Talbot that I'd stop by his office later this morning about his case, but I think I have plenty of time for this too. I can always step out if I need to."

"That sounds fine." A few seconds later, Julia heard the front door open, and then Carmen came to her office.

"Ms. Clarke is here."

"Please show her in."

Julia and Meredith both stood when Carmen returned with the client in tow. Rayna Clarke was a slender young woman in her midtwenties. Julia was five foot nine, but Rayna was taller, maybe five eleven. Her honey-blond hair was bobbed, curled under at her square jawline, and held in place with a navy-colored headband that coordinated with her navy-and-white sundress. Her earrings perfectly mimicked the daisies on the dress's trim.

"Won't you sit down, Ms. Clarke?" Julia asked.

"Thank you. But please call me Rayna."

"All right, Rayna. And you call me Julia. This is my partner, Meredith Bellefontaine."

"It's nice to meet you," Meredith said as they all sat down.

Rayna looked around the office, taking in the needlepointed Louis XV chairs, the antique piecrust table with its tall vase of lilies, and the Aubusson rug.

"This is nice. I didn't quite know what to expect."

"Private investigators have come a long way since Sam Spade," Meredith said with a smile.

"Oh, of course. Uh, I'm not quite sure where to start about all this."

"First let me get some information from you so I can start your file," Julia said.

She asked Rayna questions and filled out the form they used for new clients with all the pertinent information.

"Now," she said as Carmen brought in three steaming cups of coffee, "let's get started with why you're here."

"Thank you, Carmen," Meredith said.

"Yes, thank you," Rayna added.

Carmen smiled and then left them alone.

"Don't be nervous," Julia said to Rayna, noticing she didn't seem very comfortable yet. "We're just here to help you, okay?"

Rayna nodded and let out a slow breath. "I'm sorry. I don't quite know what I'm doing or what's going on. I wanted my grandmother to come with me. She's the one who found the egg in the first place."

Julia held up her hand. "Before you get started, tell me where the egg is now. I understand that the video of Madison finding it has gone viral, and the Boys & Girls Club, not only in Savannah but nationwide, has been getting calls and emails about it. If you haven't seen to it already, we need to put the egg somewhere safe."

"I understand. My grandmother is personal friends with the manager of the bank we use. He let us put it in her safe-deposit box on Saturday night, so it's in good hands."

"Excellent. Now why don't you tell me what happened. You said the egg belongs to your grandmother? My partner and I have been wondering if it's Fabergé. It certainly has that look about it."

"I've heard of them," Rayna said, "but I didn't know anything about them until I read some articles yesterday after the newspaper mentioned the egg might have been created by them. It doesn't make sense to me. How could something this valuable, something that was designed for Russian royals over a hundred years ago, have ended up in my family?"

"That's a good question," Julia said. "What does your grandmother say about it?"

"As far as she knows, it was passed down from her mother-in-law—my grandpa's mother, but I have no idea if it was originally hers or not. Nanny didn't know about the egg until just recently, and there are no older members of the family left to ask."

"But you said it was passed down to her. I'm not sure I understand. If it was left to her—"

Rayna put her mug on the table. "She had it, but she didn't know she had it until last Friday."

"But how could she have had it for so long and not known it?"

"I'm not sure even I believe it," Rayna said. "Ever since I can remember, my grandmother, Jean Clarke, has had what she called a treasure box. It really belonged to my grandfather, but he died not long after Uncle Skip was born. Skip is my dad's younger brother, and so Nanny was the one who ended up with the box. She says she's leaving it to me, though, because, well, Uncle Skip..."

She shrugged uneasily, and Julia didn't press for information about him. It was probably some long-standing squabble that had nothing to do with the egg or the box.

"And you don't know if anyone in your family had the box before your father's grandmother?" Meredith asked.

"Nanny always said Granddad had it from his mother, and his mother, Patricia, said it was her mother's. But her mother and father died young, and she was raised mostly by her grandmother. I don't know about anything before that, and I don't think Nanny does either. She only said that the treasure box was something they were supposed to take care of."

Julia jotted down some notes. "And the egg was in the box."

"Well, yes, but we didn't know it."

"Why not?"

"It's just a wooden box. Nanny always kept her jewelry and other keepsakes in it. Anyway, she called me Friday afternoon and told me she dropped the box and it broke open. There was a bunch of cotton wadding packed in this little compartment on one end of it, and the egg was inside. It was like somebody had made it to hide the egg in."

"And nobody knew it was there?"

"I can't imagine they did," Rayna said. "I mean, besides whoever put it there in the first place. Otherwise somebody would have displayed it or sold it or something years ago."

"Probably. I'd like to see this box. It sounds very interesting."

"I thought about bringing it with me. I thought about bringing Nanny too, but then I decided I'd see what you thought about taking the case, whether there's something you can do to help us, before I got you involved."

"We can probably find out more about your family history for you," Meredith said. "And, of course, more about the egg itself."

"There are some lost Fabergé eggs," Julia added. "It's quite possible this is one of them. Then the big question would be how it got into your treasure box and whether or not your family has any right to it."

Rayna nodded. "Nanny and I were wondering about that. If somebody hid it in the box because it was stolen, then we don't want any part of that. But if it's ours, we'd like to know that too."

"Of course. Tell me what happened with the Easter egg hunt. How did this egg end up in the park on Saturday?"

"It's kind of silly," Rayna said. "Jordan Montoya is a high school boy who mows Nanny's lawn and runs errands for her and whatever else he can do to help out. On Friday, when Nanny found the egg, she called me, wanting me to see it, but I was visiting a friend in Atlanta and I wasn't going to be home until Sunday afternoon. She didn't know what the egg was and whether it was valuable or not. She sounded a little worried about keeping it at her house, though I couldn't imagine that it could possibly be a big deal, so I told her to give Jordan my key and have him put the egg inside my house and

I'd look at it when I got home and then we could talk about what to do next."

"That sounds fairly straightforward," Meredith said, taking a few notes of her own. "Obviously, something went wrong."

Rayna took a sip of her coffee before continuing. "She had bought some candy and small toys for the egg hunt and sent Jordan to take those to the Boys & Girls Club too. He must have mixed up the boxes, because I got the toys and the charity got the egg. Of course, I didn't realize I had the wrong box until I got home Sunday afternoon. By that time the egg hunt had already happened. Then we saw the news and heard them say the egg might be very valuable, and Nanny was really upset about everything."

"I can imagine," Julia said.

"But before we could decide what to do about it, the club called her and told her they had the egg and someone would bring it to her right then. It's a good thing your granddaughter found it and gave it back."

Julia smiled. "Madison is my great-niece, but yes, we're glad it was returned to you. I see the club didn't have any problem tracking you down."

"It's funny. It turns out that a girl who goes to school with Jordan was the one who got the egg from him and put it in the Easter egg for the hunt. She thought it was just a plastic toy." There was a sudden twinkle in Rayna's eyes. "I think she has a little crush on Jordan, so she definitely remembered him dropping off the box. There never was any dispute about it."

"That's a relief," said Julia.

"The bad thing is that now everybody in the world knows about the egg and that it was returned to us."

"At least it's in a safe place," Meredith said. "Even if we find out it's not Fabergé, it could still be very valuable."

"Yes. And if it does belong to someone else, I want to make sure nothing happens to it."

Julia put her pen down. "Very good. So there's nothing urgent for us to do at this point."

Rayna bit her lip. "Well, yes, I'm afraid there is. Or at least something you ought to be aware of right away."

"Yes?"

"Nanny had a letter delivered to her by messenger yesterday afternoon. It was from an attorney's office here in Savannah, but it was on behalf of a man named Christian Kirkland-Wright."

"And he would be...?"

"According to the letter, his father is the Duke of Prescott, somewhere in the north of England."

Julia raised her eyebrows. "And?"

"He says the egg belongs to him and his family and he would like to have it back."

Chapter Four

JULIA LOOKED AT MEREDITH AND then at her client.

"Are you saying he has proof that the egg belongs to him?"

Rayna shrugged. "I'm not sure what's involved. The letter says that Mr. Kirkland-Wright is coming to talk to Nanny about the egg, and they're asking that we don't do anything with it until he can confirm that it's the one he thinks it is."

"I knew the video of us finding the egg went viral pretty quickly, but why would someone in England watch it?"

"I guess somebody who works for the duke must have heard about it and let him know," Rayna said, "and now his son is coming to take care of the matter. So, yes, I think it's important to find out as quickly as possible whether or not we have any legal claim to it."

"Okay, are you ready to start now? And do you think we could go talk to your grandmother right away? I'd like to get some information from her about your family and have a good look at that treasure box."

"Nanny has a group of friends she quilts with on Monday mornings, but I can ask her to meet us at her house afterwards. If she's not home by the time we get there, you can still see the box and our family Bible too. That has some birth and death information in the front. I'm not sure how far back it goes, but it's a start."

"That sounds like a good idea. She lives alone?"

"Yes. She doesn't drive anymore, but between me and her friends, she gets around okay. Let me give her a call and let her know we're coming."

Meredith looked at her watch. "I don't think I'm going to have time to go along. I have a client to see." She shook Rayna's hand. "It was good to meet you. I'll be looking forward to hearing what Julia finds out, and we'll both be working on your case."

"Thank you," Rayna said. "I feel much better about the whole thing already."

"I'll catch up with you when I get back," Julia said.

***

Julia followed Rayna to a street off Reynolds not far from Forsyth Park, and they pulled up to a cute little redbrick bungalow near the corner.

Rayna knocked and then let herself in. "Nanny? Are you home yet?"

There was no answer.

"She'll be here in a few minutes," Rayna told Julia. "She had to get someone to bring her home."

Julia nodded, and then she noticed the small wooden box sitting on the coffee table. It was obviously old, but it had been well cared for. The cherrywood was highly polished and smooth as glass.

"Is this the one?"

Rayna nodded. "I'm not sure where the egg was hidden, but Nanny said—"

She broke off, and they both turned toward the back of the house.

"What was that?" Rayna asked in a whisper, her eyes wide.

Julia put a finger to her lips.

Rayna's eyes got even wider. "What are you going to do?"

"Be still for a minute."

Neither one of them moved or spoke. Julia barely breathed. For the longest time, there was total silence. Then there was the sound of a door very quietly closing.

"What's back there?" Julia murmured.

"Kitchen," Rayna breathed. "Utility room. Door to the garage."

"You stay here."

Rayna nodded jerkily.

"If anything happens, get out the front door and call 911."

Again Rayna nodded.

Julia took a deep breath and moved toward the kitchen. Once she was there, she peered around the doorframe. It was empty, but from where she was, she could see that one of the panes of glass in the back door was broken. Obviously, someone had been able to get in that way. Had he gotten out the same way? Or was he still in the house?

Julia was about to turn around, get Rayna out of there, and call the police, when she heard a crash from inside the pantry.

"We'd better get out," she called, forcing her voice and her hands to stay steady. "Hurry, Rayna, and call the police."

Then a man's voice came from behind the pantry door. "Wait a minute! Wait a minute!"

Rayna came into the kitchen. "Oh great." She put her hands on her hips. "Don't worry. It's Uncle Skip. I recognize his voice."

The knob on the pantry door slowly turned, and then the door swung open, revealing a tall, pale man with sparse, blondish hair and a thin mustache. He was lanky except for a pronounced beer belly.

His wide mouth wobbled into a smile when he saw his niece. "Rayna. Hey. Tell your friend who I am. I'm not a burglar or anything."

"It's all right, Julia," Rayna said. "This is my uncle, Skip Clarke. Uncle Skip, this is Julia Foley."

Julia watched him warily. "Are you the one who broke the window?"

Skip shrugged his bony shoulders. "Heh, uh, well, yeah, but it's not what you think. My mother lives here. I came for a visit, but she wasn't home, so I thought I'd come in and relax for a while until she got back."

Rayna gave him a hard look.

"No, now, it's true, Raynie. A hundred percent true. Come on. My own mother? Come on. I'm going to fix that window. I promise you. For now, I'll put a board over it. Mom won't mind. You can ask her when she gets in. You didn't want me sitting on the street waiting, did you?"

"Do you want to get the police out here?" Julia asked Rayna.

Rayna sighed. "No, I guess not. Nanny wouldn't like that, no matter what he did. Uncle Skip, why are you here?"

"Can't a guy come see his family without there being a lot of questions?"

He pushed past them, and Rayna and Julia followed him into the living room.

"I know I haven't been around a lot lately," he added, "and I was feeling bad about that, so I thought I'd come see Mom. And you, of course, Raynie. Nothing wrong with that, is there?"

"Nothing except you haven't talked to me or her since Aunt Liz died."

"So?"

"That was nearly six years ago."

Skip winced. "I know. I'm terrible, but it's not because I don't care. I had…things I had to do."

Rayna's eyes were hard. "People make time for what's important to them."

"Don't be that way, Raynie. You know it upsets Mom when everybody doesn't get along. You wouldn't want to upset her, would you?"

"No, but I don't want her to be hurt either. I'm not going to let you or anybody take advantage of her. Don't even try."

"Mom does what she wants," Skip said, his expression cool and a little smug. "She's a competent adult. You can't tell her who's allowed to come to her house or what she can and can't do with her own money."

"You came because of that egg, didn't you?"

Skip didn't answer.

"Admit it. It's been all over the news."

"Okay, maybe so. But only because it reminded me of how long it's been since I've been home. Is that so wrong?"

"Skip!"

The three of them turned toward the front door. A tall, rather frail-looking woman with stooped shoulders and tight gray curls stood at the open front door. Her gray eyes were wide behind her gold-rimmed glasses.

Skip gave her a lopsided grin. "Hi, Mom."

"Oh, Skip honey." Mrs. Clarke rushed to him and pulled him close. "Where have you been? I've missed you."

"Like I was telling Rayna, I heard about what was going on, and it reminded me of how long it's been since I was home." He gave her a squeeze. "Since I saw my mom."

"And Rayna let you in?"

He looked appealingly at Rayna, but her stern expression didn't change. Finally, he ducked his head.

"I know I did wrong, Mom, but when you didn't answer the door, I, well, I got in through the back. I'll put in new glass, I promise. I shouldn't have, but then I started wondering if you might be in here all alone and you *couldn't* come to the door. God forbid something might have happened to you, but I wasn't sure. I had to check."

Rayna's grandmother put her hand up to his cheek. "Oh, Skip, I'm sorry. I wouldn't have worried you for the world. You know I have my sewing group on Monday mornings. I have for years."

"Right. Yeah. I guess I forgot."

Rayna's glance heavenward said she knew Skip was well aware of his mother's routine even after so long an absence, and had wanted to take advantage of it.

Mrs. Clarke smiled, misty eyed. "It's just glass. I don't want you to worry about it. I can have Jordan fix it. He's very handy around the house."

"Sure," Skip said, shrugging. "You know I was never much about fixing stuff anyway."

"Come sit down, honey. Have you eaten?"

"Nanny," Rayna said, "I brought Mrs. Foley from the detective agency with me. We were going to talk to her about what we need to do."

Mrs. Clarke put out her hand. "I'm sorry, Mrs. Foley. It's so good of you to come."

Julia shook hands with her. "Please call me Julia."

"And you must call me Jean. I'm sure I need to fix my son some breakfast. He really doesn't eat enough. I'd be happy to fix you something too. I thought I'd make scrambled eggs and hot dogs. It's Skip's favorite."

"That's very kind of you, but I already ate this morning," Julia said, glad for the good excuse.

"Nanny," Rayna said, "Uncle Skip can fix his own breakfast if he's hungry. Julia has a very busy schedule, and we need to stop wasting her time."

"I'm sorry, Mrs. Foley," Jean said. "I mean, Julia. It's only that I haven't seen my son in over six years. You understand."

"Certainly," Julia said, and she did. It had to be hard for a mother to be away from her son for so long, no matter what he was like.

"This is about that egg, isn't it?" Skip asked, his pale eyes narrowed. "What are you planning to do with it, Mom?"

"I'm not sure yet, Skip. Rayna thought we ought to keep it at the bank until we know more about it. We don't want anything happening to it in case it's not really ours."

"Not ours?" he protested. "You found it, didn't you? Why wouldn't it belong to us?"

"It belongs to Nanny," Rayna told him sharply. "*If* it was in the treasure box by mistake, then it belongs to whoever is the legal owner. But we are certain about one thing. It doesn't belong to you."

"And why not? I'm Mom's only living son. Her only living child. Why shouldn't it come to me someday?"

"Because Nanny—"

"Now, you two," Jean interrupted. "We don't know who it belongs to at this point. And Rayna is right. Julia's time is valuable. Skip, honey, I'm so happy to see you, but I have to deal with this right now. The food is in the refrigerator. If you don't want eggs, you can help yourself to whatever's in there."

Skip snorted and shuffled off to the kitchen. His mother looked longingly after him.

"Why don't we sit down?" Rayna urged, glancing back toward the kitchen door. Then she turned to Julia and lowered her voice. "I don't know if it's a good idea to talk here."

"Why can't we talk here?" her grandmother asked.

"Nanny," Rayna hissed. "Uncle Skip is probably listening."

"That's all right. There's nothing he can't hear."

"We can go to my office if you both would like," Julia said. "I don't absolutely have to be back there until four o'clock, so besides that, whatever works for you is fine with me."

"We can talk here," Jean said, giving her granddaughter a pat. "Let's sit down."

She sat on the floral couch, and Julia and Rayna settled on either side of her.

"We were looking at that box before your son came in," Julia prompted when neither of the others said anything. "Can you tell me about when you found the egg?"

"It's kind of funny really. I mean, having it all these years and not even knowing the egg was there. I can't imagine why nobody ever said anything." Jean picked up the treasure box. "I've known about this since I married my husband. He told me it was his mother's and her mother's before that. I never dreamed there was anything hidden in it. I polished it on Friday, and I suppose it was a little slick, because it slipped right out of my hands. It hit carpeting and not tile, thank goodness, but that was enough to make the side of it pop open."

She pointed to a split on one side of the box. It was hard to see.

"I tried to push it back into place after I got the egg out," she explained. "And really, it wasn't very much wider when I first noticed it. Maybe about a quarter of an inch. But there was some cotton wadding poking out of it, so I tried to pull that free, and the side panel popped right off."

She opened the side, revealing a compressed and yellowing clump of cotton. She removed it and lifted off the top layer. Inside was a hollow that would have fit the crystal egg, pedestal and all.

"I can see why it didn't rattle all this time," Julia said as Jean put the cotton back into place. "Do you think it would have opened without being dropped if someone knew how?"

"I was wondering that," Rayna said, picking up the box and turning it in her hands. "But I haven't been able to figure it out."

"I could figure it out," Skip said through a mouthful of sandwich as he came into the room.

He set his plate on the coffee table and grabbed the box. He poked and prodded and examined but didn't come up with a solution. Finally, he opened his pocket knife and jammed it into the narrow slit near the end.

Chapter Five

"OH, HONEY, DON'T!" JEAN CRIED.

Rayna grabbed the box from Skip, barely giving him time to pull back the knife he had jammed into the side of it. "You're going to ruin it."

Skip glared at her, but his mother reached over and patted his arm.

"Why don't you sit down with us now, honey? I'm going to have somebody find out how the box works, so you don't have to worry about it."

"I could have opened it," Skip grumbled.

"If you'd like," Julia said, "I know someone who could examine this and figure out how it was supposed to operate. It would be nice to know if the egg was sealed up in there permanently, or if this is some kind of puzzle box that opens only if you know the secret."

Skip rolled his eyes. "I don't—"

"Would you like me to show the box to my friend, Jean?" Julia asked pleasantly.

"Don't you think that would be best, Skip?" Jean asked. "An expert would know a lot of things we don't."

He shrugged and grabbed his plate again. "Whatever. I came back to try to help, but if you don't need me around..."

"Skip, honey—"

"No, it's all right. I deserve it. I should have stayed in touch. I've been trying to make something of myself all this time, trying to make you proud of me, but I guess it didn't happen quick enough for you."

Jean looked as if she was about to cry. Rayna's mouth was clamped tightly shut. Skip was obviously not above playing on his mother's emotions to get his way. He was a real piece of work.

"I'm sure it's no reflection on you," Julia told him smoothly. "And your mother's right. An expert could help us a lot in this case. After all, if that egg is as valuable as we suspect and your family has a right to it, we ought to find out as soon as possible, shouldn't we?"

"Yeah, well." He took another bite of his sandwich. "I guess that makes sense enough." He grinned around his food. "You're the pro."

She checked the time on the clock above the television set, careful to not make it obvious. Time was ticking by, and she wasn't getting much in the way of answers.

She turned her attention to his mother. "You were telling me about when you found the egg."

"Oh yes," she said. "When I took it out of the box, I had no idea what it was. It seemed to be very old, and I was almost sure those were real pearls on the base of it, so I thought Rayna ought to look at it. All I can think is that Jordan mixed the boxes up, and we didn't know until she got home that anything was wrong. Thank goodness the Boys & Girls Club gave it right back to us."

"We have it back for now," Rayna said. "But then there's this English guy who says it belongs to his family."

"Yes, I'd like to hear about that," Julia said.

Rayna took a legal-sized envelope from her purse and handed it to Julia. "That was delivered to Nanny yesterday afternoon by special messenger."

Julia opened the envelope and unfolded the letter inside. It was from a Savannah attorney she was acquainted with. She read it over.

Dear Mrs. Clarke,

My office has been contacted by His Grace William Kirkland-Wright, Duke of Prescott, regarding the crystal figurine you discovered yesterday. A valuable art piece fitting its description is known to have been in the possession of one of His Grace's ancestors until sometime in 1893 and has since then been believed to be lost.

It is the duke's desire that I represent him in this matter and in determining what claim, if any, either you or he may have to the piece you found. He also wished us to inform you that his son, the Honorable Christian Kirkland-Wright, Marquess of Prescott, will be coming to Savannah in order to meet with you on the duke's behalf to discuss the matter in full.

Please contact me at the above number at your earliest convenience so arrangements can be made for all parties to meet. The Marquess is scheduled to arrive tomorrow.

Sincerely yours,

Roy Keller

Attorney at Law

"Hey, that's today." Skip grinned. "A duke. That's pretty impressive. That egg, whatever it is, must be pretty valuable. And this marquess guy ought to be willing to pay for it."

Rayna didn't respond to him. "What do you think, Julia? Would you be able to come with us to meet him?"

"That would be a good idea," Julia said. "If I can talk to the marquess directly, I'll be able to find out a lot more than if I only got your report on what was said. I take it you haven't talked to Roy Keller's office yet about when they want to meet."

"I wanted to give you as much information as I could about what's happened so far and then see if you were willing to join us at the meeting. But I don't have any plans for the rest of the day. What about you, Nanny?"

"Oh no," Jean said. "I'd like to get Skip settled in his old room and make sure he's comfortable, but I'm sure I can go any time that's convenient for everyone else."

"Very good." Julia scanned the letter again. "It sounds like Roy is eager to talk right away, Jean. I think it would be a good idea for you to call him now and try to schedule something."

"Don't you have clients you have to see today?" Rayna asked.

"Not till very late this afternoon and then probably not for long, but the sooner we set a time for this meeting, the better I'll know how to arrange the rest of my day."

"I can go," Skip told them. "I have some pretty important business to take care of, but I guess I can put that off for a while. I mean, family, am I right?"

Rayna looked away from him, her lips pressed tightly together.

Julia handed the letter to Jean. "He said for you to call the number on their letterhead."

"Yes, all right." She dialed and waited for a moment. "Hello," she said finally. "This is Jean Clarke. Mr. Keller sent me a letter yesterday, asking me to call to arrange to meet with him."

She listened.

"Six thirty?" She motioned for Rayna to hand her the pencil and notepad on the end table beside her. "Oh, all right. Yes, seven would be better." She scribbled out what she had written and wrote down something else. "The address on your letterhead, isn't it? Yes, we'll be there. And tell Mr. Keller thank you. Goodbye."

She hung up and gave Julia a slightly bewildered smile. "We're set for seven o'clock at Mr. Keller's office. I can't believe I'm going to meet English royalty!"

"Not royalty, Nanny," Rayna said, "just nobility."

"Well, a duke anyway."

"No, his father's a duke. For now, he's a marquess."

"Whatever he is, Mom," Skip said, standing up with his now-empty plate, "you can't let him push you around. People like that think they own the world and peasants like us have to do whatever they say. Well, possession is nine-tenths of the law and stuff. And I say that egg belongs to us." He grinned. "Of course, we could give him a good deal on it."

"It doesn't belong to *us*," Rayna said, getting up too.

She was as tall as he was, maybe even slightly taller, and he shrank back.

"It's Nanny's. If it was legally passed down to Granddaddy, then she inherited it from him, and it has nothing to do with either of us."

He scowled at her. "Then why are you in the middle of everything?"

"Because I want to make sure nobody tries to take advantage of her." She looked him straight in the eye. "Nobody."

He didn't move for a moment, and then he huffed and slouched toward the kitchen, muttering something about wanting to know who had died and left her in charge.

Rayna sat down again. "I'm sorry, Julia. I just get so frustrated with him. It's not like this is anything new. Even after all these years, he hasn't changed in the least."

"Don't be that way, Rayna," Jean said. "He's trying to do better. I know it's been a long time, but he did come home. He missed us."

"Nanny, he came home because he heard about the egg and hoped you'd end up with a lot of money. He's probably already got half of it spent."

"Rayna."

Rayna took her grandmother's hand. "I'm sorry. I'll try to be more patient with him, but honestly, when do you ever hear from him unless he wants something?" She looked up at the ceiling, took a steadying breath, and then gave Julia a tight smile. "What do we need to do now?"

"I'd like to get some general information about your family. Didn't you say you have a family Bible with births and deaths in it?"

Julia got as much family history as she could from Rayna and her grandmother. She also took several pictures of the Bible's faded flyleaf where the marriages, births, and deaths were recorded.

"And you know for sure that your husband's grandmother passed the box down to his mother?" she asked finally.

"As far as I know," Jean said. "Dalton always said his grand-mama Willow left it to his mother when Willow and Granddaddy Elliot died of influenza. Willow was a Brenton, and they lived in a big house, but her folks lost everything in some kind of crash around the turn of the century."

"So the treasure box was hers."

Mrs. Clarke nodded. "But whether it was passed down to her or made for her, I don't know. Dalton's mother, Patricia, wasn't very old when her mother died, so she couldn't tell him much about her. I always meant to find out more, but I guess I never got around to it."

"We've done a lot of this kind of research," Julia said with a nod toward her notes. "I'm sure we can find out more. Whether that will lead us to an explanation for why the egg was in the box and who it belongs to, we'll have to see." She looked at Rayna and then at her grandmother. "Is there anything else you think I should be aware of before I start looking into the case?"

Jean shook her head.

"I'm not even sure what questions to ask at this point," Rayna said. "But you can always call me if there's something you want to know. If I can't tell you, I can try to find out."

"Or you can ask me." Skip came out of the kitchen, wiping his mouth on a paper towel. "Could be I heard something from back when I was a kid that might help you."

"I'd be interested in hearing about that," Julia said, picking up her pen expectantly.

Skip shrugged. "I can't think of anything right now. But you can always ask and I could think about it."

His mother patted his arm. "That would be so helpful. Maybe there's something your father said way back when that could be useful."

Rayna didn't look so sure, but she didn't comment.

"I can always use good information," Julia said. "If you'll give me your number, I'll contact you if there's something you might be able to help me with."

"My number," Skip said. "Yeah, heh, you'd better call me here at Mom's for now. I need to get my number taken care of."

"That'll be fine," she said pleasantly. "I have your mother's number in my case information. Is there anything else any of you have for me to work with? Letters? Diaries? Photographs?"

"There are pictures of my husband and his parents," Jean said.

"I can email them to you, if it would help," Rayna added.

"I think we have a pretty good grasp of who was in the family to that point," Julia said, "though I might ask you for them later."

Rayna nodded.

"What about Willow and her husband? Do you have anything more about them? Marriage records? Death certificates? Anything at all?"

"No," Jean said. "I'm sorry. I never saw anything like that. I've always wondered with them both dying so suddenly if all of their personal papers might have been lost or thrown away."

"That's possible," Julia said. "But I have resources. I'll see what I can turn up. It may take a little time."

"But we don't have time," Rayna said. "Our meeting is in a few hours."

"Then I'd better get to work." Julia stood up. "Just remember, this doesn't have to be settled tonight. Everybody involved has the right to gather as much information as possible. We're not going to be rushed."

Still, Rayna had a point. They didn't have much time before they met with Christian Kirkland-Wright. Not much time at all.

Chapter Six

Savannah, Georgia
September 1893

"It's horrible."

Willow Brenton tossed her father's newspaper onto the breakfast table, earning his disapproving glance.

"I beg your pardon, young lady."

"I'm sorry, Papa, but it is horrible. All those people dead and injured and homeless. It's been over a week, and the Red Cross hasn't come. What are they going to do?"

His expression softened slightly, and his brown eyes, so like her own, warmed. "There will be help. There is help already. Some of my business associates and I have sent a good deal of money to help them recover, and I'm sure we aren't the only ones."

"Money to whom?"

"Well, to the Red—"

"The Red Cross! Oh, Papa, I know they do a lot of good, but they're still dealing with the hurricane that hit in June. Are the Sea Islands people supposed to wait for help for another two or three months?"

"Who's supposed to wait for help?" Mama asked as she sat down at the table opposite Papa, looking sweet and fresh in a soft pink morning dress. Evie, in her tidy black dress and white apron, poured out Mama's coffee and filled her plate with ham and poached eggs.

"The people who were in the hurricane at the end of last month," Willow said. "One of the ladies at the church social was talking about how terrible it is for them. Miss Cunningham. She's going to go and help."

Mama looked startled. "Herself?"

"She was a nurse during the War between the States," Willow said, looking down at the blue and cream stripes in her silk skirt. "She said it was very hard, but she was glad that she had done what she could to ease the suffering of brave men. But now it's not only men. They're women and children too. They were very poor to begin with, but now they have nothing. Their crops were washed away, their homes were blown down. Many of them were killed. Maybe a thousand or more. Those that are still alive are starving."

"Lucas," Mama said to Papa, "is that so?"

Papa took the newspaper from the table and folded it to cover the headline about the hurricane that said "That West Indian Monster" and the photograph that showed the destruction the hurricane had left behind.

"It is a tragedy," he said, "and of course, we should all do what we are able to help those less fortunate. But I cannot agree that genteel ladies ought to go to such places and expose themselves to dangerous conditions, dangerous situations.

Let them make clothing and prepare foodstuffs to send. Let them sell their fancy goods to raise money for the cause. That is the part of a lady in such circumstances."

"But during the war—" Willow began.

"That was war. Miss Cunningham, I am sure, is a fine Christian lady with noble intentions." Papa fixed her with a look. "Spinster ladies of a certain age," he said gravely, "need causes to occupy themselves in their waning years. A young lady of your delicacy and position has no business putting herself and her reputation at risk by haring off to tend to who knows what sort of people. What would young Sheffield say?"

"Oh, Elliot." Willow huffed and picked up her spoon to put sugar into her tea. "What do I care what he thinks?"

"You know he's asked Papa for you," Mama said gently.

Willow scowled. "So?"

"He's been waiting a long time."

"Well, I never told him to." She blew out her breath, making one of her dark curls bob. "I know. He's a very nice young man, and I should be honored. Well, he is a nice man, and I am honored. But I've known him all my life."

"So then you know he has a good family and a good character and won't do anything to wrong you," Papa said. "There's many a roué who'd find you and your money a dainty feast to be enjoyed and the bones cast aside."

"Lucas!" Mama scolded.

"Well, the girl's not a child anymore. If she's determined to have her way, she ought to know what may lie ahead." Papa reached over and took Willow's hand. "You know I

want only what's best for you, honey. What would you do in the middle of all that want and destruction?"

"Well, I'd help."

Willow hesitated, knowing she hadn't examined the idea so thoroughly as to know for certain what that help would entail. Miss Cunningham had spoken of holding soldiers' hands and holding cool compresses to their fevered brows. Of writing letters to their wives and mothers. Of reading to them from uplifting books. She could do those things.

She squeezed the hand that held hers. "Papa, I want to know I've done something that makes a real difference to someone. You know I've never really been anywhere or done anything but enjoy myself. I want to do this. I want to go with Miss Cunningham and the other ladies to Beaufort and help."

"Nonsense," Papa said. "You take food and clothing to the mission every Wednesday. Your circle of young ladies makes quilts for the unfortunates down there. You help your mother's friends make baby clothes for the poor women who have need of them."

"But I never even see those people, Papa. I never talk to the ones in need or get to know what they're like. They're only words to me."

"Willow dear," Mama said in her gentle voice, "we know you mean well, but I can hardly think it wise—"

"To go unchaperoned? I know, Mama. But what if I take Hannah with me and Silas to drive us?"

"Your maid and our yardman?" Papa barked. "Out of the question."

"But I would be with Miss Cunningham and all the other ladies who are going. I wouldn't be alone. Papa, please let me do this. I don't want to go away forever, but I do want to do something, at least one thing, that is more than for myself. Papa, please."

"Out of the question," he said again, and he picked up the discarded newspaper, shook it out, and held it up in front of his face. The terrible picture showing the ruin in the Sea Islands was visible again.

"Mama," Willow pled softly.

Mama merely shook her head and turned her attention to her poached eggs.

Willow looked down at her own plate, knowing that, as usual, she would eat less than half of what was there and the rest would be thrown away. How much would the people in Beaufort appreciate even what she had left over?

She looked at Mama again, wondering if that little shake of her head meant no or merely wait. She knew Uncle Reynold and Uncle Kit had credited getting through the war with all their limbs to the kind ladies, the genteel ladies, who had been willing to leave their sheltered homes and care for the wounded. Mama had heard their stories time and again. No doubt she had worried and prayed for her brothers until they had at last come home. Was it possible that she would speak to Papa on Willow's behalf?

I want so much to go, she wrote in her diary that night. Papa is probably right that I don't realize what I will find when I reach Beaufort. Miss Cunningham says she cannot describe the conditions she has seen, in the war and at the other tragedies to which she has been witness. She once saw a steamboat explosion and tended the wounded there. She said it was, in that moment, much worse than the war had been. But at the least, she knows she is strong enough to face whatever it is she encounters. I know no such thing about myself. But somehow I will find out. Somehow, I will go to Beaufort.

Chapter Seven

JULIA PARKED HER CAR BEHIND the office. By then Meredith was back from meeting with Mr. Talbot, and Julia went to discuss the new case with her.

"How'd it go?" Meredith asked as Julia sat in the chair across from her and set her coffee cup on the desk.

"It was interesting. A little more going on than I thought. First tell me how it went with Talbot."

Meredith smiled. "All taken care of. How about the Clarkes?"

"The duke's son is supposed to get in tonight. They asked Roy Keller to represent their interests locally."

"At least he's somebody we know." Meredith gazed through her office's floor-length windows and on to Forsythe Park across the road. "I wonder what he has in mind. Is he talking lawsuit here?"

"I don't know. It doesn't seem like it at this point. All he wants to do is meet with the Clarkes."

"Yes. You met the grandmother?"

"She seems like a nice lady, but she lets her son manipulate her."

"That's Uncle Skip, right?"

"Right. When we got to her grandmother's house, he had broken in through the back door." Julia grinned. "I think I gave Uncle Skip a bit of a scare saying we were going to call the police."

"He really goes by Skip?"

"Really," Julia said. "He's fiftysomething and acts fourteen. Hasn't been around the family for years until now."

"Because he heard about the egg."

"If you ask me," Julia said, as she checked her watch.

"We're scheduled to meet with Roy at seven tonight. I suppose the Clarkes ought to get themselves an attorney too."

"I don't know if they need to jump into that right away," Julia said. "If it gets down to an actual suit, then yes, of course. But if we can find out enough on our end that definitively shows Mrs. Clarke either does or doesn't rightfully own the egg, a lawsuit and a lawyer might not be necessary. It's very early in the process. We ought to get more information first. The Clarkes can hire an attorney at any point along the way."

"Good. I don't think they have much money as it is. The more groundwork we can lay, the less they'll have to pay a lawyer to do."

Julia picked up her mug. "Are you available tonight? I'm not sure when this duke's son will be here."

"I'll be glad to come." Meredith's eyes twinkled. "GK won't mind."

GK was her Russian Blue cat, her only housemate since her husband, Ron, died.

"For now, I'll tie up all the loose ends I have for the day," Meredith continued. "Then let's see what we can find out before the meeting."

"Perfect. I'll make a copy of my notes so you can get caught up on the details."

Julia made the copies, dropped them off on Meredith's desk, and then went into her own office and reviewed the notes herself. Then she picked up her phone.

"Julia," Maggie Lu said when she answered. "How are you?"

"Oh, good. Do you have a minute to talk?"

"Sure. What's going on?"

"It's about that egg Madison found at the egg hunt."

"Mmm, you have really stirred up something, haven't you?" Maggie Lu laughed softly. "That news is all over the country."

"All over the world," Julia said, and she told Maggie Lu about Mr. Kirkland-Wright.

"You're not kidding. And he's coming here already?"

"Tonight. I'm doing a little research on the people who hired us to try to figure out how they got the egg and if it's rightfully theirs. They think it goes back to a woman named Willow Sheffield. Have you heard of her?"

"Sheffield," Maggie Lu mused. "I can't think of any Sheffields straight off, but I can check into it. Do you know anything else about her?"

"The lady who actually had the egg all this time is Mrs. Jean Clarke. Her husband was Dalton Clarke, and he's deceased. She's got to be in her late eighties, I think. Willow Sheffield was her husband's grandmother and was married in 1894, so I'm assuming she was born sometime in the 1870s or so. Her maiden name was Brenton."

"Oh, all right. I've heard of some Brentons that lived in one of the exclusive areas of Savannah. I don't know if those are the same ones, but I'll see what I can find on them. I suppose you're in a hurry."

Julia chuckled. "I'm sorry to ask it, but the duke's son will be here later today, and I'd like to find out how the Clarke ancestors happened to get the egg. At least some possibilities. If you don't have time for this, I completely understand. I wouldn't bother you if everything wasn't happening so fast."

"No, now, it's not a bother. It's kind of exciting, to tell the truth, and I'm glad to help. That name Brenton is tickling something in the back of my mind. Granny Luv had a neighbor who used to work for a family named Brenton or maybe Brendon or Braydon, but that was after the Civil War, and they sure didn't live anywhere near the exclusive areas of town. They were well off enough to have a maid, obviously, but she was the only help they had, as far as I remember. I'm sorry I can't give you anything certain right now, but I can look."

"You've helped a lot already, Maggie Lu. If those are the same Brentons, and they went from living lavishly to someplace not so luxurious, I'd like to know why that was."

"And if they lost their money for some reason," Maggie Lu said, "why didn't they sell that egg? From what they're saying on the news these days, it might be worth a lot of money, especially if it's a Fabergé."

"Exactly. Of course, Jean didn't realize she had it, and it seems fairly likely that her husband didn't know about the egg and neither did his mother. That's why I have to start with Willow Sheffield. Willow Brenton, I mean."

"All right," Maggie Lu said. "Well, this is a good time for me to do a little research. Baby Jake is with his mama right now, and all I was planning on doing is a little knitting."

"Thank you, Maggie Lu," Julia said. "I'm going to see what I can find in the public records about the Brentons, but you always seem to get down to the interesting little details that tell the whole story."

"It's like solving a puzzle. When's your meeting?"

"Seven tonight, so anything you can find out before that would be a big help. I can't thank you enough."

"No problem. I'll call you if I discover anything useful."

"Talk to you soon, Maggie Lu."

Julia hung up with a shake of her head. She didn't know what she and Meredith would do without Maggie Lu's knowledge of Savannah history, especially the things that weren't in history books and newspaper articles. After a moment's thought, Julia went to talk to Carmen.

"I need you to check for records on a Willow Brenton or Willow Sheffield. Preferably Willow Brenton Sheffield. Marriage records. Deaths. Births. Anything you can find. I'm guessing, but I think she was born in the 1870s or so. Married in 1894."

"I'll check."

"And for a Dalton Clarke and a Jean Clarke. Her maiden name is Gray. Dalton was born in 1928."

"Got it," Carmen said. "I'll let you know what I find out."

Julia's phone was ringing when she got back to her desk. It was Rayna Clarke.

"I'm still at Nanny's," she said, "but I wanted to ask you a favor."

"We're still on for seven this evening, aren't we?" Julia asked.

"Yes, seven's great."

Julia could hear Rayna's grandmother talking in the background. She sounded eager to get the matter settled. Then she heard Skip say he was available at seven too.

"Oh boy," Julia said under her breath.

Rayna got back on the phone. "Nanny's ready to go. Uh…" She dropped her voice. "Can you tell Uncle Skip that there isn't room for him to come or something? He's going to try to run everything, and it's going to be terrible."

"I'm sorry," Julia told her, "but that would be for your grandmother to decide. She's really the one who owns the egg, unless it's proved to belong to someone else. I realize you're the one who hired me, but she's the one the duke's son wants to talk to. It's up to her to bring whoever she wants unless you can convince her otherwise."

"Okay," Rayna said. "Then you'd better expect three of us, because Nanny has never told Uncle Skip no about anything, and I can't imagine she's going to start now. And I'm not sending her over there without somebody to make sure she doesn't get run over by him."

"That's probably a good idea. I'll try to keep things on track as much as I can, but this is just a preliminary meeting. We want to find out what basis the duke has for his claims about the egg, and I want to get a feel for how reasonable this Christian Kirkland-Wright is."

"I looked him up on the internet."

"Oh good," Julia said. "I was about to do that myself. Anything particularly noteworthy in what you found?"

"For some reason, I thought he'd be older, but he's only three years older than I am. Nice-looking in an English sort of way. He was in the military. The best schools. He went to Eton and Cambridge."

"Impressive."

"That doesn't mean he's not a nitwit."

Julia chuckled. "I suppose not, but it makes it less likely, I think. Anyway, I'll look him up too. Meredith will be coming with me, by the way. And a friend of mine is trying to find out what she can about Willow Brenton. You don't happen to have any additional information on her, do you? Addresses where she lived? An actual birth date? Parents' names and birth dates? Anything?"

"I'm sorry, no," Rayna said. "The Bible we showed you must have been Willow Brenton's when she got married, and that's where the page with the family history starts. Before that, I don't know anything. I guess I should have had someone trace my ancestry before now, but it was never really an issue until this point."

"We'll find out what we can," Julia assured her. "But anything you can come up with will make our job easier and faster. We don't have a lot of time today to get our information together, but again, this is just preliminary. It's not like we're going into court expecting a final determination on the egg's ownership."

Rayna exhaled. "Yes, you're right. I think we're all a little bit nervous and excited. I mean, except for Uncle Skip. He thinks we're going to walk in there, say the egg is ours, and immediately get tens of thousands of dollars for it."

"I'm sorry to disappoint him, but I doubt it's going to work out that way."

"Good. Maybe he'll lose interest after that and disappear again."

"Maybe he really does want to get back in touch with your grandmother and even you," Julia suggested gently, though her less-charitable side was skeptical.

"Maybe. Anyway, should we meet up at your office, or go directly to Mr. Keller's?"

"We'll meet you there," Julia told her. "If you come up with any additional information about your family, give me a call. And it would help if you all got there just a few minutes early. If we find out anything you ought to know, that will give us a chance to tell you about it."

"All right. We'll see you a little before seven at Mr. Keller's."

"Good. Oh, and make sure you bring the box with you. So far that's really all we have that shows that the egg has been in your family for a very long time."

"Should we bring the egg too?" Rayna asked. "Nanny would have to get it out of her safe-deposit box before the bank closes."

Julia considered for a moment.

"Let's leave it where it is for now," she said finally. "Mr. Kirkland-Wright must have seen the video from the Easter egg hunt by now. He has a good idea what it looks like. If he would like, we can take him to see it tomorrow. Tonight we need to talk."

***

During the afternoon, Julia did some research on Savannah deed records. She didn't find anything in the name of Willow Brenton or Willow Sheffield. She did find a house in a once-fashionable neighborhood that was deeded to Elliot Sheffield in 1894 and then to someone else in 1909. She found another home a few blocks away from that one that was deeded from a Mrs. Lucas Brenton, widow, in 1911. Lastly, she found a deed dated that same day to Mrs. Lucas Brenton for a house in a considerably less fashionable neighborhood. She didn't find anything else under that Mrs. Brenton's name.

She glanced at the list of names and dates she had taken from Jean Clarke's family Bible. Patricia Louise Sheffield had been born to Elliot and Willow Sheffield in 1895. She had married Claude

Clarke in 1921. Julia checked the records for the name Claude Clarke. There was no record of a deed in his name until 1929. That property had then been deeded to Dalton Clarke and his unnamed wife in 1961. Dalton Clarke was Rayna's grandfather. Julia smiled when she realized that this was the deed to the house Rayna's grandmother still lived in.

Carmen came in a little while later, bringing her a copy of the marriage certificate for Elliot Raymond Sheffield and Willow Alice Brenton in 1894 and their death certificates in 1909.

"They died only two days apart," Carmen said. "It's sad."

"Yes, it is. And it's sad about their daughter." Julia glanced at her notes and did a quick calculation in her head. "So their daughter, Patricia, was only fourteen at the time. That must have been really hard on her."

"Do you think she lived with her grandmother after they died?" Carmen asked, reading over Julia's shoulder.

"That would be my best guess until we find out something different, though I'd like to know what happened to the house that was deeded to Mrs. Brenton in 1911." She gave Carmen the address. "It looks like she moved down in the world when she moved there, and the next thing we know about Patricia Sheffield is that she and her husband bought a house in 1929."

Carmen looked thoughtful for a moment. "So Patricia was thirty-four years old when they bought the house. How long they were married before that, or where they lived, is anybody's guess."

"You're right, unfortunately. I'm going to go talk to Meredith about what we've found so far. Do me a favor and see if you can track down the owners of the house Mrs. Brenton sold in 1911."

Julia gave Carmen the address. "And see if you can find anything else on Patricia or her husband until they bought the house Rayna's grandmother lives in now."

"Okay."

"Oh," Julia added. "See if you can find out anything about Skip Clarke. Going by the family Bible, I assume that his real name is Dalton Randal Clarke, after his father. Born March 2, 1972. I want to know if he has any current wants or warrants and if he's done any prison time."

Carmen clicked her tongue, pretending to be shocked. "I'll find out."

Julia followed her out of her office and into Meredith's. By the time they discussed Julia's case so far and the ones Meredith was working on, it was time to leave for the day. Julia wanted to get home and have dinner before she went to Roy Keller's office.

She found Beau in his armchair drinking Cheerwine and reading an old detective novel.

"Hey there, Julie-bean," he said, smiling as she leaned down to kiss his cheek. "I guess I lost track of the time."

"I wanted to get home and get dinner so I can make an appointment at seven." She looked around. "Where's the drama princess?"

Beau chuckled. "Probably sacked out somewhere. She was bouncing around like an overcaffeinated squirrel about an hour ago, attacking one of her catnip mice. I figure she's passed out by now."

Julia shook her head. "Must be nice. Have you gotten the mail yet?"

"No."

He started to get up, but Julia held up one hand.

"Don't worry about it, I'll go."

She went out the front door and down the walk. It was so pretty outside, she wished she and Beau could relax for the evening on the porch. Too bad she had a meeting to go to, but that was the job.

There wasn't much in the mailbox. A couple of bills. A couple of ads. Hardly anybody sent real mail anymore, and that was kind of a shame, but she couldn't deny that the electronic stuff was quick and efficient.

She took a minute to freshen herself up for tonight's meeting, and then, while she tossed a garden salad with Italian dressing, Beau whipped up some turkey sandwiches, a quick meal they both enjoyed.

"I'm surprised we don't have company," Julia said as they sat down. "Bunny's usually trying to bum a taste of turkey when there is any."

Beau shrugged. "She hasn't smelled it yet. She must really be worn out."

"What a life." She checked the clock and hurried to finish her meal. "I don't plan on this taking very long, but if it's more than an hour or so, I'll give you a call."

"Thanks. Be careful."

"Always. Would you please get the trash out before it gets dark? The truck comes in the morning."

"I'll take care of it."

She gave him a quick peck on the cheek and went out to her car. It was going to be good to get more information about where the egg had come from, but she liked the Clarkes, especially Jean. She hoped she didn't have to tell that sweet lady that one of her ancestors was a thief.

Chapter Eight

UNLIKE THE COMFORTABLY ELEGANT OFFICES of Magnolia Investigations, the offices of attorneys Keller, Maxwell, and Miles were sleek and gleaming and utterly modern. Julia and Meredith spoke briefly with the Clarkes, who were waiting for them, and when they all went inside, Roy Keller greeted them himself.

"I didn't want to keep my assistant late," he explained as they walked to the conference room.

Julia was never quite able to reconcile his rich baritone voice with his small stature and mild expression. He always said it gave him an advantage over his legal adversaries who underestimated him.

"All Mr. Kirkland-Wright wants to do at this point is find out where your side stands," he said.

"What's he like?" Julia asked him, her voice lowered.

"Seems like a reasonable guy. Very polite. Very British. You can judge for yourself."

"He might as well know now that he can't push us around," Skip said, clearly making no effort in the least to not be heard.

Rayna pressed her lips together but didn't say anything. Jean merely looked distressed.

"Here we are," Roy said, all smiles as he opened the conference room door.

There were two men standing at the far end of the conference table. Earlier that afternoon, Julia and Meredith had done a search for Christian Elman Kirkland-Wright and found not only basic biographical information but a recent photograph, so Julia was able to rule out the man on the left at once. The one on the right was about thirty, maybe not quite. He was over six feet tall, had an unmistakable military bearing, and was dressed with an almost-offhand elegance. His skin was fair but ruddy, and he looked as if he spent at least part of his time outdoors.

"I suppose we ought to make introductions," Roy said. "I'm Roy Keller. I'll be representing Mr. Kirkland-Wright as we try to figure out our particular little problem." He nodded toward Julia. "Mr. Kirkland-Wright, this is Meredith Bellefontaine and Julia Foley. They are investigating the matter on behalf of the Clarkes. They run Magnolia Investigations."

"Ms. Foley," Kirkland-Wright said with a slight bow. "And Ms. Bellefontaine."

Julia smiled and moved to Jean's side. "This is Mrs. Jean Clarke. She's the one who originally found the egg."

"It was in here," Jean said, a slight quaver in her voice as she held out the treasure box.

Kirkland-Wright's dark eyes warmed. "Ah. I see. That looks very old, doesn't it?"

She nodded.

"This is Mrs. Clarke's granddaughter, Rayna," Julia said.

"Mr. Kirkland-Wright," Rayna said, offering her hand. "I hope we can get this all worked out soon."

"As do I," he assured her, and then he looked expectantly at Skip.

"I'm her son," Skip said, jerking his chin toward his mother. "You can call me Skip."

"Skip then," Kirkland-Wright said, shaking hands with him too.

Skip crossed his arms over his chest. "Who's your buddy?"

There was an almost indiscernible twitch at the corner of Kirkland-Wright's mouth. "I beg your pardon. This is Mr. Lumley. He's assisting me while I'm here in Savannah."

"Good evening," Mr. Lumley said in a low voice.

He was a sturdily built man of average height with curly black hair around a bald dome of a head. Julia judged him to be in his midforties.

"Now that we know who's who," Roy said, "why don't we all sit down. Coffee, anyone?"

Julia helped him fill cups and pass them out while everyone except Lumley took seats at the table. Lumley stood expectantly at Kirkland-Wright's side.

"Mrs. Clarke," Roy said, "why don't you tell us about when you found the egg? We've heard the story about the Easter egg hunt, but we'd like to know how you came to have it in the first place and how it came to be in that plastic egg."

"I, uh…" Jean looked at Julia. "Maybe you could tell it best."

"I know this must be quite awkward for you, Mrs. Clarke," Kirkland-Wright said, "but it would help me a great deal to hear you tell it. I've found at times that details can be lost in translation as it were."

He gave her a smile that was equal parts understanding and appeal, and she seemed to relax a little.

"Well," she said, "it started with this." She pushed the treasure box over to him. "It belonged to my husband's grandmother. You can see there's a small compartment built into it. I didn't know about that until I happened to drop it and it came open. If you look at the cotton wadding inside, you can see where the egg was and that it was packed in so tightly that it never rattled."

Kirkland-Wright nodded as he looked at the cotton. "Do you know how old the box is?"

Jean shook her head. "I know it was in the family before my husband's mother was born, and that was before the turn of the twentieth century."

"1895," Julia supplied from her notes.

"I see." The Englishman continued to examine the box. "And how did the egg you found, Mrs. Clarke, end up at the hunt?"

Jean gave him the details with Rayna and sometimes even Skip adding to the story.

"It seems you were very fortunate in having it returned to you," Kirkland-Wright said. "What a pity after all that if you shouldn't end up with it."

Skip looked up, his expression belligerent. "Listen—"

"Uncle Skip, please." Rayna looked coolly at Kirkland-Wright. "We don't want anything but the truth. But, as you can see, the egg has been in our family for well over a hundred years. If it had been stolen, wouldn't someone have mentioned that some time ago?"

"It would seem so, Miss Clarke, but my understanding is that the egg wasn't stolen but lost."

"Lost?"

Kirkland-Wright nodded. "Let me show you something. Lumley?"

"Yes, sir."

Lumley picked up the briefcase that was on the chair in the corner behind him and opened it. He took a file folder out of it and handed the folder to Kirkland-Wright.

"Thank you." The Englishman opened the folder and spread out a number of photographs on the table. "This is Fabergé's Renaissance Egg. It's currently in the vault at my family estate in Yorkshire."

The images showed a large pearlescent egg elaborately decorated with gold and gems and enameled flowers. Two of the pictures showed the egg opened up.

"It's beautiful," Meredith said, and Jean and Rayna nodded in dumb agreement.

"That oughta buy a few lottery tickets," Skip added.

Kirkland-Wright's pleasant expression didn't change.

"It was created in 1892, a commission from Alexander III of Russia for his wife, the Empress Maria Feodorovna. As you can see, the egg is empty. Fabergé eggs are known for the wondrous surprises they contain."

Julia nodded. "And you think the egg Mrs. Clarke found is what is supposed to go inside this one."

"It or something very like it," Kirkland-Wright said.

"If this belonged to the Russian royal family," Rayna said, "how is it that you think your family has a claim to it?"

"Because we happen to have ties not to Russian royalty but to Russian nobility. Six generations before me, there was a Countess

Katarina Radulov who happened to be great friends with the empress, who gifted the egg and its contents to her at Christmas."

"That was a very generous gift," Meredith said.

Kirkland-Wright nodded. "The countess had no children of her own, but she was very fond of the two sons of her younger sister, Alexis and Nikolai Voronin. When Alexis decided to travel to America, I'm told that the countess removed the Resurrection Egg—that's what the inner egg was called—from its hiding place inside the Renaissance Egg and told him to keep it with him always. She said it was to remind him of her prayers and of his faith and that he must one day return it to its rightful place along with himself."

"Oh." Jean sighed. "And he never came back, did he?" She clutched her son's sleeve. "It's too sad."

"What happened to him?" Rayna asked coolly.

"There was a hurricane," Kirkland-Wright said. "In a place called...?"

"Beaufort, South Carolina," Lumley supplied. "I believe it's roughly forty miles from Savannah."

Julia nodded. "I know the place. What year did Alexis die?"

"1893," Kirkland-Wright said. "He was twenty-five."

"So sad," Jean breathed.

"We thought the Resurrection Egg was lost with him, but it seems now that it wasn't."

"If what Mrs. Clarke found is in fact the Resurrection Egg," Julia said. "Are there any photographs of it?"

"Only a description from a letter, dated March 19, 1893, that the countess sent to her sister telling her she had sent the egg with her nephew. It describes the egg in detail, and every detail fits the egg that Mrs. Clarke found."

Kirkland-Wright took another photograph from the folder and put it on the table. It showed a yellowed, nearly crumbling piece of paper filled with faded writing in what Julia was certain was Russian.

"The translation is on the back, if you'd care to read it," he said. "You may keep that copy if you'd like. Feel free to have it translated for yourself."

Julia quickly scanned the translation. It perfectly described the egg in Jean's safe-deposit box. *It is a miracle in miniature*, the countess had written after the description. *All of the Gospel small enough to fit easily in the hand and large enough to fill the heart.*

"Thank you," she said. "This will be very helpful."

She didn't say so, but yes, she would have the letter independently translated. Just in case.

"May I ask," Meredith added, "how you are related to this countess and to her nephew?"

"Certainly. My great-great-grandmother was Honoria Kirkland-Wright, née Voronin. Her father was Nikolai Voronin, younger brother of Alexis. Their aunt was the Countess Katarina Radulov."

For the first time, Rayna's expression softened as she looked at the Englishman. She seemed fascinated. "I knew Queen Victoria was related to many of the European royal families, including the Russian one. I never considered that an English duke would be of Russian descent."

"We're an inbred lot," Kirkland-Wright said with a twinkle in his dark eyes.

Mr. Lumley pursed his lips.

"You can be related to the pope if you want," Skip snapped. "That doesn't mean you get everything your way all the time. Not here in the US."

"By no means," Kirkland-Wright said affably. "As was mentioned, we want only to find the truth."

"I think we all agree on that," Julia said. "The question now seems to be how the egg got from Beaufort and into the box and how the box came to belong to the Clarkes."

"Precisely. Might we be able to see the egg?"

Rayna glanced at Julia.

"It's in Mrs. Clarke's safe-deposit box right now," Julia explained. "I suppose you could see it when the bank is open tomorrow."

She looked at Jean for confirmation.

"Yes, of course," the older woman said. "I didn't want to keep it in the house when it might be very valuable."

"I understand completely, Mrs. Clarke." Kirkland-Wright looked around the table. "We've laid out the case for both sides. Is there anything else we ought to discuss this evening? Or shall we resume sometime tomorrow?"

Lumley moved a little closer to his side. "Perhaps an exchange of contact information, sir?" he asked quietly.

"Good idea." Kirkland-Wright turned to Roy. "Would that be a problem? Or would it be best to have all contact go through you?"

Roy shrugged. "We're all getting along well. There's no reason both sides can't stay in touch. Unless the Clarkes object. Julia?"

"Is that all right with you?" Julia asked her clients.

"Well, sure," Jean said, and she gave Lumley her phone number and address.

Kirkland-Wright looked expectantly at Rayna. "Do you live with your grandmother?"

"No," she said, "but I live near her. Close enough to take care of her."

Jean beamed at the Englishman. "She's a sweet girl."

"I live with her," Skip said. "With my mother, I mean. I'll be taking care of things for her."

Kirkland-Wright raised one eyebrow. "What about you, Mrs. Clarke? Would you prefer to have someone deal with us on your behalf? Or should we contact you directly? The decision is entirely yours."

Jean looked from her son to her granddaughter. "I suppose it's up to me now, isn't it? After all, I was the one who inherited everything of my husband's."

"Very true, ma'am. Very true. And I'm sure your family and Mrs. Foley and Mrs. Bellefontaine here are well able to advise you if you feel in need of help. Above all, I want to make sure that, whatever the final disposition of the egg may be, you are satisfied that it was fairly taken care of."

"That seems fair," Jean said. "Doesn't that seem fair?"

Rayna glanced at Kirkland-Wright as if she were wondering how far she could trust him, but she nodded. "The only thing I want to do is to make sure my grandmother isn't taken advantage of. By anyone."

"I think we all want to make sure of that," Julia said, though she wasn't quite sure if everyone present was actually on board with that. Skip certainly looked annoyed at this point.

"Well," Roy said brightly, "is there any other information anyone would like to bring to the table before we adjourn? Mrs. Clarke? Christian?"

Kirkland-Wright shook his head.

"I don't know what it would be," Jean said.

"I'd like you to have my information, Mr. Kirkland-Wright," Julia said, passing him her business card. "In case there's anything you need from me. And of course, Roy has my information too."

"Thank you," he said, tucking the card into his coat pocket and holding out one of his own. "And do call me Christian. Kirkland-Wright can be rather a mouthful."

Julia took his card with a smile. "And you must call us Julia and Meredith."

Everyone stood up then. Christian shook hands with the Clarkes and gave each of them one of his cards too.

"It's been a pleasure meeting you all," he said, his eyes particularly on Rayna.

She turned pink and looked away.

"It's such an honor, your lordship," Jean gushed. "I don't know what to say."

He took her hand and bowed over it. "The honor is mine, ma'am, but really, you must call me Christian. As long as I'm here in your country, it seems only fitting."

"Christian then. What time did you want to come to the bank?"

Christian turned to Roy. "Is there a particular time that would suit everyone? I have nothing scheduled on this trip besides dealing with this matter. Practically nothing anyway."

"Does anyone have a particular preference?" Roy asked the group. "What about ten o'clock?"

Everyone agreed on ten, and Rayna gave Christian the name and address of the bank.

"You'll want to take this with you," he said, handing her the treasure box. "It certainly would be interesting to know where that came from too."

"It would be a big help," Julia agreed.

"And," Meredith said, "that's something we're going to try to find out."

"Very good. Until tomorrow then. It was good meeting all of you. Lumley?"

"Coming, sir."

Lumley gathered up the photos from the table and began putting them into the briefcase.

"Could we possibly get copies of those too?" Julia asked Christian.

"Certainly. You can have those, in fact. I can always have more printed out."

Lumley handed him the pictures, and Christian passed them along to Julia.

"Thank you," she said. "We'll meet you at the bank in the morning."

She and Meredith herded the Clarkes out of the office ahead of them and walked with them out of the building.

"I think that went well," she said when they reached Rayna's car. "Christian seems to be a reasonable man. I hope we can come up with a solution to this problem that everyone can live with. I'm not sure that, even if it did once belong to his family, he has a legal claim to it by now. Not unless he can prove something criminal has happened."

"I also hope we can resolve it," Rayna said.

Meredith considered for a moment then said to Jean, "Maybe it's time you got the egg appraised and hired an attorney too."

"I don't know," Jean said. "I don't think I'm ready to have a lawyer yet. Not until we know how that egg got into the treasure box."

"Christian is a little too smooth, if you ask me," Rayna said, glancing back at the building.

Her grandmother gave her a look. "Now, he's a perfectly nice young man. Very handsome too."

Rayna rolled her eyes.

"Thinks a lot of himself," Skip said with a look of disgust.

His mother patted his arm. "Come on. Why don't we go home and do something fun? It's not late yet. We could put on a movie and even have popcorn. Won't that be fun?"

He shrugged grumpily.

"Julia and Meredith, you're invited, of course," she added.

"Thank you," Julia said, "but I really have to get home. My husband will be wondering where I am."

"And I'm sure my cat is waiting up for me," Meredith said with a twinkle in her eye. "But we'll see you tomorrow at the bank, all right?"

"Ten o'clock," Jean said with a wave.

She got into the passenger seat, Skip got in the back, and Rayna got behind the wheel.

"There are some papers in my grandfather's old desk," Rayna told Julia. "I'll go through them tonight to see if there's anything helpful there."

"That would be great," Julia said. "If you find anything, give me a call, will you? We'd rather you tell us about it without Christian and Roy hearing at the same time."

"Okay," Rayna said. "See you tomorrow."

"Anything else for now?" Meredith asked after the Clarkes had left.

"I think that's it. I'll see you in the morning." Julia watched her drive away and then headed toward home.

"I'm back," she called as soon as she came through the door. "Beau?"

She looked into the living room, but his chair was empty.

"Beau, are you home?"

It wasn't like him to just leave and not say anything. She stepped out into the yard and called again, but still there was no answer. She had just gone back inside when the front door opened.

"Beau," she said, smiling. "I was wondering where you'd gone." Her smile faded at the troubled expression on his face. "What's wrong?"

"Bunny's gone."

Chapter Nine

"WHAT DO YOU MEAN BUNNY'S gone?" Julia asked. "Are you sure?"

"I've looked all over the house and outside for over an hour," Beau said miserably.

"She's got to be somewhere," Julia said. "When did you see her last?"

"When she was playing with that catnip mouse of hers, before you got home. I don't remember seeing her after that."

"You didn't go outside around that time, did you?" she asked him.

"No, I'm sure I didn't. I was reading my book till you got home."

She mentally retraced her steps from the time she had come in from work. There wasn't much to remember. She had made a salad for dinner while Beau fixed sandwiches. She had freshened her makeup and hair. She had gone out to get—

She squeezed her eyes shut as she remembered. The mail. Had she shut the door behind her? She couldn't remember. She remembered locking it after she came back inside, but had that been too late?

There was pain and pleading in Beau's eyes. She loved Bunny dearly, but Bunny and Beau had a special bond. How was she going to tell him it might be her fault that the cat was gone?

"We've got to keep looking," she said. "Maybe she has a hiding place we don't know about."

"I tried everything. I shook her bag of treats. I even opened a can of tuna. She never came out." He mopped his face with one hand. "She's gone."

"Oh, Beau."

Julia wanted to cry. She'd have to tell him what she'd done, but she couldn't do it right now. They'd just have to find Bunny, and then nothing else would matter.

"I'll get her bag of treats, and we'll look around outside again," Julia said with what she was sure was an unconvincing smile. "You know how she is. Just one little rustle of that bag and she comes running."

After a fruitless search, Beau put his arm around her, looking as miserable as she felt. "Come on. It's getting late. We'll put a bowl of food out for her. That ought to bring her back, don't you think?"

Julia nodded. She couldn't tell him. She knew she ought to, but she couldn't make herself do it. Tomorrow. Tomorrow, no doubt, Bunny would be outside the door before the sun was up, yowling to be let in.

They left out a bowl of cat food liberally laced with treats and then reluctantly went inside. Julia tried to make small talk as they watched television, mostly telling Beau how the meeting had gone, but neither of them had much to say. Every once in a while, he would jump up and go to the door to see if any of the cat food had been eaten.

It was late when they finally went to bed. Julia prayed that God would send Bunny home quickly and watch out for her while she was away. And she prayed that Beau would forgive her for being careless enough to let the cat get out and for being too much of a coward to admit it.

***

It was barely dawn when Beau slipped out of bed. She heard the faint rattle of the front blinds and knew he was looking outside.

"Honey," he called to her, his voice low. "Honey, come quick."

She got up and padded into the living room, but by the time she got to the window, he had turned around.

"Never mind," he said, shaking his head.

She looked out onto the porch and caught a glimpse of something gray and furry hunched over the cat food bowl stuffing itself. Her heart leaped, and then she realized why Beau had been disappointed.

"A raccoon." She went to him and gave him a hug. "I'm sorry. I guess we have no way of knowing if Bunny came back during the night and ate something."

"No telling," he said. "I'm going to get dressed."

He went into the bathroom, and she sank down into the chair next to the bed. She felt worse this morning than she had last night. What could they do now besides wait for Bunny to come home?

"We can put up signs," she suggested as she and Beau sat over their breakfast of oatmeal with a side of fresh fruit. "We can offer a reward for her. Somebody will find her."

Beau gave her what she was sure was supposed to be an encouraging smile. "That's a good idea. She can't have gone too far yet. I'll make some flyers and put them out around the neighborhood. And I'll keep looking."

She squeezed his hand. "I wish I could stay home and help you, but I have to meet the Clarkes at the bank at ten, and before that I need to go into the office and look up a few things. All those Russian names Christian Kirkland-Wright was tossing out there ought to be easy to research. And I need to see if we can find a Russian translator for that letter he gave us a copy of."

"I understand," he said. "You've got a lot of obligations to take care of. I'll see what I can do while you're gone."

"Oh, Beau." She got up and went to him, putting her arms around him from behind and pressing her cheek to his. "I wish I could spend the day with you and look too. I hate it that she got out."

He shook his head. "It was an accident. You know how sneaky she is. How many times has she gotten locked in a closet or closed in a drawer because we didn't see her get in?"

"I know. But we've got to get her back." She brightened suddenly. "I just thought of something. She was microchipped when we adopted her. If somebody finds her and gets her scanned, they'll know she belongs to us."

"Right," he said. "That's right. In the meantime I'll keep looking for her."

"Text me if you find her, okay?" Julia said. "I don't care what I'm doing. I want to know."

She felt bad as she left the house, bad for not staying to help him, bad for not being there to comfort him, bad for not telling him what she had done. But all the guilt in the world wasn't going to bring Bunny back.

"I'm sorry," Meredith said when, as they shared coffee in Meredith's office, Julia told her about Bunny. "But her collar has your phone number on it, doesn't it?"

Julia winced. "We have a tag with our phone number on it, but Bunny wasn't wearing her collar."

"What?"

"She's an indoor cat. We weren't planning on her going out."

Julia shrugged helplessly.

"I know this is upsetting for you," Meredith said, "and scary too, but accidents happen. It's nobody's fault."

"No, that's not true. Not in this case."

"What do you mean?"

In spite of Julia's attempt to hold them back, hot tears welled up in her eyes.

"I'm afraid I let her out when I got the mail yesterday."

"Oh no. Are you sure?"

Julia wiped her eyes. "No. I didn't see her get out. I've tried to think about it over and over, and I can't be sure that she didn't get out then."

Meredith bit her lip. "What did Beau say about that?"

"I haven't told him yet."

"Maybe you'd feel better if you talked to him about it," Meredith suggested.

"I'm hoping she'll be back by the time I get home this afternoon, and then it won't be an issue."

"You don't think he'll be mad at you, do you? Beau?"

"No," Julia admitted. "I don't think so, but he's awfully upset."

"That's why you should talk to him about it," Meredith urged.

Julia squeezed her eyes shut and rubbed her forehead. "I'll think about it. Right now, though, I've got to put that out of my mind and deal with the Clarke case. I need to do some research on the place where Alexis Voronin ended up when the hurricane hit the Sea Islands in 1893."

"Wasn't that area mostly inhabited by formerly enslaved people trying to start their own independent farms?" Meredith asked.

"I don't know. That's part of what I need to find out."

"I don't know much about it myself, but I've always had the impression that it was a fairly poor area until the resorts moved in." Meredith jotted down a few notes of her own. "Seems an odd place for a Russian nobleman to be back then."

"Right," Julia said. "If he was here, why was he here?"

"I can do a little checking on that, if you like," Meredith said. "I can trace this countess down to your English duke and see if I can find evidence that their family actually is in possession of the larger egg."

"The Renaissance Egg. It ought to be fairly well documented, even if the Resurrection Egg is considered lost."

"I thought I'd track down a translator for us and verify that."

"Good idea. Okay," Julia said, getting to her feet. "I've got to tackle a couple of things before we meet Christian and the Clarkes at the bank."

"I'll see what I can find out too." Meredith's expression softened. "And try not to worry too much about Bunny. I'll be praying that she'll come home. And then you and Beau can talk."

Julia went to her office, scanned the Russian letter Christian had given her the night before, and saved it in the Clarke file. Then she found a translator and forwarded a copy to her.

Before long, it was time to head to the bank.

"We'll be back around lunchtime," Julia told Carmen on their way out. "We'll call you if that changes."

"Have a good time," Carmen said mischievously.

Julia rolled her eyes. A good time was at the bottom of the list of what she was expecting from her visit to Jean Clarke's bank.

Chapter Ten

MERIDIAN PREMIUM FINANCIAL WAS ABOUT a five-minute drive from the office, on Bay Street near the river. The Clarkes were waiting for Julia and Meredith inside the busy lobby.

"Good morning," Jean said brightly.

She wore a knit top with a string of pearls and was sitting in a green wingback chair. Her son and granddaughter were standing beside her. Skip looked as if he was wearing what he had slept in. Rayna, on the other hand, looked comfortable in slacks and a coordinated jacket with a silk blouse underneath.

"Good morning," Julia said. "How is everybody?"

"Eager to get this over with," Rayna said. "I'm getting more and more behind on my work."

"I meant to ask you before," Meredith said. "What kind of work do you do?"

"I'm a technical writer. I write manuals and process documentation and that sort of thing."

"Interesting," Julia said.

"I work remotely, which is great, but it means when I'm dealing with something like this during the day, I have to make up for it by working late at night."

"I'm sorry, honey," her grandmother said. "I know you have better things to do than see to my problems."

Rayna's eyes warmed. "Don't you worry, Nanny. I'm glad to help."

"You know," Skip said, "now that I'm here, I can take care of all this. I can drive Mom around and stuff."

Rayna put one hand on her hip, looking as if she couldn't decide if she was annoyed or amused by the offer. "How are you going to do that, Uncle Skip? You don't have a car."

"Well, I figured I could use yours while I'm in town. When you don't need it and everything. Like when you're working and it's just sitting in your garage."

Jean looked at her granddaughter uncertainly. "It might be a little more convenient for you, Rayna. I mean, if you didn't have to help me all the time. I don't like to be a bother."

Rayna shook her head. "I'm glad to do everything I can to take care of you, Nanny. You're not a bother. And I want to make sure everything goes right when you're dealing with business matters. It can be a little confusing sometimes, but I think between the two of us, we can figure it out."

Skip looked annoyed, but before he could make any objections, Christian Kirkland-Wright and Mr. Lumley came into the bank, accompanied by Roy Keller.

"We're not late, I hope," Roy said.

"Right on time," Julia told him.

"And ready to get going," Roy said.

"Quite," Christian said, glancing around the bank. "How do we go about seeing the egg?"

Jean got to her feet. "I'll have to show my ID and sign in, and then Mr. Jeffers will take me into the vault to get the box. Then we can all go into the little office they let me use when I need to see something I've put away here."

"Is there room for all of us?" Roy asked her.

She glanced at the seven people around her. "I think so, if no one minds standing."

They all followed her to one of the tellers, and she asked to see Mr. Jeffers. A moment later she was welcomed by a large, gray-haired man who exuded the professional trustworthiness of a physician or a clergyman.

"Mrs. Clarke, how are you?"

"Very well, thank you, Mr. Jeffers. I'd like to open my safe-deposit box."

"Ah," he said with a smile. "I thought you'd be back about that. I understand you've gone viral."

"Isn't it the most amazing thing? Anyway, I have several people who would like to have a look at my little treasure, if you don't mind helping me get my box. Could they wait for me in the office I usually go to?"

"If you'd like," Mr. Jeffers said. He nodded toward the rest of the group. "If all of you would please follow me, I'll show you where you can have some privacy, and then I'll take Mrs. Clarke into the vault."

The "little office" was no more than ten feet on either side. It had a pair of chairs in it and a small table and that was all.

"I expect Mrs. Clarke will want to sit down," Christian said once they were inside and Mr. Jeffers had taken his client away. "Would either of you like to take the other chair, Julia? Meredith?"

Meredith turned to Rayna. "Would you like to sit down?"

"Oh no, thank you. You go ahead."

"I don't mind," Skip said, plopping himself into the chair, "if nobody else wants to."

"I'm sorry," Rayna told Julia and Meredith with a touch of embarrassment and a disapproving glance at her uncle.

He blinked at her. "What?"

Julia only shook her head, trying to keep the amusement out of her eyes. Uncle Skip was quite a character.

Lumley was standing in the corner next to his employer, his sensibilities having clearly been offended, but Christian's expression, apart from a distinct coldness, was unchanged.

"Would you like me to ask for another chair, ladies?" he asked.

"Really, we're fine," Julia said.

He seemed to relax a little at that. "Have you two been in investigation very long?"

"Two years now," Meredith told him.

"It seems rather an exciting profession. Or ought I to say dangerous?"

"Sometimes a little touch-and-go," Meredith admitted. "But I've enjoyed it."

"And what about you?" he asked Rayna.

"She's a writer," Skip said.

Christian nodded appreciatively. "I've always admired writers. How they create people and places out of nothing quite amazes me."

"I'm not that kind of writer," Rayna said, blushing faintly. "I do technical writing, but I do write fiction sometimes. Not anything published though."

"I'm a businessman," Skip said, not waiting to be asked.

Christian kept his eyes on Rayna. "I see. What sort of business are you in?"

"Oh, I have a lot going on," Skip told him, "though right now I have to make sure I take care of my mom, see that she gets treated right. I'm sure you understand."

Christian looked at him, his expression mild but keen understanding in his eyes. "Naturally. No one likes to be taken advantage of."

Behind him, Mr. Lumley narrowed his eyes, no doubt appraising the upstart American with disapproval.

"But I have a lot of irons in the fire," Skip went on. "Lots of ideas that'll turn the world on its ear. Once I get them into production, you know."

"Of course," Christian said.

"That takes money, but I'm always on the lookout for somebody who isn't scared to take a chance on the next big thing. I mean, some of those start-ups forty or fifty years ago, you could have bought into cheap, and now those companies are worth billions."

Christian nodded. "Your ideas are that good then."

"All they need is a little cash to turn them into reality. Now, if my mother sells that egg of hers, she could—"

"Here it is," Jean said, her eyes alight as she carried the gray metal safe-deposit box into the room.

Mr. Jeffers escorted her to the table, waited for her to be seated, and then left them alone, shutting the door behind him. Everyone leaned in a little closer, their eyes on Jean as she put her key into the box's silver lock and turned it.

"I haven't needed this box much since my husband died," she said as she lifted the cover. "But I'm glad now that I have it. I would worry way too much if I had kept this at home. It seems everyone in the world knows it's here."

"She's had several calls about it," Rayna said. "And people have come by. Reporters and bloggers and I don't know who all. And then there are people we haven't heard from in years."

She fixed her eyes on Skip, but he was staring at the small package his mother had just taken from the box. Jean unwrapped the crystal egg and held it up.

"Ah," Christian said, smiling. "May I?"

"Oh, of course." Jean handed it to him.

"May we take some photographs?"

"Certainly."

Christian set the egg on the table and nodded at Lumley. Lumley took his phone from his pocket and began snapping pictures of it from all angles. Then he took out a ruler.

"If I may, madam," he said, making a slight bow to Jean.

She nodded, a little flustered.

"As I mentioned last night," Christian said, "we believe this could be the Resurrection Egg. I'd like to send these pictures and measurements to the man who tends to that sort of thing for my father to see if it would fit inside our Renaissance Egg."

"That seems like a smart thing to do." Julia looked at Rayna. "Don't you think?"

"And if it wouldn't fit?" Rayna asked Christian. "Would that end any claim your family might make on it?"

"We don't want to make any kind of statement on that ahead of time," Roy said before his client could answer. "Right now, we're all trying to uncover the facts in the case, aren't we?"

"That seems fair," Julia said on behalf of her clients. "Would it be possible for us to have a copy of those pictures and the measurements too?"

"We'd be happy to oblige," Christian said. "Would it be best to send them to the email address on your card, Julia? Or would you prefer we arrange to have physical copies delivered to your office?"

"Email would be fine. Thank you."

"Are you done?" Skip asked when Lumley slipped the ruler back into his pocket.

"Yes, sir," Lumley said with a hint of disdain in his clipped tone.

Skip grabbed the egg and whistled low between his teeth. "There's not much to it, but what's there is choice."

"Hand me those photos of the Renaissance Egg, if you would, Lumley," Christian said.

With a haughty glance at Skip, Lumley brought out copies of the pictures Christian had given Julia last night.

"Look at the enamel work on this one and on ours." Christian pointed out the base of the egg in the picture and the one Skip was holding. "Except for differences in scale, they look quite similar to me."

They were very alike in color and style, and the pearls set into the pedestal that held the crystal egg seemed a lot like the ones that were around the top half of the Kirkland-Wright egg. It was hard to tell from nothing more than a photo, but it did seem that the two eggs must be connected in some way. Julia didn't say that aloud though. It was far too early in the game to start giving away points to the other team.

"Might I have a look now?" Christian asked, holding out his hand to Skip. "If you've quite finished."

"Oh yeah. Sure."

Skip gave him the crystal egg, and Christian examined it closely.

"Lovely, isn't it? Really quite amazing. And to think it's been in your family all this while, Mrs. Clarke."

He spoke to the older woman, but his eyes were on the younger.

"We had no way of knowing it was there," Rayna said firmly.

"No, of course not." Christian handed the egg back to Jean. "I have no doubt of that in the least."

"Right," Julia said.

But, she wondered, who would end up with the egg?

Chapter Eleven

Willow clutched the side of the buggy as it jolted into yet another rut in the sludge-filled Beaufort street. She didn't know what she had expected to find here, but it wasn't this. Not a town full of nothing but mud, debris, and chaos. Refugees from the hurricane were crowded into whatever shelter they had been able to find.

The two weeks since the disaster had taken their homes and livelihoods had brought them little relief. Willow had seen several places swarmed with people—men, women, and children—being given a ration of the food and supplies that were available.

"One of the distribution centers," Elliot Sheffield said from the back of the tall bay mare, who picked her way daintily through the mud. His white linen suit was spattered with the stuff. "I understand there are several of them so far," he told Willow. "Your father and mine and several other gentlemen from Savannah have sent supplies out here. It doesn't seem like enough yet."

From his seat in the front of the buggy, Silas clutched the reins more tightly and frowned at him. "Just don't be saying anything about what we got with us yet, Mr. Elliot, or we'll never get it through to the hospital."

It had taken Willow a goodly amount of pleading and wheedling, and the threat that she would sneak out of her window in the middle of the night and go to Beaufort completely alone, to get her mother and father to give their grudging blessing on her mission to help the people injured by the hurricane. But they had given that blessing only under very precise conditions.

She had to go with Mrs. Cunningham's group of ladies, she had to let Silas drive her and stay to help in any way he could, and she had to allow Elliot Sheffield the privilege of being her knight and champion until she was brought safe home again. Both of her watchdogs, she was sure, had strict instructions to never show their faces in Savannah again if anything were to happen to her.

She was glad to have Silas with her. He was a touch of home in a strange place, and she knew she could count on him to be practical and levelheaded no matter what he ran into here in the Beaufort pandemonium. And, she admitted to no one but herself, it was good to have Elliot here too.

He had a genius for smoothing the way for her even when she wanted to do things he didn't really want her to do, things her mother claimed were scandalous. Oh, nothing truly scandalous, of course, just little things that weren't as quiet and demure as Mama expected of her. Like coming to Beaufort. It was an absolute miracle that she was even here at all, and she vowed to make the most of it. She vowed that, at least for a while, she would make her time count for something or someone besides herself.

"Just drive steady, Silas," Elliot said, keeping his voice low and even as they moved past a corner where a tattered group of men eyed them warily, as if they knew food and blankets were packed inside the buggy.

In the seat at Willow's side, there was a precious store of laudanum and bandages in a bag that was under her shawl, and if nothing else they brought got through to the hospital, that bag had to. Willow hadn't let it leave her sight the whole forty miles from Savannah.

Elliot had to stop a couple of times to ask directions to the hospital. When they finally arrived at the address, they found it wasn't a hospital at all but a three-story Georgian house with a hastily patched roof and upper windows that were mostly boarded up. Miss Cunningham was coming out the front door with a pail.

"Miss Brenton!" she cried, seeing the buggy. She pitched what looked like dirty water into the already-overflowing gutter. "You're the last to arrive. The others are getting settled. Come in."

"Hello, Miss Cunningham," Willow said as Elliot dismounted. He lifted her from the buggy, over the muddy curb, and onto the house's front step. "Thank you, Elliot. Miss Cunningham, this is Mr. Elliot Sheffield. Elliot, this is Miss Eliza Cunningham."

Miss Cunningham was, as her father had said, a lady of a certain age. Her blue eyes behind the wire-frame glasses were small and set close to her nose. What there was of her graying brown hair was set in a severe bun on the top of her head, but there was warmth, intelligence, and determination in her expression. Willow firmly believed there was nothing that Miss Cunningham couldn't do once she put her mind to it.

Elliot bowed. "Good afternoon, Miss Cunningham. I do believe we've met before."

"Why, yes, Mr. Sheffield, we have. It was at your mother's garden party some years ago when our ladies were raising funds for the widows and orphans of our fallen soldiers."

"It was indeed. I'm sent here to assist Miss Brenton in any way I am able, and I would like to extend that assistance to you and all your ladies while we are here."

"Thank you, sir, and God bless you. We can certainly use a gentleman's help with our poor unfortunates."

"And I brought Silas from home," Willow told her. "He's eager to help."

"Yes, ma'am, Miss Cunningham," Silas said as he got down from the buggy. "I'm ready to do whatever needs doing."

He wasn't exactly young anymore. His hair was a wreath of fluffy cotton against his dark skin, though Willow thought he was only somewhere in his fifties. She knew he would be a greater asset to the relief effort than the half dozen young ladies Miss Cunningham had brought with her.

"Beg pardon, Miss Cunningham," Silas said, taking the bag that Willow had been watching over, "but Mrs. Brenton told me to give this bag to nobody but you and nowhere but the hospital. It's mostly laudanum and some carbolic for infection, all we could get back in Savannah, and as much bandaging as would fit in there too."

"There's also as much food as we could pack in the buggy," Elliot added. "I have two wagonloads coming after us too."

"Oh, thank you." Miss Cunningham beamed at Silas as she took the bag from him. "Please come in. All of you. You haven't arrived a minute too soon."

The front parlor of the house had been turned into a ward with as many cots as possible stuffed into it. Every cot was full. Some of them, Willow saw, had more than one occupant in them. Some were mother and child, she assumed, and some contained two or three small children. All of them looked hungry, sick, and poor.

"It's terribly sad," Miss Cunningham said as they walked through the parlor and into what had been the dining room, which was also filled with ill and injured refugees. "So many of these men and women have come out of slavery. They've worked their small farms, and many of them had done very well. Now in a moment all of it is gone, not just the crops but the homes and the animals and even the people in their families." She forced a smile and moved quickly through to another large, patient-filled room. "Even some of those who tried to help have been killed or injured or have fallen ill.

Between the damage done by the storm and the overcrowding, the sanitation is atrocious."

Willow slowed for a moment as did the others with her, taking time to look around what must have been the home's grand ballroom. It was dominated by an enormous chandelier, and through the floor-to-ceiling windows that lined the back wall—the ones that weren't boarded up anyway—she could see what was left of a formal garden. A gazebo, roofless and broken, stood in its center, its one remaining trellis hanging by a few tenacious vines and swaying lazily in the breeze.

"Whose house is this?" she asked after a moment.

"It was left to the town by a widow who died this past winter. She had no family, and she put in her will that she wished her home to be used in some way that would benefit as many people as possible. The town council was planning to make the house into a meetinghouse and library, but the hurricane has set back that plan. It seemed only logical that it would be used now as a temporary hospital, especially since the real hospital is full up."

"And you're in charge here?" Elliot asked, his dark eyes full of admiration.

Miss Cunningham laughed. "Oh, good heavens, no! That would be Mrs. Murphy. She's head of the Ladies' Aid Society here, and she has a veritable army of workers all around the city. But she's made me one of her lieutenants. It's my job to keep all my young ladies"—she smiled at Willow and then at Elliot and Silas—"and gentlemen, of course, occupied in relieving those who are suffering, comforting the bereaved, and maintaining good spirits."

"I am at your command, ma'am," Elliot told her. "I may not have a gift for nursing, but I would be pleased to do all I can in the way of heavy work or in acquiring and distributing the necessary supplies. My father does business with a number of Savannah's wholesalers and large merchants. He told me to send him word of what is most needed here, and he will arrange to have it brought in."

"My father too," Willow said. "He's already sent some money, but if there's something in particular he can send, I know he will."

Miss Cunningham hugged her. "Oh, bless you. Bless you both. There's so much we need, I don't know where to start." She clutched the bag of medical supplies to her chest. "This is what we need most. I'll show you where the other girls are camped out. You'll be packed in with them like a sardine, and there are no cots up there, but I'm sure you can manage. And..." She glanced at Elliot and Silas and lowered her voice. "I'm sorry I had to tell you to not bring your lady's maid, but I trust you can manage your personal matters alone."

"I can," Willow said, though she knew very well it was going to be awkward until she got used to it.

Miss Cunningham beamed. "Excellent. There's not much room, certainly not for any nonessential personnel, but I think we can clear out a storeroom off the kitchen and lay down a nice pallet for you, Silas, if that will be agreeable."

"Yes, ma'am. That will be most kind. And I can do most any kind of work you need."

"Thank you. Mr. Sheffield, you may be a difficulty."

"Not at all, ma'am," Elliot said. "A blanket under a roof of any variety will suit me."

"Perhaps one of the local families could take you in. You'll be gone most of the day, and they wouldn't be required to give you your meals. So I think—"

"Forgive me, ma'am, but no. I appreciate your consideration, but I gave Mr. Brenton my solemn oath that I would look after his daughter, and that I mean to do. I can hardly do that if I'm asleep on the other side of town."

"Mr. Elliot, sir," Silas said, "you had best take that room off the kitchen. I can—"

"Nonsense," Elliot said. "I'm young enough that camping out is still an adventure. I spent almost two weeks last summer sleeping on the ground during a hunting trip, and it did me no end of good. And this time of year, I'll certainly be warm enough." He looked out into the garden. "What about there in the gazebo? I don't think it would take long to put a few boards up for a roof, and I wouldn't need much more. What do you think, Silas?"

Silas looked guiltily at Willow. "Now, I don't know, sir. It's hardly right—"

"Are you saying you won't lend me a hand?" There was a twinkle in Elliot's eyes. "Miss Willow, you'd best speak to him."

"No, sir," Silas said. "I'm not about to be contradictory with Miss Willow. I learned that lesson when she was about four years old."

"Then it's settled," Elliot said. "I saw plenty of spare lumber in the streets. I think we can find enough to make do."

Willow took his arm. "Thank you. You're always so nice."

"Your servant, Miss Willow," he said with a slight bow. "Always. Now I will leave you to settle into your boudoir. Silas, if you'll come along with me, we'll see if the wagons have arrived and, if not, find some wood for my little palace."

"First things first," Miss Cunningham said, holding up her hand. "We need the things in the storeroom moved into the kitchen and stacked up wherever else we can find so we can lay out a bed. Miss Brenton, you go on up to the attic. My young ladies are all at the top of the second flight of stairs under the dormer windows. I'll send Miss Denning to help you get settled. Tell her to take one of the blankets from my bed and one from the wash that's hanging outside."

"I won't need that," Willow told her. "I brought my own bedding from home. We all did."

She didn't admit that it was her mother who had insisted on that, having heard more than once Uncle Reynold and Uncle Kit's tales of wartime and hospital lice.

"Excellent. Good thinking." Miss Cunningham looked around and leaned in confidentially. "You'd be surprised, after all I said during our meetings back in Savannah, how many of my young ladies came with nothing but a variety of dainty outfits more suited to a barbecue or afternoon tea. Miss Trelawney actually brought a ball gown."

"Oh my," Willow said, glad she had packed nothing but two everyday skirts and three plain blouses with her.

Miss Cunningham harrumphed. "Don't think I didn't have her send it right back home. Now come along."

Silas carried in Willow's bag, and then he and Elliot went with Miss Cunningham to clear a place in the storeroom. Willow made her way up the stairs and was met along the way by Victoria Denning, a rather wispy blond she knew from church.

"Victoria, how good to see you. I'm so glad to finally be here."

Victoria hugged her dutifully. "Isn't it terrible? So many people crammed into such a small space. There'll be six of us now packed into a place not larger than my maid's closet."

"The good thing is we won't be spending much time there." Willow was determined to be cheerful as she continued up the second and far-narrower stairway that would take her to the attic room. "Just while we sleep."

"Don't expect much of that either. There's always something needs doing."

"That's why they need us, isn't it?"

Miss Cunningham hadn't been far wrong when she mentioned sardines. Three sets of bedding filled one end of the narrow room, side by side with no room in between. On the other end, there were two, but Victoria helped Willow move them to one side so her own could be fitted in. As far as Willow could tell, their feet were meant to be turned toward the center of the room, and there was only enough space for a narrow walkway in between.

"*How are we meant to dress in the morning?*" *she asked as she set her bag on top of her blankets.*

"*One at a time,*" *Victoria said.* "*And there's a pitcher and basin down in the kitchen for us to use.*"

"*What about the rest of the attic? Doesn't it go over the whole house?*"

"*That's where Mrs. Murphy and her ladies stay, and then there's storage at one end. I haven't been in there, but Caroline Hamilton says they're packed in worse than we are.*"

Willow bit her lip, determined not to complain, determined not to be intimidated. This is what she had wanted. She could do this. Lord, help me do this.

"*Come on,*" *she said.* "*We're not such helpless ninnies that we can't do what needs to be done. Look at Miss Cunningham. She's ever so much older than we are, and she never seems to run out of energy.*" *She took Victoria's arm and turned her to the stairs.* "*We might as well get started.*"

Miss Cunningham caught them just as they got to the bottom of the grand stairway.

"*There you are. Now, Silas is settled in the storeroom, and he's gone with Mr. Sheffield to bring in the things from the wagons and see to your horse and buggy. Victoria, I need you to go see to Mrs. Davis and her baby. I know the little one needs changing and feeding. I already warmed the milk.*"

"*Yes, ma'am,*" *Victoria said meekly, and she hurried away.*

"*Willow, come with me. I have a patient who needs constant watching right now. Dr. LeClaire says he may have a skull fracture. Effie Taylor's been sitting with him since four this morning, and she really must have some sleep."*

"Oh yes, certainly," Willow said. "What do I need to do?"

Miss Cunningham led her to a small room at the back of the house. Willow thought perhaps it had been someone's office at one time. Now, it housed five male patients. All were asleep except for one. Effie, a young woman Willow also knew from church, was nodding off in a ladder-back chair.

Miss Cunningham looked them all over, her expression cheerful and searching all at once.

"Good day, Miss Cunningham," *the man said in a low voice, the crinkles around his old eyes deepening as he smiled.* "I don't want to wake Miss Effie."

"How are you today, Mr. James?"

"Not too poorly, ma'am. I'm thinking I ought to give up this bed to somebody as needs it."

"Not yet, Mr. James. When the doctor says you may."

"Well, I could—"

"Not yet. You lie down and let those ribs heal, you hear?"

"Yes, ma'am, I will." *Mr. James winced as he lay back on his cot.* "But if you need this bed, you just say."

"All right. Mr. James, this is Miss Brenton. She's come to help us now."

"Hello, Mr. James," Willow said. "I hope you're well soon."

"Thank you, miss. Thank you kindly."

"She's going to look after our Russian gentleman," *Miss Cunningham said,* "so Miss Effie can rest a while."

Mr. James nodded. "Miss Effie tried hard to stay awake, ma'am, but it was more than she could manage."

"That's all right." Miss Cunningham gave Effie's shoulder a gentle shake. "Come along now, dear. It's time you went up to bed for a spell."

Effie started awake and pushed back the twist of brown hair that had fallen down her neck, her hazel eyes blinking in confusion. "Oh, Miss Cunningham!" She leaped to her feet and then grabbed the back of the chair to steady herself. "I—I didn't mean to fall asleep."

"It's all right." Miss Cunningham looked over the muscular, black-mustached man on the cot beside her. "He seems to be resting well for now. Go on upstairs."

Effie nodded and then seemed to notice Willow for the first time. "Oh, Willow. I'm so glad you're here."

The two girls embraced.

"We'll talk more when you've gotten a chance to sleep," Willow told her. "I want to hear about everything. Oh, and Elliot's here too. Mama and Papa wouldn't let me come without him."

"Good. There's so much to do." Effie smiled sleepily. "I'll see you soon."

"Now," Miss Cunningham said once Effie was gone, "you'll be in charge of this room. Mostly you need to watch over Mr. Voronin and come get me if anything changes. And if any of our other patients need anything, you'll be the one to get it."

Willow stared at her, bewildered. She was going to be left to care for a room full of men with no more instruction than that?

"Don't worry, dear," Miss Cunningham said, pulling out the chair for her. "Just come get me if you don't know what to do. I'll check on you after I've made sure Victoria has changed Mrs. Davis's baby. If the bottle is ready, I might have you feed him. Can you do that?"

"Yes, ma'am," Willow said.

She had fed her cousin's baby last Christmas. She hoped this one didn't cry as much. She didn't want to wake all these injured men.

Miss Cunningham patted her shoulder as she left the room, and Willow sat down next to the cot that held the man with the black mustache. The Russian gentleman, Miss Cunningham had called him. She thought as she looked at him that, despite his heavy mustache, he was younger than she had first assumed. Maybe only a little older than herself.

He was a handsome man, unlike any she had ever seen, unlike any of the young men she knew. This seemed an odd place to find a foreigner, especially one from so far away. How had he ended up in a hurricane off the South Carolina coast? And what would she do if he or any of these men took a sudden turn for the worse?

"Please don't die," she said under her breath. "Don't die."

Chapter Twelve

"I ALREADY HEARD FROM THE translator," Carmen said when Julia got back to the office. She handed Julia a printout of an email. "It looks just about the same."

"Just about?" Julia asked her.

"*Más o menos*," Carmen replied. "More or less. Like here, he says part of the enamel is red. The translation on the back says crimson. Near enough, sí?"

"Near enough," Julia agreed, scanning the email and then looking over the one from the photograph again. "I'd say this is a reliable translation. Thanks for taking care of this. Anything else I should know about?"

Carmen handed her some messages, and Julia took them into Meredith's office.

"Any luck on the Russian countess?" she asked, sitting down.

"A little." Meredith pushed a page of notes and a couple of printouts across the desk to her. "There was definitely a Countess Katarina Radulov. She had no children, and her sister had two sons, Nikolai and Alexis Voronin. Nikolai's great-great-great-grandson is Christian Kirkland-Wright, whose father is William, Duke of Preston."

"Okay, so far Christian's batting a thousand. Any support for the czarina giving the countess the Renaissance Egg with or without the surprise inside?"

"That's less obvious so far," Meredith said. "The countess was a member of the court and, it seems, a friend of the royal family, so there's that. And Carmen told me that the translation of her letter backs up the story that she had the Resurrection Egg."

"Seems to."

Julia took her phone out of her purse, checked it for messages, and then sighed.

"What's wrong?" Meredith asked.

"Oh, nothing. I was hoping Beau had texted me."

"Why don't you call him?"

"I did on my way here, but it went to his voice mail. He must be out looking for Bunny."

"Wouldn't he take his phone with him?"

"Most of the time he would," Julia said, "but he might not have thought about it if he was only going to walk around the neighborhood."

She stared through Meredith's office windows, deliberately turning her thoughts to what her next steps ought to be in finding out who owned the egg. But, despite her best efforts, her mind went back to Bunny and Beau.

With Bunny's street smarts, surely she knew how to take care of herself. But that wouldn't protect her from other animals or mean people or any number of accidents. That wouldn't make Julia feel any better if Bunny never came home.

"Julia?"

She started and then smiled. "Sorry. I guess I was miles away."

Meredith's eyes were kind. "Why don't you go home? I know you're worried about Bunny. And about Beau."

Julia shook her head. "Beau can handle it. There's nothing I can do about Bunny that he can't, and I've got work to do." She stood up. "I'm going to see if I can find out more about Rayna's family, especially Willow, her great-great-grandmother. I'd like to learn more about her activities at the time Alexis Voronin was in this area and if they may have met."

"If she was upper-class," Meredith said, "they could have met at any number of social functions. Those ought to be in the society pages of the newspaper."

"Especially if there was a mysterious Russian nobleman attending. I'd like to find pictures if I can too."

"Have you mentioned this to Maggie Lu?" Meredith asked. "She discovers some pretty amazing things given enough time."

"I have her on the lookout for anything she can find. I was hoping, by some miracle, that she'd come up with something before our meeting last night, but I guess she didn't. I'll call her back and tell her what Christian Kirkland-Wright had to say, and that you've verified at least his family history. I'll let you know what I discover."

"Good luck," Meredith called after her as she went down the hallway to her own office.

Julia buried herself in research, and the afternoon went quickly. It was nearly five when she came back into Meredith's office with her notes.

"Look at this."

She showed Meredith a picture she had printed from an ancestry website. It was of a petite young woman with a sweet face and wide brown eyes. She wore a dress of white silk and lace, and a long lace veil covered her curling dark hair. She cradled a sheaf of white roses in one arm. Her other arm was curled around the elbow of her groom, a lanky-looking young man with gentle eyes and brown hair parted in the middle and curling at his stiff collar. He wore a black cutaway coat, a white silk waistcoat, and a white bow tie, and carried a stovepipe hat.

"Who are they?" Meredith asked.

"That is Mr. and Mrs. Elliot Sheffield on their wedding day, June 2, 1894."

"Very nice. And they are?"

"They are the great-great-grandparents of our client, Rayna Clarke. And Mrs. Sheffield, the former Willow Brenton, is the person who once owned the box the Resurrection Egg was hidden in."

"1894?" Meredith frowned. "And when was the hurricane?"

"That was on August 27, 1893. It's possible that the box was passed down to her at some point before that, or she could have had it made especially for the egg. But it doesn't seem likely that she could have had the egg before Alexis Voronin brought it with him out of Russia, and that was in the spring of 1893, according to the countess's letter."

"Dated?" Meredith asked, looking at her own notes.

"March 19," Julia supplied, checking the email of the translation Carmen had gotten for her. "So sometime after that but before he died in the hurricane, he must have met Willow Brenton and given her the egg."

"Or she took it."

"I guess that's a possibility. Though it seems from everything I've found so far she was from a wealthy family. It doesn't seem likely that a young upper-class lady would steal, especially a religious icon. I mean, if I were going to steal something, it wouldn't be that."

"It does seem like a bad idea," Meredith agreed. "So how do you think she would have gotten it?"

Julia set one elbow on Meredith's desk and then leaned her chin on her fist. "There aren't that many possibilities. He gave it to her. He sold it to her. She stole it from him. She found it and didn't know who it belonged to. She found it and decided to keep it and not search for its real owner." She raised one eyebrow. "Somebody else found it or stole it and hid it in her box, and she never knew it was there."

"That last one is an interesting theory. That could explain why it sat there all those years and nobody ever tried to sell it or display it or anything."

"Going by the deed records I found for the family, it looks like they had a downturn in their fortunes in the early 1900s. They could have used a windfall like that egg, if only they had known it was there."

"Christian didn't say it was ever reported stolen or anything?"

"No," Julia said. "At least not that he told me. We can ask him if he's sure Alexis had the egg until his death."

"That might be hard to prove or disprove." Meredith tapped the rim of her coffee cup with her pencil, thinking. "Maybe he wrote to his aunt or his mother or brother and told them the egg had been lost or stolen? It seems likely that Mr. Kirkland-Wright would have supplied that piece of proof if he had it."

"Exactly. They've maintained all along that Alexis had the egg until the hurricane and it was lost then."

"You don't suppose someone could have taken it off his body." Julia shuddered. "I hope not."

"Me too. You didn't find any information about how he died, did you?"

"No, not yet. That's something else we need to ask Christian. If they knew Alexis died in the hurricane, someone must have written to the family at some point. Maybe he can get us a copy of that letter or at least a reference to it."

"That would be helpful." Meredith checked her watch. "I'm sorry to have to leave you with this, but I have to go."

Julia gave her a knowing glance. "Quin?"

Meredith nodded. Quin Crowley was a local attorney, Beau's sometime golf partner, and Meredith's boyfriend. Julia didn't know of any serious plans between them, but she couldn't help hoping there would be.

"Well, you two have fun," she said, and then she felt a sudden weight drop into the pit of her stomach. She was going to have to go home now too.

Meredith must have seen the dread she was feeling.

"Are you going to talk to Beau?"

"Oh, I don't know. Maybe Bunny's home by now."

"He'd have called, wouldn't he?"

Meredith was right. He would have called.

Julia gathered up everything from the Clarke case and put it back into the file. "I'll let you know if there's any news. Tell Quin I said hi."

"Sure," Meredith said. "Call me, okay?"

"Yeah, okay."

Julia checked her schedule for the next day, and then she went home. She found Beau on the front porch with a bag of kitty treats. He didn't appear as if he had good news.

"Nothing?" she asked, coming to stand beside him and looking out at the trees and hedges in their neighbors' yards.

Beau shook his head.

Julia felt a prayer well up inside her aching heart. *Send her home. Please send her home.*

She took a deep breath. "Why don't I fix us some dinner, and then we can look some more, okay?"

"I've walked all around," Beau said as he followed her inside. "I put up signs wherever they'd let me."

He showed her what he had printed out. It was a picture of Bunny lounging on the couch, and beneath it in large letters was written, MISSING. FEMALE TABBY CAT, NINE YEARS OLD, CHIPPED. NAME BUNNY. REWARD. Beau's cell phone number was listed below that.

"Nothing yet," he added.

"We'll keep trying."

They ate in front of the TV. Julia could tell Beau wasn't much in the mood to talk, and neither was she. They caught each other up on how the day had gone, she gave him an update on the Clarke case, and that was pretty much it. Once they had eaten, they cleaned up the kitchen and then went back outside. The sun was going down, streaking the sky with oranges and purples, and throwing long shadows from trees and houses.

"She could be anywhere," Beau said, and he shook the bag of treats again. "Bunny!"

They took a slow walk around the block, searching every shadow and corner, talking to anyone they saw on the street or in front of a house. Everyone was sympathetic and promised to look out for Bunny, but none of them had seen her.

"It takes only a second for a pet to get out," Beau said as they reached the house again. "A second or two of letting your guard down, and then it's too late."

"It doesn't take much," Julia agreed.

Maybe this was the perfect opening. She could tell him what she had done. He would know it was an accident.

They stopped on the porch, taking one last look around, and then went inside.

"I thought if she ever got out, she wouldn't go far," Beau said, and he got himself a bottle of Cheerwine from the refrigerator and sat down at the table. "I can't believe she's gone. Just like that."

Tears burned behind Julia's eyes. "Beau, I'm so sorry. I think I must have—"

"No, now, we can't worry about how it happened at this point. She's out, that's all we know and that's all that matters. We'll just have to keep looking until we find her."

He was right. She knew he was. But why did she still feel so guilty?

Chapter Thirteen

JULIA WAS EARLY GETTING TO the office the next morning, meaning to start to work on the list of things she needed to accomplish. But so far all she had done was sit and stare at her coffee cup. Who was she kidding? She had left early because she didn't want to stay home knowing how disappointed Beau was that Bunny had still not returned. She didn't want to deal with her own disappointment. Her own worry. Her own guilt. Better to keep her eyes on business.

Carmen hadn't arrived yet when the phone rang. Julia picked it up on the first ring.

"Magnolia Investigations."

"Is this Julia?"

Julia paused for a moment, trying to place the voice she was sure she had heard before, and then it clicked.

"Rayna. Good morning. What can I do for you?"

"I'm sorry to bother you so early," Rayna said. "Actually, I didn't expect anyone to answer. I was going to leave a message."

"Is everything all right? You sound a little flustered."

Rayna huffed. "Mad, more like."

"What happened?"

"Uncle Skip tried to get the egg out of my grandmother's safe-deposit box yesterday afternoon."

"You're kidding." Julia had to force herself not to laugh at the man's brazenness. "What was he thinking?"

"He told Nanny that he wanted to make sure he couldn't get it out. You know, like a test of the bank's security."

"He said that?"

"That was after Mr. Jeffers called Nanny and told her what happened. Uncle Skip had helped himself to her key and thought he could open her box because he's her son. They turned him down, of course. Now Uncle Skip is trying to make Nanny sign something that says he can get into the box anytime he wants. So far I have her convinced that's a bad idea, but I can't promise that will last long. He's always been good at talking her into things."

"Did she get the key back?"

"Yes," Rayna said. "As a matter of fact, I have it now. I convinced her it would be safer with me and that she didn't want to be held responsible if the egg ended up belonging to the Duke of Preston and it was missing. She was terrified that she'd have to pay for it."

Julia chuckled. "I don't think all of us together could afford that."

"That's why I'm calling. I want to ask your opinion about something."

"Sure."

"Is there any reason I shouldn't put the egg in my own safe-deposit box?"

Julia thought for a moment. "Do you bank at the same place your grandmother does?"

"No. And I don't have a box either, but I could get one. What do you think?"

"Your uncle doesn't know where you bank?"

"I'm sure he doesn't," Rayna said. "Nanny doesn't even know."

Julia thought a moment longer. "Do you think your grandmother would agree to that?"

"That's why I wanted to get ahold of you as soon as possible. She's pretty upset with Uncle Skip right now for taking her key, but he's already working on her like he always does, telling her he didn't mean any harm and that he was only trying to make sure the egg was safe, and all the other garbage he tries to pull on her. I think if I can ask her about it this morning, she would agree."

"She did seem a little nervous about being responsible for the egg," Julia said. "Maybe that wouldn't be a bad idea at all."

"Would we have to let Mr. Kirkland-Wright know about it?"

"Not necessarily, unless you'd like to let him know it's been moved and that it's in a secure place."

"Okay," Rayna said. "Um, one other thing."

"Yes?"

"I don't like moving something that valuable on my own...."

"You want me to go with you? Sure, I can do that. Let me know what time, and I'll be there. Not a problem."

Rayna exhaled. "Thank you. I'll talk to Nanny and then call you back."

After she hung up, Julia got herself a fresh cup of coffee and started doing more research on Willow Brenton and Alexis Voronin.

There was a mention of an Alexis Voronin in the New York papers, describing him enjoying the city's nightlife. That article said he had recently come from Montreal, so she checked the Canadian

papers too, and found another mention there that included his connection to the Russian royal family.

When she turned up nothing else on Alexis, she moved on to
Willow and found "the charming Miss Brenton" mentioned in an
1892 article about a cotillion held by the mayor of Savannah and his
wife. Another article, one detailing the good works of a local mission, noted that among the ladies who donated their handwork
included "the daughter of Lucas Brenton, local financier." And there
was a photograph showing a semicircle of young ladies in white
dresses standing in front of the fountain in Forsyth Park at a city-
wide picnic in honor of Independence Day. "Miss Willow Brenton"
was the dark-eyed girl third from the left holding a lace parasol.

Then Julia struck gold. She found an article titled "Angels of
Mercy Minister to Hurricane Victims."

*A number of our Savannah belles have laid down their dance
cards and ivory fans and taken up bandages and medicine bot-
tles. A small group of young ladies, encouraged by Miss Eliza
Cunningham, a member of the First Baptist Church, have traveled to Beaufort, South Carolina, our neighbor to the north, to
bring aid to the thousands suffering from the effects of the devastating hurricane that destroyed so many homes and farms in the
Sea Islands.*

*The young ladies, Miss Janet Weekes, Miss Elsie Newman,
Miss Caroline Hamilton, Miss Victoria Denning, Miss Effie Taylor, and Miss Willow Brenton, have gone to assist Miss Cunningham under the larger efforts of Mrs. Reba Murphy of the Beaufort
Ladies' Aid Society and the many medical doctors who have*

volunteered their time and skill to help those in need. Mr. Elliot R. Sheffield, son of wholesaler, E. B. Sheffield, has also offered his aid to the mission.

Miss Cunningham invites anyone of good character and with a willingness to work to join her party and, failing that, to donate any amount of money or goods to ease those who are suffering and to help her and her ladies do as much good as they are able. Donations may be taken to the First Baptist Church, Bull Street.

Julia hurried into Meredith's office, grinning from ear to ear. "She was a volunteer."

Meredith blinked at her. "Excuse me?"

"Willow Brenton. She was a volunteer in the relief effort in Beaufort after the hurricane. She went with a group of ladies from her church to take care of the injured, and Elliot Sheffield went too."

Julia handed Meredith a printout of the article.

"Wow," Meredith said, scanning it. "That could certainly explain her connection to Alexis Voronin. Did you find anything about him yet?"

"Nothing but a couple of mentions, though that reminds me. I need to contact Christian about any information he has on Alexis's death. That would help a lot." Julia glanced at her watch and saw that it was nearly eleven. "Huh," she said.

"What?" Meredith asked.

"Rayna was supposed to check with her grandmother about moving the egg, and I thought she would have called me back by now."

"Moving it? Why?"

Julia told Meredith about Skip trying to get the egg from the bank.

Meredith rolled her eyes.

"I'd better call Rayna and see what the plan is."

"Would you like me to see if I can find anything else on Alexis?" Meredith asked.

"Yeah, if you would. That would be a big help. I'll be back."

Julia went into her office and called Rayna.

"Hey, I was about to call you," Rayna said. "I'm over at Nanny's right now, and we've been discussing moving the egg. She'd like to talk to you about it."

"All right," Julia said. "Put her on."

"Julia. How are you?" Jean sounded a little breathless. "I'm so sorry to bother you about this."

"It's no bother," Julia told her. "The reason Rayna hired me is to help you get through this with as little trouble as possible. She said she talked to you about putting the egg in her bank."

"Yes, and I want to make sure you think that's the right thing to do. I know so little about this kind of thing, and I don't want to make a mistake."

"I don't think it would be a mistake," Julia assured her. "Rayna told me about what your son tried to do."

"Well, yes," Jean said uncertainly. "That did bother me quite a bit, but I think he was only trying to help. After all, it would be a terrible thing if the egg was actually stolen. He's made me feel better about the bank having strong safeguards in place."

Julia forced herself not to give her opinion on what Skip had done. No doubt Rayna had already been over that in spades with her grandmother.

"Yes, their systems are usually very safe," Julia said. "But since you don't want to have anything happen to the egg, especially if it turns out that it doesn't belong to you, I think it's a good idea to put it somewhere safe. Do you feel comfortable having Rayna put it in her bank?"

"Oh yes. She and I already talked about that and about her getting a safe-deposit box. I told her she should have one anyway. I'm just the tiniest bit worried about carrying the egg from one bank to the other, but Rayna says you'll go with us."

"I'll be happy to do that. I do think it's a good idea. Even people who mean well can sometimes be led astray by something as magnificent as a Fabergé egg."

Jean was silent for a moment, and then she said, "Yes, I think it's not right to tempt people past what they can bear. Let's put it in Rayna's bank, and then I won't worry about anyone being bothered about it. Yes."

"Good. Now when do we want to do this?"

"I'll let you talk to Rayna about that, all right? She's much better at the practical things than I am, and I'm busy only on Mondays, unless I have to see the doctor about something. Here's Rayna."

"Julia," Rayna said after a moment's delay. "We're set then? I already discussed it with my bank manager, and he can meet with us at four this afternoon, if that's all right."

"That should be fine. Meanwhile, I'm going to call Christian and see if I can get some more information about his Russian ancestor who he claims was the last legal owner of the egg. What time would you like to meet this afternoon?"

"Would three thirty work? My bank is only about ten minutes from Nanny's."

"That'll be perfect. I'll be there."

Julia hung up and then dialed the number she had for Christian. Someone picked up on the second ring.

"Good morning."

"Hello," Julia said. "I'm trying to reach Mr. Kirkland-Wright."

"May I say who's calling?"

"This is Julia Foley from Magnolia Investigations."

"I'm sorry, ma'am, but His Lordship is out attending to some business matters at the moment. This is Lumley speaking. May I leave a message for you?"

"Yes, please, Mr. Lumley. Let him know that I have some questions I'd like to ask him about Alexis Voronin as soon as possible."

"I'll give him your message right away, ma'am," Lumley said. "Can he reach you at the number you gave him last night?"

"That's the best one, even after hours."

"Very good, ma'am. I will tell him. Good morning."

Julia ended the call. She'd feel better when the egg was in Rayna's bank, out of Skip's reach.

She got to the bank at about twenty-five minutes after three, glad that the drizzling rain had stopped. The Clarkes were just coming up to the door. All three of them.

"Hello, Jean," Julia said. "Rayna. Skip, what a surprise."

Skip gave her a little smirk. "I want to make sure Mom's safe while this is going on."

Jean gazed at him adoringly. "He hasn't left my side all afternoon."

"Yeah," Rayna deadpanned. "So brave of him. It had to be pretty risky for you to be in your own home in the middle of no danger whatsoever."

"Now, honey," her grandmother said, not quite scolding.

"I thought you didn't want your uncle knowing where your bank is," Julia said to Rayna in a low voice as they entered the lobby.

Rayna scowled. "I was outvoted."

"Well, let's get this taken care of," Julia said cheerfully to everyone. "Before it starts raining again."

"Yes," Rayna said, her expression softening. "I'll feel better when I don't have to worry about this."

"I don't know why you have to move the thing anyway," Skip said as they walked up to one of the tellers. "I already proved that it's safe here."

"It's for the best," Jean assured him. "We'll all worry less."

Skip grumbled but didn't argue anymore.

Rayna ignored him. "We'd like to see Mr. Jeffers," she told the teller.

The young woman nodded. "I'll get him for you."

Mr. Jeffers came out of his office a moment later. "Well, I didn't expect to see you all here again." He looked at Skip a little warily. "Everything all right?"

"I need to get into my box again, if that's all right," Jean said.

"Certainly. Come this way."

He escorted them to the little room they had been in before, and then he took Jean into the vault. A moment later they came back with her safe-deposit box, and as before, the bank manager left them alone.

Jean put her key into the lock, turned it, and opened the box. Then she caught a startled breath.

Julia looked into the box.

The egg was gone.

Chapter Fourteen

JULIA STARED AT THE CLARKES, and they stared back at her. No one seemed to be able to move. It was gone. The Resurrection Egg was gone.

"Nanny," Rayna said, her face ghost white.

Jean had both hands over her mouth. "Oh no."

"You should have let me get it and bring it back home," Skip fumed, shuffling through the legal documents that were still in the safe-deposit box as if the egg might be stuck between their pages. "I could have at least kept my eye on it."

"You'd better get Mr. Jeffers," Julia told Rayna. "He needs to be aware of this."

Rayna nodded and hurried out to the bank lobby.

"And he needs to tell us what happened to our property," Skip bellowed after her.

Jean sat down suddenly. "Oh no. Oh no. What am I going to do? If the egg really does belong to the duke's family, I'll never be able to repay them. Oh no."

"It's all right," Julia soothed. "We're going to find out what happened. I promise we will. And maybe Mr. Jeffers knows something we don't. Let's see what he has to say about it."

Just then, Mr. Jeffers bustled into the room, his round face flushed.

"Tell me what's happened, Mrs. Clarke," he said, going immediately to Rayna's grandmother. "I understand something from your safe-deposit is missing."

"Yes," Jean said, almost sobbing. "It was there yesterday when I opened my box. I know I put it back in and locked it up. Everyone saw me do it. It should still be there."

"What is it you're missing?" the bank manager asked her.

She described the egg in detail while he removed everything from the box and even shook out the papers that were in there.

"I thought that might be it," he said gravely. "Clearly it's not there now." He put the papers back into the box and then studied the lock. The key was still in it. "It would be better if nobody touches the box now, though I don't see any sign that it's been tampered with." He glanced at Skip. "I realize we had a...misunderstanding yesterday afternoon about who was allowed access to the box, but since the proper protocols were not met at that time, the box was not removed from the vault."

"Is it at all possible that someone else might have gotten Mrs. Clarke's key somehow and removed her box?" Julia asked. "For example, someone who might have access to another box?"

"No," Mr. Jeffers said firmly. "No one goes into the vault without me or one of my employees. And we make sure that we remove only the box the person has requested and signed for."

"I don't understand what could have happened to it," Jean said.

Rayna put her arms around her. "We'll find out, Nanny. Try not to worry."

"Can we determine how many people have taken out their boxes since Mrs. Clarke was in the vault yesterday?" Julia asked.

"I suppose you can't tell us who they are, but maybe knowing how many there were would give us an idea about what we're dealing with."

"I think we can at least do that," Mr. Jeffers said. "Why don't all of you stay here, and I'll be right back."

Once he had closed the door again, Rayna turned fiercely to Skip.

"What did you do?" she demanded. "How did you get the egg out of the vault?"

Skip held up both hands. "Whoa, whoa, whoa. They didn't let me within fifty feet of that vault, remember? How was I supposed to get in there? *When* was I supposed to get in there?"

"I don't know," Rayna said. "You tried. We know that much."

"Please," Jean said, looking from Rayna to Skip and back again. "This isn't helping anything."

"I'm sorry, Nanny," Rayna said, after giving her grandmother a kiss on the cheek. "You're right. We need to focus on what happened. Uncle Skip, I owe you an apology too. I know you've been with Nanny all day."

"I have," Skip said. "Look, I know what I did yesterday didn't look very good, and I'm sorry about that. But I couldn't have taken it today, and I'm sorry it's gone." His expression softened. "I want to help get it back, Raynie. Really."

She smiled. "Okay. We'll all do what we can."

Mr. Jeffers came back in with a register book in one hand and a concerned look on his face. "Were you in the bank earlier today, Mrs. Clarke?"

Jean's forehead puckered. "No. Not until just now. Why?"

He put the register book on the table and opened it up. It was the record of people who had signed in that day to access their safe-deposit boxes. Her signature was the second from the top.

"Yes," Jean said, "I signed that a few minutes ago."

"And this?" Mr. Jeffers asked, flipping back one page.

He pointed out the third line from the bottom. It showed that at 2:49 p.m. someone had signed in to look at a box with the same number as the one on the table. And the signature read *Jean G. Clarke.*

Jean looked bewildered. "But—"

"Is that your signature?" Mr. Jeffers asked her.

"It—it looks like it, yes. But I wasn't here. My son and my grand-daughter can verify that. I was with them."

Rayna leaned close to the book, scrutinizing the signature. "It does look like yours, Nanny, but Mr. Jeffers, she's right. Uncle Skip and I were with her. She didn't leave the house until we all came up here together."

"And she has her key with her right now," Julia said. "So no one took it." She refrained from adding "again" to her comment.

"This is troubling," Mr. Jeffers said. "An employee wouldn't be able to access the box without Mrs. Clarke's key either."

"You usually accompany your clients into the vault to get their boxes, don't you, Mr. Jeffers?" Julia asked.

"If I'm available, I do." He nodded toward Mrs. Clarke. "Especially for the special ones who have been with us a long time."

"But you didn't show anyone into the vault at 2:49 today?"

"I would have remembered Mrs. Clarke, of course, if I had. But this afternoon I was occupied with a visitor from about a quarter to three until about ten after. In fact, it was the English gentleman you had here with you yesterday. Mr. Kirkland-Wright."

Julia could tell that was as much of a surprise to the Clarkes as it was to her.

"What was he doing here?" Rayna demanded.

"He wanted to know that our vault was secure and that the appropriate safeguards were in place," Mr. Jeffers said. "I was happy to show him around and explain our procedures to him. He seemed quite satisfied with everything."

"So you didn't see the person who signed in at 2:49," Julia said.

"I did not. But I can find out who did."

Mr. Jeffers left the room again, and a few minutes later, he came back with a very young-looking blond wearing thick glasses.

"This is Terry Reed," Mr. Jeffers said. "She was the one who took care of the person who came in today at 2:49. Please tell us about that, Terry."

Terry winced. "I'm sorry, Mr. Jeffers, but I don't remember that much about it. Since you were busy, Brian told me to take care of the woman. I did everything I was supposed to do, didn't I? I think I did."

"Just tell us about it," Julia said, trying to put her a little more at ease.

"Well, she came in and said she wanted to open her box, so I checked her ID and had her sign the log. Then I checked her signature. After that, I took her to the vault and got her box for her and brought her in here so she could open it in private. After a couple of minutes, she called me back in, and we put the box back in the vault. That's all." Her lower lip trembled. "Did I do something wrong, Mr. Jeffers?"

The bank manager shook his head. "It sounds as if you did everything you should have done."

"Do you remember what she looked like?" Julia asked.

"Not really. It was drizzling out, so she had a scarf over her head. A dark blue one, if I remember right. And she was wearing a light raincoat, one of those that look like cloth but repel water."

"You have a good memory," Julia said, encouragingly. "What else do you remember about her? Hair color? Age? Height?"

"She was an older lady," Terry said, glancing at Jean. "I'd say about her age, and her hair was gray and permed like hers."

"Was she short or tall?"

"Tall. Taller than me, but a little stooped. And she wore glasses."

"What did her glasses look like?" Julia asked.

"I don't know. Glasses. I didn't really pay that much attention. She had her ID and her key, and the signature matched, so I didn't think about it."

"Is there anything else you remember?" Rayna asked the teller. "Anything at all? What did she sound like?"

"She had just a normal voice. I mean, she sounded like she was from here."

"From the US," Julia asked. "Or from Savannah specifically?"

"From Savannah, I think." Terry exhaled. "I don't know. Maybe it could have been from anywhere in the South, but I usually notice if people sound like they're from somewhere else. She sounded like she was from here."

"Like me," Jean said.

"Yes, ma'am," Terry said miserably. "I'm so sorry."

"It's all right. You did everything you were supposed to do. I don't blame you at all."

"She's right, Terry," Mr. Jeffers said kindly. "You followed the protocol correctly. There's nothing else you could have done. Now go back to work and don't worry about it."

"Thank you, Mr. Jeffers," Terry said, and she slipped out of the room.

"So, someone had your key and your ID," Julia said.

"But I have them," Jean protested, digging them out of her purse. "I had to use my ID when I signed in just now, and I had to use my key to open the box."

"And there's not a duplicate key?"

"Oh no," Mr. Jeffers said. "Clients don't have duplicates, and they can't have them made. And we don't have keys to the clients' boxes."

"Clearly someone was pretending to be Mrs. Clarke," Julia said. "What about your security footage? Would we be able to see that?"

"Certainly. We don't have cameras in here, but the vault is always monitored as well as the entrance and the lobby. Specifically, our tellers' stations. Let me talk to our security chief and find out what we can do."

Mr. Jeffers disappeared again, and once more, Rayna turned on her uncle.

"You had the key and Nanny's ID yesterday."

"And I put them back yesterday," Skip said. "You saw them, Mom."

"He did give them back, honey," Jean said. "I checked on them this morning, and I just used them. They're right here."

"What about that English guy being here right at the same time the box was opened?" Skip asked. "That sounds a little fishy to me."

"That is quite a coincidence," Julia agreed. "I definitely want to ask Christian about that, among other things. It's possible too that the teller is lying. It would be worth a sizeable bribe to get access to that egg."

Jean gathered up the papers that were still in the box. "Rayna, I think I want you to take all this and get a box in your bank for me. It's things like my will and power of attorney and the deed to my house and such. You're my executor anyway, and I'd feel safer if they weren't in here anymore. I don't like the idea of somebody getting in here so easily without me knowing about it."

"All right, Nanny." Rayna took the papers from her and then glanced at her watch. "We're supposed to be at my bank at four anyway, so we'd better leave pretty soon. Julia, can you take care of getting the information about the security footage from Mr. Jeffers for us?"

"No problem," Julia said. "I'll let you know what I find out."

"Thanks. I'll get somebody to put your box back into the vault, Nanny."

One of the tellers helped her return the safe-deposit box, and then the Clarkes left. Julia waited where she was until Mr. Jeffers came back.

"They had an appointment they had to get to," she explained. "They asked me to get the details about seeing the security footage."

"All right. Mr. Waters, my security chief, said it won't be a problem to review the footage from the time period in question, from all of our cameras, but obviously we won't be able to release any of it to you without a subpoena. We can arrange for you and the Clarkes to see it though, if that would be helpful."

"Very helpful. When can we do that?"

"What about tomorrow morning?" Mr. Jeffers offered. "That will give us time to collect the pertinent footage and copy it into one file for you to see. Would that work?"

"That will work. What time? I'm sure the Clarkes will make themselves available whenever is convenient for you."

"How about eleven? That will give Waters a chance to capture everything. And, of course, we'll keep the footage protected in case Mrs. Clarke wants to file a report with the police."

"Oh, I'm certain she will," Julia said. "She claims her son has been with her all day, and I can't imagine her not wanting to press charges against anyone else."

"That son of hers," Mr. Jeffers said with a shake of his head. "He was fairly blatant about wanting to get into his mother's box yesterday, as if he had the unqualified right."

"But you don't know that the egg was in there before or after his attempt, do you?"

"I didn't know what was in there at all," Mr. Jeffers said. "What people keep in their safe-deposit boxes is entirely their business. Naturally, I had heard about the egg being found, and it didn't at all surprise me that Mrs. Clarke had put it in her box, but I can't honestly swear when it was or wasn't in there or whether it was in there at all."

"I did see it there yesterday," Julia said. "Now all we have to do is figure out who took it out."

Mr. Jeffers nodded. "I hope we'll find out tomorrow."

"See you at eleven."

Chapter Fifteen

As soon as she left the bank, Julia called Rayna. The call went straight to voice mail, so Julia assumed the Clarkes were already at Rayna's bank getting her a safe-deposit box. Julia left her a message saying they could review Mr. Jeffers's security footage at eleven the next morning. After that, she called Christian. Again Mr. Lumley answered.

"Good afternoon, Mrs. Foley. Yes, His Lordship is in. One moment, please."

"Julia," Christian said, a cheerful contrast to his lugubrious assistant. "Hello. How are you?"

"Things have taken a decided turn for the worse," she told him. "Do you have time for me to come talk to you for a few minutes?"

"Certainly," he said, concern in his voice. "What has happened?"

"I'd really like to tell you in person, if I may. Is now good?"

"Of course." He gave her the address of his hotel and the suite number.

"I'm only five or ten minutes away. I'll be right there."

Christian was staying at the Andaz Savannah on Barnard Street. Julia thought the suite might be modest by ducal standards, but it was a luxurious two-bedroom unit with a full kitchen, a fireplace, and a balcony that overlooked Ellis Square. The clouds had broken by the time she got there, and the balcony doors were open, letting in the cool, rain-scented breeze. Too bad the reason for her visit wasn't a more pleasant one.

Christian was sitting on the cream-colored couch, but he got up when Lumley showed her in.

"Do sit down, Julia. May we get you something? Coffee?"

"Coffee does sound good," she said, taking the navy-and-cream-striped wingback chair he offered. "It's turned cool after the rain."

"Would you rather have the door closed?" Christian asked with a glance toward Lumley, and Lumley immediately headed toward the balcony.

"Oh no," Julia assured him. "I love how fresh it smells after a storm. Please leave it."

"Just the coffee then, Lumley, please."

Lumley bowed. "Very good, sir."

He went across the room to the kitchen, and Julia watched him for a moment.

"Does he cook for you too?" she asked.

Christian smiled. "Lumley is a jack of many trades, which is why I brought him with me on this trip, but cooking isn't one of them. He is good enough to serve coffee or tea when required. I didn't want to bring an entire staff with me when I had to travel in such a hurry, and we've done well enough as we are. The staff here is excellent. Now, what's this news you have for me? It doesn't sound at all good judging by what you said on the telephone."

"I'm afraid it's not good," Julia said. "The egg is gone."

The crash of china from the kitchen area made them both look up.

"I beg your pardon, sir," Lumley said, using a dish towel to try to clean up the coffee and smashed cups on the floor. "I couldn't help overhearing."

"It's quite all right, Lumley," Christian said. "I'm a bit shaken myself. Why don't you have housekeeping come up and see to it and bring us some coffee from the kitchen."

"Yes, Your Lordship."

Lumley went into the other room, and Christian turned to Julia.

"What happened to the egg? I thought it was in the bank vault."

"It was. It's not there anymore."

"I can hardly believe it."

"The bank is looking into the matter, but there's not much more I can tell you about it. Just that Mrs. Clarke opened her safe-deposit box and it was gone."

"Just like that?" Christian asked. "That's outrageous. Have they notified the police?"

"Not yet. We're going to look at security footage in the morning. That might help us know who could be responsible for the theft. And I would like to know why you were there."

Christian frowned. "At the bank?"

Just then there was a knock at the door.

"'Ousekeepin'."

Julia noticed the woman had an English accent. Not the posh accent Christian had, but something broader and slower.

Lumley went to the door. "Come in, please."

The woman was probably fortyish, tall and thin, and was dressed in a neat navy-colored uniform. Her ash-blond hair was in a tidy bun at the nape of her neck, and she kept her eyes on her sensible shoes. "You need summa tidied up, sir?"

"Over here," Lumley said, walking over to the kitchen area.

She followed, pulling her cart behind her.

"His Lordship is entertaining company at the moment," Lumley told her. "So please be as quick as possible."

"Yes, sir. Righ' away. Ah won't faff about."

She got to work with Lumley standing, arms folded across his chest, watching her.

"Anyway," Julia said, "why were you at the bank?"

"I wanted to know how secure it was," Christian said. "How did you know I was there?"

"You just happened to be there right when our thief got access to the vault and the safe-deposit box. The bank manager said he was showing you the bank safeguards at the time."

Christian frowned. "Are you accusing me of being involved?" he asked.

"No. I'm just telling you what I know."

"I'd like to see that security footage too. Do you think the Clarkes would object?"

"I'd be happy to ask them, if you'd like. I don't think Mrs. Clarke would mind at all."

"Her granddaughter might," Christian said. "She seems rather wary of me, don't you think?"

Julia smiled to herself. She'd seen the spark of interest in Christian's eyes when he looked at Rayna. She'd picked up on Rayna's grudging interest too.

"I think she's very protective of her grandmother."

"With that uncle of hers around, I can see why."

"Whoever actually did get in was a little more sophisticated than Uncle Skip," Julia said. "We'll know more about it tomorrow."

"This all seems quite suspicious." Christian turned toward the kitchen. "Lumley?"

"My Lord?"

"Have I any appointments in the morning?"

"I'll check your calendar, sir."

Lumley disappeared again.

"I should very much like to go along with you tomorrow," Christian told Julia. "Do you think you could contact Mrs. Clarke about it now? Or should I speak to her directly?"

"Excuse me, sir," the housekeeper said hesitantly.

Christian turned to her. "Yes?"

"Ah'm done, sir. Is there owt else ah can do?"

"No, I don't believe so." He stood and took a folded bill out of his pocket and handed it to her. "Sorry about the mess." He squinted at her name tag. "Gwenda. You've tidied up for us before, haven't you? You've been a great help."

She tucked the bill into her pocket. "Thank you, sir."

"Uh, we were to have some coffee brought up."

"Ah'm sorry, sir, but ah know nowt about that. Shall ah ask at the kitchen?"

"If you would, thank you very much."

"Yes, sir." She hurried out with her cart and shut the door after herself.

"Now where were we?" Christian asked Julia.

"You were asking if you should talk to Mrs. Clarke about going to see the security footage tomorrow."

"Ah, yes. What do you think?"

"I don't mind asking her. That will let you make whatever changes to your schedule you need to." She called Mrs. Clarke and got her voice mail. "I'll try Rayna. Maybe they're together."

Rayna picked up right away.

"Julia, hi. Did you find out anything about us seeing that security footage?"

"Yes, that's one of the reasons I'm calling. But first I wanted to ask you how it went getting a new safe-deposit box at your bank."

"It was fine. I put all of Nanny's papers in it. I wish I had thought about this when she first found the egg. Then Skip wouldn't have even tried to get it out."

"At least the system worked at that point, and he didn't get it," Julia said.

"Thank goodness for that. Now, what about that security footage? I really want to have a look at whoever it was that got into the box."

"Mr. Jeffers thinks his security chief will have something for us to review tomorrow morning at eleven. Do you think you and your grandmother could come back to the bank then? I tried to call her first, but she didn't answer."

"She's with me," Rayna said, "but I'm sure eleven will be fine. Let me ask."

She must have put her hand over her phone then, because for a moment Julia could hear only the muffled sound of her voice and her grandmother's.

"Nanny says that's fine," Rayna said after a moment. "We'll be there."

"Good," Julia told her. "I have something else to ask you both too."

"Okay."

"Once I finished talking to Mr. Jeffers, I came over to Mr. Kirkland-Wright's hotel to give him an update about the egg and find out where he was when it was taken. He's asking to come to the bank with us in the morning."

"I think Nanny wants to see that security tape before she does anything else. He'll just complicate things."

Christian was just across the coffee table. Julia hoped he couldn't make out what Rayna was saying.

"I'm only telling you that he'd like to be there. I'm not telling you what to do. Why don't you ask your grandmother? Or if you'd rather, I'd be happy to talk to her myself."

"I'll let you speak to her."

Julia heard Rayna and her grandmother talking in the background again, and then Jean came on the line.

"Hello? Julia?"

"Hello, Jean," Julia said. "Did Rayna tell you what I called about?"

"Yes, she did. And I think Mr. Kirkland-Wright ought to come if he'd like to. I don't want him to think we have anything to hide or that we're trying to make a claim on anything that isn't rightly ours."

"I'll let him know."

"Good. And, Julia," Jean said confidentially, "don't mind Rayna. She's upset about what happened with the egg. I think she's afraid Mr. Kirkland-Wright is going to think we're not honest."

"Neither of you should worry about that," Julia said. "We'll make sure everything is completely aboveboard."

"That's good. I'm afraid my son didn't appear at his best to Mr. Kirkland-Wright when they met. Sometimes people don't understand how Skip is. He means well, but he doesn't always express himself as he should, and they get the wrong impression."

If the impression people got was that he was a small-time hustler, then they probably weren't far off the mark. But then again, Julia wasn't looking at the man through a mother's loving and hopeful eyes.

"I know you want to be totally honest," Julia said. "And I'm sure Mr. Kirkland-Wright will appreciate it. I'll let him know we're on for tomorrow."

"Thank you, dear. You've been so helpful."

"You're very welcome," Julia said. "But I won't feel like I've done anything until we find that egg and figure out whose it is."

"Well," Jean said, "you've made me feel much better about the whole thing anyway. We'll see you tomorrow."

"I take it I'm allowed?" Christian asked once Julia ended the call.

"You're allowed. If you're available."

Lumley was standing at Christian's side holding a tablet. "You're supposed to meet with Mr. Danforth at the shipping office at ten, Your Lordship, but that's all you have scheduled until one-thirty at Mr. Keller's office. Shall I try to set another time for Mr. Danforth?"

Christian considered for a moment. "I don't think so. I'm just stopping in because my father asked me to. It shouldn't take long for me to have coffee and a short chat with him."

"Very good, sir."

Lumley gave a slight bow and began tidying the room.

"Now," Christian said to Julia, "Lumley tells me that you have some questions about Alexis Voronin. What would you like to know?"

"You said that he died in the Sea Islands hurricane in 1893. Do you happen to know the exact date of his death?"

"No, I'm sorry, I don't. But it's possible we have something in our family records that would give that."

"Maybe in his aunt's letters?" Julia suggested.

"The countess was a prolific correspondent. We have many of her letters in our archives along with her diary. It's quite probable that she would have made note of something as affecting as Alexis's death. Of course, it would all be in Russian."

"I'm sure. But we have some very good translators."

Christian nodded. "Of course. Would you like me to find out what we have from the fall of 1893? You don't happen to recall the exact date of the hurricane, do you?"

"It was August 27th," Julia said, "but I would expect it to take some time for a letter to get back to the countess after that, given the state of emergency in the disaster area."

"And the sheer distance between here and there. Unless someone telegraphed, of course."

"I'm very interested in knowing when he died and how his family was informed," Julia told him. "It wasn't uncommon for a nurse or other attendant to write letters home for a patient or to write the family to inform them that the patient had died."

"And you think that might give us some information on what happened to the egg?" Christian asked.

Julia wasn't quite ready to tell him about Willow Brenton being a relief volunteer after the hurricane. She wanted to see what came up from the information he could access without prejudicing him beforehand.

"I hope so," she said. "But anything you have, anything at all, would be helpful. Anything that might show why he was here, who he was in contact with, what his plans were. Do you think he would have written to his brother?"

"Nikolai? He might have. We have some of his papers too, I believe. I can certainly have someone look into that for you. I should have thought of that earlier."

"I know you didn't have much time to plan this trip, so that's perfectly understandable."

"To be honest," Christian said, "I'm not all that familiar with what we have from the Voronin branch of the family, but I can certainly have someone look into it. And our answers ought to get here much more quickly than they would have back in their day. I'll have Lumley take care of it right away."

"I'll see to it, sir," Lumley said. "And again, I apologize about the mess."

"It's not a problem."

"It sounds like the housekeeper is from your part of the world, Mr. Lumley," Julia said. "Is that a Liverpool accent? Like the Beatles?"

"That's Yorkshire," Christian said. "Right, Lumley?"

"I wouldn't know, sir."

Lumley's voice was stiff and carefully upper-class, like the pronunciation of a BBC commentator.

Christian gave Julia a wink. "Never mind, Lumley. Why don't you go ahead and contact Barrows about that information we were talking about? And tell him the sooner the better."

"Right away, sir," Lumley said, and he disappeared again.

"I'm afraid you hit the man in a sensitive spot," Christian said to Julia. "He's as Yorkshire as they come and has worked hard to bury his accent. He has the occasional slip, but for the most part you'd never know where he was from."

"I'm sorry. I had no idea I said something wrong."

"Of course you didn't. And I'm sure he'll recover nicely. Don't let it trouble you."

"I've always been fascinated by accents," Julia said. "I was in a play in high school that was set in England, and the different characters were from different parts of the country, so they each had a particular accent. We tried so hard to get them all right, but you would probably have laughed hearing it."

"You must have a good ear for it to recognize some of the subtleties. I'm afraid I can't very much tell a Midwestern accent from a New England one, but I always notice when someone is from somewhere down here. I find it charming," he said gallantly. "Miss Clarke's is particularly appealing."

Julia couldn't help wondering if Rayna found upper-class English accents attractive too.

She didn't realize they had never gotten their coffee until after she and Christian had finished their talk and she was making her way through the hotel lobby. She saw the woman who had cleaned up the broken china pushing her cart toward a storage room, and she decided to find out if she was even close about the woman's accent.

"Gwenda!" she called, hoping to catch her before she was out of sight.

The woman turned. "Yes, ma'am?"

"I'm sorry to bother you, but accents always interest me. I was just up in Mr. Kirkland-Wright's room, where you cleaned up the broken dishes."

"Aye, ma'am."

"I was wondering where you're from. I first thought it was Liverpool, but he says Yorkshire. Would you mind telling me?"

The woman paused for a moment then said slowly, "I'm sorry, ma'am, I'm from Exeter in Devonshire. That's the south of England."

"Oh." Julia was a bit taken aback by the abrupt change in Gwenda's pronunciation. "I guess I was really off. Thank you."

"You're welcome, ma'am," she said. She pushed her cart into the storage room and shut the door.

Julia walked out to her car, replaying in her mind what the woman had said earlier, listening for the cadence and the lilt of the words. She would have sworn the woman was at least from somewhere in the north of England, but if she was, why would she lie?

The question bothered her all the way home.

Chapter Sixteen

Beaufort, South Carolina
September 1893

"Miss Willow?"

Willow drew a quick breath and shook herself awake. Mr. James had gotten out of his bed and was standing beside her, his kindly eyes filled with concern.

"Do you want me to look after the gentleman so you can sleep a few minutes?"

"No. I'm sorry." She wiped her eyes with both hands, pushed herself out of the unforgiving ladder-back chair, and managed to smile. "And you ought to be asleep."

"You tell me that every night, miss, and every night I can't hardly do it. Not that I'm not grateful for having a place to rest and for you ladies' kindness in tending me, but Miz Cunningham don't always understand about old folks. We don't need no eight or ten hours of sleep most nights. That's why you and me end up sitting and talking like we been doing these past few nights while you look after us all."

"I've enjoyed it, Mr. James," she told him. "I've hardly been anywhere but Savannah and done anything but go to cotillions up till now. It's amazing to hear about all the things you've done during your lifetime."

"Pshaw, Miss Willow, nothing but working from can to can't and watching the world change round me. Sometimes I think it's gone too fast, and we lost too many of the good things in our hurry to be moving on. Not to say some of the old rightly ought to have gone too." He looked down at the Russian lying unmoving on his cot as he had since Willow had come to the hospital. "This gentleman come from all the way on the other side of the world, they say, some kind of royalty or something."

"Nobility, I think," Willow said.

Mr. James shrugged. "Whatever he was, he ended up with a bunch of us poor farmers trying to stay alive. Just like us. Sometimes the change comes too quick to give a man a chance to brace up against it."

"I suppose it does."

Willow wondered how she would have "braced up" if something as devastating as a hurricane had taken from her everything she had and the life she knew. She knew she wasn't strong, not like these people who had every day struggled to live and who had triumphed over insurmountable obstacles on all sides to make something decent for themselves and their families. She hoped that, somehow, she could grow stronger by stepping away from her sheltered life, at least for a time.

"You think he'll wake up again?" the old man asked, his dark eyes fixed on the other man's face. "Or you think he'll just slip on off to his reward?"

"I don't know," Willow said.

The other men she had been caring for had been steadily improving. Two of them had pneumonia, from near-drowning she had been told, but they were some better now. A third had a broken leg and would also be confined to bed for a while, but he was eager to get up and get back to his land, where he and his family could start over again.

Mr. James was healing more slowly, due to his age Dr. LeClaire said, but he was getting better, and his good spirits seemed never to flag.

"All the time you been here, Miss Willow, you seen this gentleman move?"

Willow shook her head. "Not on his own. Why?"

"I thought maybe I did. Just now."

"Really?" Willow grabbed the candle that sat on the little table next to her and held it closer to the young man's face, but he didn't seem any different from when she had first come to the hospital. "Maybe it was just the flicker of the light. Anyway, it's very late, Mr. James. You ought to rest even if you can't sleep."

"No, miss, look there. Look at his eyes."

She brought the candle closer still and saw what looked like rapid movement behind the young man's eyelids and a flutter of his thick, dark lashes. She caught a breath, but before she could think what to do, his eyes opened.

"Don't—don't try to get up," she said, thinking she sounded very stupid and looked equally so as she waved her hand.

He said something in a language she didn't understand, and then he said, "Where am I?"

"You're in the hospital. I'm going to get the doctor."

"Hospital? Where?"

He had a heavy accent, but he seemed to have no problem understanding and speaking English.

"This is Beaufort, South Carolina. You were in the hurricane."

"Ah."

"What happened to you?" she asked. "How were you hurt?"

He looked puzzled. "I do not know. My friend, he took me on his boat and we were trying to reach the harbor before the storm came." He put one hand to his head and flinched. "I cannot remember after that. Where is my friend? His name is Oliver. Oliver Brownwell. He is here?"

"I'm sorry, I don't know. I'd better get the doctor. No, don't get up."

The Russian was struggling to push the blankets away, and Willow couldn't seem to calm him.

"Please, just rest now. Let me get—"

"Now, sir," Mr. James said in a firm, soothing voice, "you don't need to fret yourself here. You let Miss Willow get the doctor, and he'll see to you. Then we can find out about your friend."

The young man seemed to relax a little at that, and Willow hurried out of the room. She went straight to the ballroom and then to the kitchen. Miss Cunningham was standing over the stove heating some milk while the little baby she had balanced on her hip fretted and squirmed.

"What's wrong?" she asked at once.

"It's the Russian gentleman," Willow told her. "He's awake."

Miss Cunningham's mouth formed a perfect O of astonishment, and then she smiled. "Well, thank God. How is he? Is he right?"

"He was talking, if that's what you mean, but he doesn't seem to remember what happened to him."

"No bleeding from the ears or nose?"

Willow shook her head, still not quite used to Miss Cunningham's directness in nursing matters.

"No problem breathing? His eyes don't look wrong?"

"None of that," Willow said. "He was trying to get up, but Mr. James got him to stay still so I could come for you."

"Here." Miss Cunningham thrust the whimpering baby into Willow's arms. "I daresay the milk is warm enough. Make sure it's not too hot and then fill the bottle. I'll get Dr. LeClaire, and we'll go see to your patient."

As soon as Willow got the baby fed and to sleep, she took him to his mother and then hurried back to the room where her own patients were. Dr. LeClaire, in his nightshirt, robe, and slippers, had finished his examination of the Russian man and was outside the door giving Miss Cunningham his assessment.

"He does seem to be in his right senses, but he is far from well yet. Apart from the damage to his skull, he has injuries to his internal organs." The doctor gave Willow a stern look. "You've been taking care of him?"

"Yes, most nights. Effie Taylor minds the patients in this room during the day. Sometimes it's one of the other girls if we're needed somewhere else, but mostly it's us."

"All right, good. I want you to listen carefully. That young man is going to want to get up long before he should. It's been to his advantage being unconscious all this time. I had to do some surgery on him when he first came in, and that long sleep let him heal some, but only some. He's still likely to tear open some stitches or get more of a fever than he has right now. He's got to be kept still and quiet as long as possible." The doctor's heavy white eyebrows went up. "Do you understand?"

"Yes, Doctor," Willow said. "Is there something I can do to help him?"

"You mind what Miss Cunningham here has to say. That's the best advice I have for you young ladies, all of you. She knows what to do, and she can always send for me in an emergency. Now, while I'm up, I've got a couple of other delicate cases to see to. Good night."

He hurried into the dimly lit corridor, and Miss Cunningham and Willow went back into the room. Mr. James was still standing beside the Russian man's cot. The Russian's eyes were closed.

"He went straight back to sleep when the doctor left," Mr. James said with a wondering shake of his head. "I guess that little bit of talking was too much for him."

"Mr. James," Miss Cunningham said sternly, "if you are unable to sleep, I must ask you to at least rest in your bed."

"Yes, ma'am."

Mr. James made his way back to his bed without another word.

Willow gave him a sympathetic smile and a soft good night and then turned to the Russian again.

"I thought he was better," she whispered to Miss Cunningham.

"It is a good sign, his waking up, but he must be very careful now. Hospital fever can be very dangerous. It would be better for him, for all these people, to be in their own homes away from this overcrowding, but they have no homes anymore and no place else to go." She took a deep breath and then smiled wearily. "We'll do all we can for as many as we can, Willow dear, and God will make up the rest."

"Yes, ma'am. I pray He will."

Miss Cunningham patted her shoulder. "You do what the doctor says. If the gentleman wakes up again, keep him calm and as still as possible. If he seems worse, send for me or the doctor."

When she was gone, Willow pulled her chair near Mr. James's cot. He was lying down, but he had a piece of wood on the bed beside him, and he was studying it as if he were trying to charm its secrets from it.

He gave her a half-abashed smile. Just that afternoon, the doctor had told him that, if he was careful not to jostle himself too much, he could amuse himself with his whittling knife.

"Right now there seems to be a lot of wood scraps lying around," Dr. LeClaire had said. "And if it'll keep you still for a bit longer, I guess it'll be well worth it."

Elliot had come in right after that to help with the patients while their bedding was changed, and he must have overheard what the doctor said, because a couple of hours later, he brought Mr. James several pieces of polished cherry wood.

"I think it must have come from a chifforobe or suchlike," he told the old man. "Whatever it was is all in pieces, but this is the best of it. I thought you could make something fine out of it."

"That's kindly of you, Mr. Elliot, it surely is."

Elliot shrugged. "I broke my ankle when I was a boy. It was pure torment lying in bed all that while with nothing to do. I hate to see anybody in that state, Mr. James."

"Most kindly, sir. I'll see can't I make something nice from it."

He'd worked with his knife the whole rest of the day, worked until the light was gone, and now he still didn't sleep.

"What do you think you'll make?" Willow asked him softly.

"I know what I want to do, miss. It's fine wood, too fine for something commonplace, and I expect it'll take me a while to do right by it."

Before she could ask him anything more, the Russian man stirred again. She went to him immediately.

"Shh," she soothed, keeping him from sitting up. "Just lie back now. Are you hurting?"

He shook his head and turned away from her. "Bad dream."

"I'm sorry. Would you like some water?"

He shook his head again.

She moved her chair back to his bedside. "Would you like to talk awhile? I'm a good listener."

For a moment he didn't respond. Then he turned to face her again.

"What is your name?"

"Willow Brenton. I came from Savannah to help with the refugees. I'm afraid I don't know very much about nursing, but I'm learning. Mostly I try to make sure everyone is as comfortable as possible." She studied his face. "I think you must be in pain."

"It is nothing."

He shrugged, but his dark eyes flicked away from her, and she knew he wasn't telling her the truth.

"And your name?" she asked.

"I am Alexis Voronin. How long have I been here?"

"I don't know for sure," she admitted. "You were here when I first came. Would you like me to find out for you?"

"It does not matter. Where is Oliver? He was with me."

"I'm afraid I don't know that either. You said his name was Brownwell, right?"

Mr. Voronin nodded.

"If you'll lie still, I'll see what I can find out." She checked the clock on the wall near the door. It was almost three o'clock. "Actually, I think that will have to wait until everyone gets

up. Miss Cunningham will know how I can find out about him. She should know how long you've been here too. But you must be patient. The doctor says you will set yourself back if you don't lie quiet."

"Yes, so he said." He let out a long, dejected breath. "You will talk to me? Until I can sleep again, perhaps?"

"I'd be happy to," she said, relieved to see him being so cooperative. "But I'm afraid I don't know anything that's very interesting. This is almost the farthest I've been from Savannah my whole life."

That earned her a slight smile. He had a charming smile.

"You must have been just about everywhere in the world."

"No," he said, "but many places in my own country. I have visited the chief cities of Europe and of Asia. I have seen the pyramids of Egypt and sailed down the River Nile. And to get here I have braved the great Atlantic."

"How exciting!" Her exclamation ended up being more of a squeak when she belatedly tried to keep from disturbing the other patients, and that seemed to amuse him. "Will you tell me about it?"

"Where should I start?"

It was getting light and even Mr. James had fallen asleep when Willow finally had a chance to write in her diary again.

Our Russian gentleman is awake at last. I know he is grieved for his friend, Mr. Brownwell, who was very likely lost during the terrible storm, but it seemed to help him when he told me some of the adventures he's had all over the

world. He is an engrossing storyteller, and I'm glad he knows English so well. I feel as though I've seen the places he talked about with my own eyes. But I must make certain he does not tire himself overmuch with talking. Though we are yet strangers, I'm sure my heart would break if anything were to happen to him. He seems such a kind and fine-looking gentleman. He must get well.

Chapter Seventeen

JULIA GOT TO WORK EARLY again the next morning. There was no sign of Bunny, and Julia hadn't been able to tell Beau that Bunny's escape was her fault. Beau was still looking for her, still calling, still putting up signs. Neither of them was willing to admit that the cat could be gone for good. Julia was determined to be hopeful and encouraging, and she was sure Beau was doing the same thing. He never even speculated on how the cat could have gotten out, which made her feel even more guilty. It was unbearable.

She was glad when it was finally time to go to the bank again to view the security footage with the Clarkes and with Christian. She got there far earlier than necessary and decided to spend her wait time in her car mulling over the information she already had on the case. Her list of questions to research had reached two pages before Rayna pulled her car into the space next to Julia's.

Julia got out. "Good morning."

Skip hopped from the back seat of his niece's car. "Hey. We're finally going to get this figured out, right?"

"I hope so." Julia turned to Rayna and her grandmother. "Good to see you both. Are you ready to go inside?"

"I am," Jean said firmly. "I want to know who would dare pretend to be me."

"We'll find out, Nanny." Rayna took her arm, steadying her as she stepped up on the curb. "I guess Christian's still coming."

"He's supposed to be," Julia said. "We're a little early."

She was surprised to find Christian already inside the bank waiting for them. As usual, Lumley stood behind him, a little to one side.

"Would you care to sit down, Mrs. Clarke?" Christian gestured toward a chair and then nodded to Rayna. "And I expect you'd like to sit here next to your grandmother."

Rayna gave him an arch look and sat down. The chair he'd indicated just happened to be next to the one he'd been sitting in.

"I suppose you're both eager to see who was in your safe-deposit box yesterday," he said.

"Maybe it was someone you know," Rayna told him crisply. "Since you were here too."

Christian looked for an instant as if he couldn't believe what she was insinuating, and then he managed a serene nod. "I was here, yes, but I'm afraid I didn't notice any of the bank's customers in particular. I was more concerned with the security measures they have in place. Evidently, even the most well-thought-out plans can be got round by a thief who's clever enough."

"That's Roy Keller coming in," Julia said before either of them could say anything else. "What's he doing here?"

Christian held up his hand. "I'm afraid that's my doing. I told him what happened, and he wanted to see the security footage too. I hope you don't mind, Mrs. Clarke."

"Oh." Jean glanced at Rayna. "No, I'm sure it's fine. Maybe he can help us figure out what might have happened."

"I hope I haven't missed anything." Roy checked his watch as he hurried up to them. "Not quite eleven, so we're all good. Mrs. Clarke, how are you?"

Mrs. Clarke smiled. "I'm fine, Mr. Keller, thank you."

"Rayna. Skip." Roy shook hands with Skip and Rayna and then with Christian. "Are we ready to see the feature presentation?"

"We're all assembled," Christian said.

Rayna stood up. "I'll see if Mr. Jeffers is ready for us."

A few minutes later Mr. Jeffers came out of his office and took them all into a room marked PRIVATE. There was a laptop set up at one end of a long table, and a stocky man in a dark suit was seated next to it.

"This is Curtis Waters, my head of security," Mr. Jeffers said, and he introduced everyone else. "Curtis will be showing you what we've got on our security cameras, and he'll be able to answer any questions you might have afterward. All right?"

Everyone sat down at the table except for Lumley, who stood behind Christian with his back against the wall.

"I gathered everything that showed the person who came into the bank yesterday and signed the vault log at 2:49 and put it into one file," Curtis said in a deep voice. "That will show the person coming into the bank, signing the register, and going into the vault and then into the viewing room. We don't have cameras in there, so we pick up again when the person comes out of the viewing room, goes into the vault, and then leaves the bank. The footage is from cameras located throughout the bank and in the vault, but I've arranged it to give the most comprehensive view of events."

Curtis opened the laptop and selected a file. Soon they saw the woman—tall, gray-haired, stoop shouldered, just as the teller had described her—come to the front door of the bank. Before she could reach the door handle, a man hurried up and opened it for her and then stepped aside to let her go first.

Julia caught her breath.

"Wait," Rayna said. "Can you stop it there?"

Curtis obliged, stopping the video as the woman reached the middle of the lobby.

"Now can you go back to the man who opened the door?"

Curtis did, and everyone turned to look at Christian, who seemed able to do no more than stare back at them.

"I—I didn't remember doing that," he said, and then he studied his own image, frozen there right behind the mystery woman. "Yes, that's me, but I was only being polite."

Rayna frowned at him but said nothing.

"I'm sure you meant well," Jean said uncertainly.

There was silence for a moment.

"Why don't we go on?" Julia suggested finally. "Maybe we'll get a better look at the woman from a different camera."

Mr. Jeffers nodded, and Curtis clicked PLAY again. They all watched as Christian was greeted by the bank manager and the woman waited for the next available teller. Christian disappeared from view with Mr. Jeffers, and the teller took the woman's ID card and had her sign the register. Then they walked over to the vault and went in.

The picture switched to a view from inside the vault, looking down on the rows of safe-deposit boxes and on the teller and the woman as they got Jean's box. Once the teller led the woman into the viewing room, there was a break followed by the door to that room opening again and the woman coming out with the box. The video showed the woman following the teller back to the vault, replacing the box, and then walking through the lobby and out the front door.

"Thoughts, anyone?" Roy asked when the video ended.

"Can you zoom in on anything?" Julia asked Curtis.

Curtis nodded. "What would you like to see?"

"Anything showing the woman's face. As close as you can get."

Curtis started the video again and then froze it when the woman first stepped up to the teller. "That's our best shot. The tellers' cameras are set up for ID."

"She's very like Mrs. Clarke," Christian said, and Rayna shot him a hard look.

"But I was still at home with my son and granddaughter at that time," Jean protested. "They can tell you that."

"I'm not making any accusations," Christian said quickly. "Just an observation."

"Beg pardon, Your Lordship," Lumley said, leaning a little closer to Christian, "and not meaning to offend, but the testimony of family members is not always the most reliable."

Now it was Skip's turn to glare, but Lumley didn't deign to notice him.

Julia studied the woman on the video again. She did look like Jean, but she was keeping her face tilted down, so it was hard to really tell that much about her. She had the same permed gray hair, but the scarf she had tied over it and knotted under her chin made it impossible to see her ears. Ears were always a telling feature, and they were very difficult to disguise convincingly.

The woman wore glasses that seemed very like Jean's, but there was something about them, something in the lenses maybe, that distorted the camera's view of her eyes. And the scarf looked as if it were pulled tight, so it distorted the shape of her face. That almost certainly wasn't Jean, but it was going to be very difficult to tell who it actually was.

"Is that the best view you can get?" Julia asked.

"Let's see."

Curtis tried pausing on various shots of the thief, but none of them proved to be very good. Finally, they settled on printing out the three best stills they could get.

"I suppose we can't get a copy of the footage?" Julia asked, knowing the answer already.

"Not without a court order," Curtis said.

"But you will keep that in case we need one, right?" Roy asked.

"Definitely," Mr. Jeffers told him. "Curtis, make sure that's secure until I let you know otherwise."

"All right," Curtis said. "Anything else for now?"

"I think that's all."

Everyone stood up.

"Thank you, Mr. Waters," Jean said.

"Anytime, ma'am."

"Very helpful, Mr. Waters," Christian said, shaking the man's hand. "Thank you."

They all filed into the lobby and out of the bank.

"I think we need to discuss what we've just seen," Julia said.

"I agree." Christian turned to Roy. "Might we use your office again? It's close."

"Will that work for everyone?" Roy asked.

Nobody disagreed, so they all drove over to Roy's office. They had to wait a moment for the secretary to tidy up the conference room his partner had just used to meet with his own clients, and then they all went in and sat down.

"I'd like to get copies of those still shots you got, Julia," Roy said right off the bat. "If you don't object."

"Oh, certainly."

Julia put the pictures on the table, and Lumley stepped up beside her.

"I should be happy to see to it, ma'am, if you like."

"Yes, thank you."

Lumley took the pictures and left the room.

"Well," Roy said once he had shut the conference room door. "It was a very interesting show, wasn't it?"

"It seems like quite a coincidence that Mr. Kirkland-Wright was there at the same time," Rayna said, looking mildly puzzled in a very put-on way.

"Coincidences happen, Miss Clarke," Christian replied. "And all I did was open the door for her."

"He never spoke to her," Roy pointed out. "And he didn't go with her to the vault or to the viewing room."

"But," Rayna said, "he was there at the perfect time to make sure the thief didn't have to go through the bank manager to get into the vault. Mr. Jeffers has known my grandmother for a good many years. He would have never been fooled by an imposter."

"Perhaps," Christian said coolly, "but the bank was. The thief had your grandmother's identification card and her key to the safe-deposit box. Something I couldn't possibly have provided to her. And the thief managed a quite credible version of her signature, something I couldn't possibly know how to duplicate."

"And my ID and my key were with me at home all day," Jean reminded them. "And so were my son and granddaughter." She looked pleadingly at Julia. "You don't think someone at the bank could have been behind this? Oh dear, I hope not. Mr. Jeffers would be so upset to think one of his people could have done something like this."

"I'll check it out," Julia assured her. "People have gone to great lengths for things as valuable as that egg."

"But they wouldn't have known the egg was there, would they?" Christian asked. "Isn't what you store in your box kept private? You didn't tell anyone at the bank you were putting the egg in there, did you, Mrs. Clarke?"

"Oh no," Jean said. "No one but Rayna and Skip. And Julia, of course. And you and Mr. Keller. I think that's all."

"None of your friends?" Julia asked.

"No, I'm sure. I haven't been easy about having the thing ever since I found it."

"People might have assumed though," Rayna said. "After all the publicity about the egg. And the people at the bank would know my grandmother has a box there."

"True." Julia glanced at Roy. "Maybe it's time we got the police involved."

Roy turned to his client. "Do you have any objection to that?"

"Not to the police, no," Christian said, "but I'd like to keep this as quiet as possible for now. The publicity was bad enough before the egg went missing."

Roy nodded. "Fair enough. We'll all have to agree to give anyone who asks a firm 'no comment.' What do you think?"

"Fine with me," Rayna said.

"We've got a private investigator," Skip protested. "What do we need the police for? I mean, wouldn't you rather have this handled quietly, Mom?"

"Well, yes," Jean said. "But wouldn't the police be able to do a lot more? They have resources that wouldn't be available to a private investigator."

"You were at home yesterday, weren't you?" Julia asked Skip pointedly. "I mean, until you came up to the bank with your grandmother?"

"Of course I was," Skip fired back.

"He was," Rayna said.

"Then you shouldn't have anything to worry about, right?" Julia asked.

Skip glared at her. "I've got nothing to worry about. I was just thinking the police have a lot of cases to work on. Who knows how much time they've got for this one? On the other hand, our own PI ought to be able to spend most of her time helping us. Isn't that better?"

"I think we can do both, can't we?" Jean said soothingly.

Skip shrugged. "Whatever you think."

Lumley slipped back into the room and put the printouts in front of Julia. "Your originals, ma'am."

"Thank you."

"And your copies, Mr. Keller." Lumley handed Roy a set of the pictures. "I took the liberty of making a copy for His Lordship as well, if that isn't out of line, sir."

"Oh, certainly," Roy said.

Julia glanced at the pictures and then frowned. "I think I got copies rather than the originals," she said to Lumley. "These are a little darker, if I'm remembering right."

"Oh no, ma'am," Lumley said. "I made a small mark on the back of yours so I would be sure not to get them mixed up."

Julia turned over one of the pages. There was a light checkmark in the upper righthand corner. "Oh, I see. Thank you."

"So what about the police?" Roy asked. "Mr. Kirkland-Wright wouldn't be in a position to report the theft. That would have to come from Mrs. Clarke."

Jean glanced at her granddaughter. "I've never reported a crime before."

"I'll be happy to help you with that," Julia said. "If you'd like me to."

Rayna gave her grandmother a reassuring nod. "I think we'd both appreciate that, Julia."

"Good," Roy said. "Is there anything else we need to discuss? Anyone?"

"I'll let you know what happens with the police," Julia told him.

Christian stood up. "I expect we've finished here for now. Thank you, Roy. And thank you, Julia. I don't have anything yet on that information about Alexis Voronin you asked for, but I'll contact you as soon as I do."

"Call me anytime," Julia told him.

"Thank you. I'll do that." Christian smiled. "Within reason, of course."

He approached Rayna. "I realize it's been a difficult day for everyone," he said. "I'm still interested in finding the truth here, no matter what it is. I think we both agree on that, don't we?"

She pressed her lips together, but then her expression warmed. "Yes, we do. And I'm sorry I said what I did. It was rude, and I'm not usually a rude person. And I'm not the type to accuse anyone without evidence."

"I suppose things have been a bit at sixes and sevens for you and your family these last few days. It can't be easy dealing with this kind of notoriety when you're not used to it. I was born to it, and it can still be a challenge."

"I just don't want my grandmother to be hurt, and I know she's worried about being held responsible for losing that egg."

"Especially if it turns out we don't have any claim to it," Jean said. "I don't know how we could ever repay you for it. If it turns out to be yours after all."

"I don't want you to worry yourself over that, ma'am," Christian said as he helped her to her feet. "Barring any criminal complicity on your part, which I cannot bring myself to believe, I can't imagine a situation in which you would be held liable. My family isn't so poorly off as that."

"Oh, thank you. And I promise we'll do all we can to find out what happened and get the egg back. Won't we, Julia?"

"We certainly will," Julia said. "Let's start with talking to the police."

"Do let us know what they say, Julia," Christian added, though he was looking at Rayna.

Rayna led her grandmother to the door. "Come on, Uncle Skip."

"Uh, yeah," Skip said. "I think I'd rather you drop me off at home first, okay? I just remembered something I forgot."

Rayna rolled her eyes. "Fine. Come on."

Lumley, still standing silently against the wall, pursed his lips.

Christian chuckled. "He's quite a character, isn't he?"

"Begging your pardon, sir," Lumley said, "but that one bears watching."

"Do you suspect him?" Julia asked.

"Oh no, ma'am. Forgive me. I don't feel the gentleman has the capacity for sophisticated crime. But neither do I think that he is morally opposed to it."

Julia suppressed a smile. That was her assessment of Skip Clarke too. She wouldn't bring it up to Jean, yet the police would almost certainly do a check on her son once she reported the missing egg. Clearly, Skip was trying to avoid their notice.

"We'll keep an eye on him," she assured Lumley.

He made a slight bow. "Very good, ma'am."

Julia met Jean and Rayna at the police station. She helped the Clarkes file a report and let the office make copies of the pictures she had from the bank's security cameras. The officer said he would keep them informed if there were any developments in the case and asked Julia to do the same for the department. He assured her that someone would be talking to Mr. Jeffers and to Mr. Kirkland-Wright about the theft.

Afterward, Rayna settled her grandmother in the passenger seat of her car. Julia was about to drive away, but Rayna waved for her to stop and hurried over to her car window.

"I haven't had a chance to give you this, but I'd like you to see what you can find out about it." She passed Julia a wrinkled slip of paper with a telephone number written on it in pencil. "I tried looking it up online, but everything I found just says that it's a private number."

"I might be able to find out who it belongs to. Where did this come from?"

"Uncle Skip left his dirty clothes for Nanny to wash, so I did them. That was in one of his pockets. It might not mean anything, but I'd like to find out for sure."

"Did you tell your grandmother about this?" Julia asked.

"No. Not yet anyway. Not until I find out what it is."

"Okay. I'll check into it and get back to you."

As Julia drove away, she couldn't help but wonder. Skip was obviously not above manipulation, but would he actually stoop to stealing from his own mother?

Chapter Eighteen

JULIA DROVE TO THE AGENCY, where Carmen told her Meredith was out meeting with a client. She got herself some coffee and went into her office. She really wished Christian would call with more information about Alexis Voronin, but while she was waiting for his call, she'd see what she could learn about the phone number Rayna had found. It was probably nothing, but it would be easy to research it one way or another. She did a quick internet search without helpful results, only learning that it was for a cell phone, which she'd already suspected.

Finally, she decided to take a chance and just dial the number. She'd never know anything if she didn't at least try. Someone picked up right away.

"Yeah?"

"Hello," she said, trying to sound friendly.

"What do you want?"

She paused for a moment. She had heard this voice before. She knew she had. It was the wheezy, strained voice of someone who'd had throat surgery. Maybe even a tracheotomy.

"I'm sorry," she said. "Who is this, please?"

"Who are you looking for?" the man rasped.

"I—I'm not sure. I found this number and—"

"Wrong number."

Before she could protest, the call was ended.

Who was that? She raked her memory. It hadn't been that long since she'd heard someone with a voice like that.

A moment later she had it. The phone number had a Savannah area code, and the man she was thinking of was just the kind of guy someone like Skip might know. She started to call again and ask for him by name, but then she decided she'd go out to his place and see him. It was always easier to tell if he was being straight with her if she could look into his eyes.

She checked her watch. By the time she got to her destination and back, it would be about time to go home, and she was going to have to talk to Beau tonight. For sure. A little drive would help her prepare herself mentally. It would give her an opportunity to pray for the right words. *Please don't let him be too upset with me. Please.*

She drank the rest of her coffee and then went into the reception area. "Carmen, I've got to go somewhere on the Clarke case. If Meredith comes in, would you please tell her I won't be back today?"

Carmen grinned at her. "Sure will."

Julia shifted her purse higher on her shoulder. "Do you have any special plans for tonight?"

Carmen's grin widened. "Chase is taking me to dinner, and then we're going to a movie."

Chase was Meredith's son, and he and Carmen had been going out for a while now.

"Well, you two have fun. I'll see you sometime tomorrow. And if Christian Kirkland-Wright calls, please tell him he can get me on my cell phone. If he says he doesn't have the number, which he does, you can give it to him."

"All right. See you tomorrow."

Julia drove to one of the less exclusive parts of town and pulled up in front of a little hole-in-the-wall with a flashing sign that announced it as NORM's. The door and windows had security bars on them, but they didn't obscure the variety of products that were for sale there. A neon-pink sign on the door said, MUSICAL INSTRU-MENTS 20% OFF TODAY ONLY!!! Either the sign had been used earlier, or it had been put there well before today.

She pushed the door open, and an electronic buzz brought a sagging little middle-aged man in a burgundy sweat suit from behind the overcrowded counter. He had bushy white Albert Einstein hair and eyebrows and a wad of chewing gum in his cheek. As always, he wore a white cloth tied like an ascot around his neck. It covered his scar.

"Yeah?" he rasped.

"Hi, Norm," Julia said.

He squinted at her and then smiled. "Well, Mrs. Foley. I didn't think you'd be back here."

"You were so helpful before, I thought I'd come see you again. I have another case I hope you can help me solve."

Early in their partnership, she and Meredith had traced a missing violin to this shop. Norm had started by denying he knew anything, but once he figured out that she and Meredith knew what they were talking about, he had helped them recover the instrument. She real-ized then that he took a rather fluid view of what was legal and what wasn't, and it didn't look good for Skip to have Norm's number in his pocket. Still, she didn't know for certain that this was the same man she had just talked to on the phone. She'd have to walk carefully.

"A case? What do I know about cases? I'm stuck here day and night. Nobody tells me anything."

"Somebody came to see you," Julia said casually. "I want to know what he said."

Norm snorted. "Nobody who'd be able to afford you would come see me, I can tell you that right now."

"I'm the one who called you a little while ago."

His rheumy eyes widened. "That was you? You should have said. I might not have hung up."

At least she knew she'd found the right guy.

"What did you and Skip Clarke talk about?"

Norm looked innocently bewildered. "Who's that? Skip Clarke?"

"He was here," she said, even though she had nothing but a hunch to back that up. "What did he want?"

Norm drew himself up haughtily. "What's between my clients and me is confidential."

"I know Skip came to see you."

"Don't be ridiculous. You have no way of knowing who I might have seen or why. You've got nothing to—"

"About the egg."

He gaped at her.

"Is there a reason someone would come to you with stolen goods, Norm? An honest businessman like you?"

"Oh, come on now, Mrs. Foley," he said with a ragged, unconvincing laugh. "Okay, maybe sometime, way back in the day, I might have arranged a deal here or there. Nothing big, now. Nothing big. And, come on, a guy's got to make a living."

"What about the egg, Norm?"

"I never even saw it, and that's the honest truth." He drew a raspy breath and then coughed painfully. "Okay, yeah, Skip came to see me. We had some business deals a while back. Just legit business, now, nothing shady, okay? I need to be clear about that. Anyway, he came in here and said he wanted to see if I could help him."

"When was that?"

He wrinkled his forehead. "Monday, I think. Yeah, Monday."

"And what did he say?"

"I don't know. He asked if I heard about that fancy egg that was found in the park, and I said yeah, I had. And he wanted to know if I knew anybody who could handle it for him."

"You mean find a buyer for it without asking too many questions, right?"

"Sure. All right, I know some people, but not that kind of people, you know?"

"Explain it to me."

"The kind of people who would have the right contacts. Look around, Mrs. Foley. Do I look like I ever got even a piece of something like that egg? Even one time in my life? Sure, once in a while I make a deal and I get a little cash, but I don't kid myself. I'm penny-ante, and so's Skip. I make enough to live. Once in a while, I spend a few days in a casino and see if I can't double my money. Always I end up back here. That egg—" He sighed, and then he cleared his throat again. "That egg's first-class stuff, if you ask me. Whoever handles that has to know the right people."

"Not the people you know," Julia said.

"Right," Norm rasped. "And not just anybody has the cash to buy something like that without anybody noticing. I had to tell Skip to take a hike. Whatever time I have left, I'm not spending it in Reidsville."

Rogers State Prison was in Reidsville, about sixty miles west of Savannah.

"So you turned him down."

"Honest truth, Mrs. Foley."

"And you never saw the egg?"

"No, ma'am. Just on television." He rubbed his fingertips over his thumbs as if he could feel the egg in his hands. "Pretty thing though, isn't it?"

"It's even prettier in person." She studied his sallow face until he started to squirm a little.

He held up both hands. "I never laid eyes on it, so help me."

"Do you ever hear about things like this, Norm?" she asked. "I mean the big deals."

He snorted. "Only if they're in the paper. The upper echelons don't exactly drop over for poker and beer on a Saturday night."

She believed him. He was right about being penny-ante and right about Skip too. Skip would be in way over his head trying to find a buyer for a Fabergé egg.

"Okay, Norm," she said. "I appreciate the time. I'd appreciate it more if you'd give me a call if you do happen to hear anything." She gave him one of her cards. "In case you lost the one I gave you last time."

He peered at her. "So he's got the egg or doesn't he?"

"All I'm saying is that I want to hear from you if you pick up any information about the egg. Anybody asking about it. Anybody interested in buying it. Anything at all. Okay?"

He shrugged. "Sure. I guess."

"Thanks," she said, and she went out to her car and drove away.

She believed what Norm had told her. She mostly believed it, anyway. Even with his shadier deals, he clearly wasn't breaking the bank with his pawn business. Maybe he didn't personally know any high rollers, but he had to know a few that were a little higher up than he was. They had to know some above themselves and so on. But a small-time guy like Norm ran the risk of being cut out entirely if he tried to negotiate a deal with so many moving parts.

He probably knew Skip better than he was letting on. He must at least know a number of guys like him anyway. Norm was probably right that the risk he'd be taking wasn't worth the reward in this case. Still, he was clearly tempted, no matter how he denied it.

She was about halfway home when her phone rang.

Christian's voice came through her speakers when she answered. "Julia, it's Christian Kirkland-Wright. How are you?"

"Glad to hear from you. Did you get anything for me?"

"I did. Do you want to hear about it now or have it emailed to you?"

"Both, please! Let me pull over so I can jot down a few notes." She parked in a restaurant's nearly empty lot and grabbed a pad and pencil. "Okay, fire away."

"My people in Yorkshire sent me a few things that might prove helpful," he said. "There's a letter to Alexis's mother, informing her of his death on the thirtieth of September. That one's in English, from one of the ladies at the hospital where he was, but there's a Russian translation on the back. There's a letter from Alexis to his brother, Nikolai, saying he was injured in the hurricane and that he expected to come home as soon as he was able. That's in English, but there's a Russian translation of that too."

"Oh, wonderful. I'm eager to see those."

"I'll make sure they're sent to you right away."

"Anything else?" Julia asked.

"I'm afraid they haven't been through everything," Christian said, "but they did find his aunt's diary in which she mentioned his injury and then his death. It seems it was very difficult for her to lose him."

"I'm sure it was if she had no children of her own."

"No doubt," Christian said. "No doubt. Anyway, I know you were eager to hear as soon as anything came up. My people will continue searching the diary for any references to Alexis or to the egg in particular. I'll keep you informed."

"Thank you, and I'll keep you posted on what we hear from the police about the theft."

"Hmm. I hope their discretion can be relied upon."

"They understand we want to keep the case as low profile as possible," Julia told him, "but they will have to investigate, and that means interviewing people who might or might not keep their mouths shut about it. There's very little we can do about that, but the officers have agreed to ask those people to say nothing about the case until it has been resolved, which I hope will be sooner rather than later."

"That would be a good thing. Have there been any other developments in the case?"

"Nothing to speak of."

She decided not to tell him about her visit to Norm's place. It had confirmed her hunch that selling the egg in a discreet and profitable manner was above Skip's pay grade, but there was always the possibility that he and Norm might figure something out if they did get ahold of the egg.

"If I turn up anything helpful," she said, "I'll let you know."

"Very good then. Thank you, Julia. You ought to have those letters and diary pages in your email in the next few minutes."

"Great. Talk to you soon."

"Right," Christian said. "Cheers."

She pulled back onto the road and headed for home. She definitely wanted to see those documents, but she was going to have to have her talk with Beau first. However he reacted to her confession, it would be good to get it off her chest. Maybe by the time she got home, Bunny would already be back anyway.

She sighed. No, that wasn't very likely. Beau would certainly have called her if that had happened.

"Lord," she breathed as her car picked up speed, "please don't let him be too upset when I tell him. And please send Bunny home."

Chapter Nineteen

BEAU WAS ON THE PHONE when Julia got home, but she could tell he was nearly through with his call.

"Yes," he was saying. "I appreciate your help. Let us know."

"Everything all right?" she asked him after he hung up.

He came over to her and gave her a hug, but it was clear that the call hadn't made him very happy.

"I was just checking with the registry for Bunny's microchip. I wanted to see if anybody had reported finding her."

She put down her purse. "They're supposed to call us if that happens, right?"

"Yes, I know. I was only hoping they'd heard and hadn't gotten around to calling us yet. You know how it is. Places like that have to be busy."

"I'm sure." She took a steadying breath. "Are you really hungry, or can we talk for a minute before dinner?"

"I'm not particularly hungry, no. What's up?"

"Why don't we sit down for a minute?"

He looked at her warily but sat with her on the sofa.

"What's up?" he asked again. "Are you all right?"

"No," she admitted, feeling the sting of tears behind her eyes and blinking hard to keep them back. "There's something I've been meaning to tell you for a while. I haven't been able to make myself do it up till now, and that's just made it harder to tell you at all."

"You're not sick or anything, are you?"

She let out the breath she'd been holding. "No. Oh no. I'm sorry, it's nothing like that. I'm perfectly fine."

He exhaled too. "Okay, that's good. What is it then?"

She bit her lip, but there was nothing to do but just say it. The words came in a rush.

"It's my fault Bunny got out."

Beau stared at her. "What?"

She blinked hard, the tears burning behind her eyes again. "I think it was when I went out to get the mail that night. I never saw anything, but you know how sneaky she can be. She must have run out, and I didn't notice. I'm so sorry, Beau. I don't know how it happened, and I've felt so terrible about it, and the longer I've waited to admit it, the worse I've felt."

He looked as if he didn't know what to say.

"I think you've known all along," she said miserably. "I should have just told you right away. I hope you'll forgive me."

"Forgive you?" He shook his head. "All this time, I've been wondering how to bring this up to you, because I think I know what happened."

She bit her lip again, waiting for him to go on, to tell her how careless she'd been.

"After you went to your meeting with the Clarkes that night," he said, "I took out the trash. I didn't see her either, but she could as easily have gotten out then as when you went to the mailbox." He pulled her into his arms. "I've been beating myself up all this time because I thought I let her out."

"Oh, Beau," she murmured, holding him tight. "I'm so sorry. I've thought you were upset with me all this time. I thought you knew it was my fault she got out but didn't want to make me feel bad by saying anything."

She felt the rumble his low laugh made in his chest.

"And I didn't want to tell you I must have let her out." He kissed her temple. "What a pair we are, Julie-bean." He sighed. "I thought I had a nibble today."

She leaned away from him so she could see his face. "A nibble?"

"A woman called and said she found Bunny. She's just a couple of blocks over from us, so I drove there right away. She did find a little tabby cat, but it was young, I'd say not even a year old yet, and it was a tom."

"That's disappointing. Maybe you should have brought him home anyway. Not that I've given up on Bunny coming back, but maybe she'd like a little brother to play with, and if the poor thing doesn't have a home..." Julia looked at him questioningly.

"Don't think I didn't consider it for a few seconds, but when I told the lady he wasn't Bunny, she was so relieved. She really wanted to keep him herself. I could tell she was already attached."

"Well, that settles that then," Julia said. "And I'm glad he has a good home."

"I am too. I guess we keep on hoping and waiting and praying." He squeezed her close again. "But I'm feeling hungry now. What would you like for dinner?"

"I'll go check on what we have," she said. "But I really want to get a look at the information my English client sent me about his Russian ancestor as soon as possible."

"Ah well, these international issues can't wait. What if you see what you got about your case, and I'll pick us up something to eat? Does that work for you?"

She kissed his cheek. "I knew there was a reason I like having you around. That would be fabulous."

"What sounds tasty to you?"

"You know, just about anything. You pick. Don't tell me where. Wherever you go, you know what I like. Surprise me."

"Fair enough. I'll handle everything." He stood up. "No eavesdropping, you hear me?"

"Okay."

He went into the bedroom, and she went to her computer and checked her email. Christian's message was waiting for her. Glancing over it, she saw it was basically a recap of their phone conversation, so she opened the attachments.

The first one was from Alexis to his brother, but it was written in a fine copperplate hand, a feminine hand, a hand that was different from the uneven signature at the bottom. One of his nurses must have written it for him.

I am writing to you today, Nikolai my brother, to tell you about my most recent American adventure. Do you remember Oliver Brownwell? We met him in St. Petersburg last year, and I met him again recently when I was in New York. He was on his way to a place called South Carolina, and he invited me to travel on his yacht there to meet his wife and family.

We were nearing the South Carolina coast when a great storm hit. They call it here a hurricane. His yacht sank, and I was washed up onto one of the coastal islands. I have not yet found out what has happened to Oliver. I pray he will soon be found alive and well.

I was unconscious for several days after I was rescued, and I am still recovering from my injuries. I do not want to worry you or our mother and aunt, so please know that I am hoping to be well soon and on my way home. As much as I have enjoyed my American visit, I find myself longing more each day for my home and family. Tell our countess that I am thankful for her prayers and keep close to me what she gave me in remembrance of them.

I thank my little nurse that she writes this for me until I am able myself, but I can sign,

Брат Алексей

Julia couldn't read the signature. She assumed it was Alexis's, written in Russian script. It was certainly written by a different hand than the rest of the letter. This was a bolder hand, but it was also not as steady as the other. That made sense if he was still recovering.

The comment about keeping close what his aunt had given him in remembrance of her prayers had to mean the Resurrection Egg, didn't it? So at least at this point she could reasonably assume Alexis still had it with him.

She turned over to the Russian translation of the letter, a translation that must have been made for the benefit of Alexis's family, but of course, the signature would still be in Russian there. She'd have to ask Carmen to get it translated too. If for some reason this was from someone other than Alexis, she wanted to know that up front.

She opened the next attachment. It was the letter to Alexis's family, informing them of his death. It was kind and straightforward, but it held little information except that he had died of his injuries on September 30, 1893. The only other feature of interest was the signature of the writer, a Miss Eliza Cunningham.

Julia recognized the name. She was the one who had taken the group of young women from the church to help with the hurricane relief efforts. If she had known Alexis, surely Willow had known him too. Maybe Julia ought to try to find out more about Miss Cunningham. She looked through her case notes for a moment, jotted down a couple of things, and then called Maggie Lu.

"Julia," Maggie Lu said. "How good to hear from you."

"Hi there. I hope I'm not interrupting anything."

"You know how it is," Maggie Lu said with a laugh. "Everything can be paused nowadays."

"I know. When I was a girl, we had to rush home to be sure we didn't miss our favorite TV shows."

"When I was a girl," Maggie Lu said, "we didn't have TV, but we'd sit and watch the radio."

Julia chuckled.

"But," Maggie Lu said, "I bet you didn't call me up to talk about how TV used to be."

"No. I have a couple of names I thought I'd run by you, if you have time."

"Does this have to do with that case involving Willow Brenton?"

"Yes, that's the one. Her great-great-granddaughter Rayna Clarke is my client."

"I've come up with a little more on Willow's folks, and on Willow too. I still haven't been through everything, but I don't think much of it has to do with your case in particular. It looks like the Brentons lost their money in the panic of 1907 when the stock market crashed and local banks went bankrupt. A lot of folks who had money in the market went bankrupt also. As far as I can tell, that's when the Brentons went down in the world. Willow's father died that same year. The obituary didn't say of what specifically, just natural causes."

"That's a lot of misfortune in one year," Julia said.

"I also found an article about an influenza epidemic in 1909. There was a Mr. and Mrs. E. Sheffield who died. I don't know if that would be your Willow Brenton and Elliot Sheffield, but maybe it's something to look into."

"What year did you say?" Julia asked, flipping through her notes.

"1909."

"That's probably them. All I have is that they died in 1909, two days apart. I figured it had to be an accident of some kind or something contagious. Thanks for the information. When you get a chance, could you send me those articles?"

"Sure thing," Maggie Lu said. "I was hoping to find more, but I'll go ahead and send what I have."

"No rush now. You've been nice enough to help out, and I sure don't want to be a pain."

"Oh, no problem. I enjoy it. What else did you want to ask me about?"

"I don't know anything about this man at all," Julia said, "but he might have died as he was trying to bring his boat ashore when the hurricane hit in 1893. I'm not sure if he lived in the Sea Islands area or not, but I know he was coming to South Carolina to visit his family. His name was Oliver Brownwell. A letter I have from that time says he hadn't been found yet. I'm assuming his boat sank."

"Was it his own boat?"

"It sounded like it was. A yacht."

"All right," Maggie Lu said with a chuckle. "I won't bother trying to find him in the poor side of town."

"And I was wondering if you could see what you can find out about a Miss Eliza Cunningham. She's the one who took a group of volunteers to help the refugees until the Red Cross was able to pitch in. Seems like she was very involved in causes. Have you ever heard of her?"

"Can't say I have. Do you know anything more about her?"

"Not much," Julia said. "Evidently she never married. So at least you don't have to worry about her showing up under a different name because she got married."

"True."

"So how are things going with you? How's that great-grandbaby of yours?"

"Keeping me running, that's for sure. How are you?"

Julia exhaled heavily. "Oh, Maggie Lu, I've been trying not to worry, but I'm afraid I have been."

"What's wrong?"

"Our cat, Bunny. She got out on Monday, and we haven't seen her since. Beau and I are pretty upset."

"I'm so sorry," Maggie Lu said. "I know Beau dotes on that cat."

"He does. He put signs up all over the neighborhood with a reward and everything, and we haven't heard anything helpful."

"I wish there was something I could do to help."

"We sure would appreciate it if you'd pray that she'll come home soon."

"I'll do that. Is it all right if I ask my prayer group too? We've seen some real miracles."

"That would be wonderful. Thank you."

"And we'll pray for you and Beau too. I know this must be hard for both of you."

"I really appreciate it, Maggie Lu. I never thought I'd feel this way about a pet, but she's a part of the family. And Beau could hardly sit down without getting a lap full of cat right away. We've missed her so much."

"God knows where she is," Maggie Lu said confidently. "We'll be asking Him for a miracle. Easter is a time for things just like that."

"Yes," Julia said. "And we could use another miracle too, now that you mention it."

"What's that?"

"The egg that Madison found at the Easter egg hunt has been stolen."

Maggie Lu gasped. "You're kidding me."

"I wish I were."

"But I haven't heard a word about it."

"We're trying to keep it quiet for now."

Julia told Maggie Lu about the situation with Christian Kirkland-Wright and Rayna's shady uncle and her grandmother's safe-deposit box.

"Oh boy," Maggie Lu said. "That is a mess. But God knows all about that too. I'll ask my prayer group to pray for that too, but I won't go into specifics."

"Thank you." Julia wished she could give her friend a hug. "You've made me feel a lot better about everything."

"And I'll see what I can find out about your Oliver Brownwell and your Miss Cunningham."

"You're the absolute best, Maggie Lu. I really owe you one. Or five."

"You're always welcome."

"And you're going to have to have lunch with me and Meredith soon. No matter what, agreed?"

"You know it. You say when and where, and I'll be there."

"Good. Thanks, Maggie Lu."

"You're welcome. Just remember God knows what's happening."

"I will. Thank you. Talk to you soon."

Julia sat for a moment after she hung up. She'd really needed to hear what Maggie Lu had said, and that Maggie Lu and her friends would be praying for her.

"Thank You, Lord," she whispered, "for friends like Maggie Lu."

She went into the kitchen to get herself a Diet Dr Pepper and realized that Beau must have gone to pick up dinner while she was on the phone.

She went back to her computer and heard him come in a few minutes later.

"Julia?" he called.

"Coming."

"No, stay where you are. Just go on with whatever you were doing. Let me get everything set, and then I'll call you."

She chuckled to herself. "Okay. Let me know."

She read over the translations of the pages from the countess's diary. The poor woman had been devastated by the loss of her Aleksey. There was no mention of the Resurrection Egg when she got the news about his death or when she realized that he had been buried in Beaufort, South Carolina, and would never be coming home to her and Russia again. Could she have believed the egg had been buried with him? Maybe that was why no one ever came to claim it.

A few minutes later, Beau called her and sat her down to a wonderful dinner of chicken parmesan with all the trimmings, including piping hot Italian bread and a potato soup that was delectable.

"I'm not going to be able to stay awake now," she said after they had eaten. "But that was amazing. I wasn't thinking Italian, but it's exactly what I wanted."

"Good. Are you feeling better now?"

"Much. I know nothing's changed, but it's better now that we've talked and now that Maggie Lu and I have talked. She's going to ask her prayer group to pray about Bunny and about getting the egg back. I feel like a five-hundred-pound weight has come off my shoulders."

"I'm glad, honey."

"Now let's get everything cleaned up, and I'll tell you about what Christian just sent me."

"Anything helpful?" Beau asked, starting to pick up plates and silverware.

"I don't know yet," she said. "Not a direct mention of the Resurrection Egg, but a reference to it, I think. One of the nurses wrote it for him. I'd like to find out who that was. It would be helpful if it showed a connection to my clients now."

"You mean if it was written by the woman who owned the box the egg was in? Why not get a sample of her handwriting and have it compared to the letter? Or is that out of the question at this point?"

"I can see if the family has something." Julia thought for a moment. "Maybe I can compare it to the writing in the family Bible. If I'm remembering right, Willow's name is written there with her husband's at the time of her marriage and then there's a record of their child's birth. It makes sense that she would have made both entries. It's not much of a sample, and I'd have to have it confirmed by an expert, but I can at least see if it's a possibility."

She got her laptop and brought it back to the table. She opened the photograph of the letter and the photograph of the Clarke family Bible next to each other.

"What do you think?" she asked Beau, her eyes alight.

"I'd say there's a pretty good chance it's the same person. Maybe you could get something with more of her writing on it from the family."

"I'm certainly going to ask. As soon as we get things cleaned up, I'll call Rayna."

"Go ahead. I'm nearly done anyway."

Julia carried her laptop to the sofa and then got out her cell phone. If she was right about this letter, it would at least prove that Willow and Alexis had known each other. But would it prove that Jean had any right to the Resurrection Egg?

Chapter Twenty

Willow had been in Beaufort for nearly three weeks now. Many of the refugees had started making progress in rebuilding their homes and businesses. They were all still awaiting help from the Red Cross, but despite the continuing hardships, she had great hope in what had been done and what was coming to be. The people who had lost most seemed the most determined to stand up and try again.

Many of the patients had recovered enough to be released from the hospital, though the five men in Willow's charge were still there. She wasn't the only one captivated by Alexis Voronin's tales of the places he had seen and the adventures he had experienced. It wasn't uncommon for them all to sit listening well past dark. Some of the volunteers, when they had a rare moment of rest, would visit for a while. Even Elliot came sometimes.

Willow had grown quite proud of him over the past few weeks. She hadn't said so at the time, but she had been rather *skeptical of his offer to come with her to help the refugees. She had never seen any side of him but the elegantly dressed, well-mannered son of a wealthy and long-established family, and she had been afraid that he might not be able to handle this kind of work. He had laughed at her when she finally gathered the courage to mention it.*

"What did you think? That I've never done anything but go to cotillions my whole life?"

She had seen him behind the house with his sleeves pushed up to his elbows and his shirt drenched with sweat as he chopped wood for the hospital's many fireplaces. She knew he often hunted and fished. She knew he'd been sent to a prestigious military academy when he was young. She just had never thought...

He seemed to share much of Alexis's love of adventure, and she remembered that Elliot had toured Europe once he finished his university studies. She was sorry now that she had never asked him to tell her about it. Still, that was nothing compared to Alexis's travels across most of the world.

Lately though, Willow was worried about Alexis. He seemed to tire more and more easily. Dr. LeClaire and Miss Cunningham talked in low, worried voices after they visited the room, and Willow was certain she overheard them say something about surgery. Alexis had already endured one operation. That was before she came to Beaufort. Something must be terribly wrong if he wasn't getting well yet.

She thought about it now, late in the night when every-thing was quiet and all of her patients were asleep, and realized that the pain she felt at the thought of his death must be more than sadness for the loss of a fellow creature, more than regret that her efforts to take care of him had been unsuccessful. There was only one emotion that could account for the depth of her sorrow.

She was watching him as he slept, admiring the perfection of his profile and the dark length of his lashes as they lay against his pale cheeks, thinking it a tragedy that one so young and so handsome should be lost in the sweet springtime of his youth, when his eyes suddenly opened.

"How are you feeling?" she asked softly.

The pain in his eyes made the question unnecessary, but he managed a slight smile anyway.

"Malen'kaya medsestra," he murmured.

It was what he had called her since he had first awakened. He told her it meant "little nurse."

"I must have been sleeping when you first came in," he murmured. "I did not know you were here."

"How are you feeling?" she asked again.

He glanced away from her and then looked deeply into her eyes. "The doctor has not told you? Nor Miss Cunningham?"

She shook her head. "What is it?"

"I must again have surgery. I cannot tell you everything the doctor said. The English, the medical words, they are difficult for me. But he says I have bleeding inside, and he must try to stop it."

She took his hand and forced herself to smile. "He's a very good doctor, you know. I'm sure everything will go well."

He nodded, but she knew the truth. Surgery was always risky, and the recovery was often worse, especially under such crowded, makeshift conditions as these.

"I want you to know how much I am thankful for your kindness, Miss Willow. It is beyond kind for a fine and lovely lady such as yourself to come so far to tend to the sick and injured."

"I'm happy I came," she said, holding more tightly to his hand. "If I hadn't, I never would have met you."

He shrugged, smiling ruefully. "I am sorry I could not let you show me more of the beauties of this place, of your lovely Savannah, of which I have heard much."

"It will still be there when you are well. And you can meet my mama and papa and my friends, and I will—"

"It is very kind, but I will, if I am able, return home after this. You remember the letter you wrote for me to my brother Nikolai. He and all my family will be eager for me to come."

"But that was before," she said, feeling a sudden heaviness in the pit of her stomach. "Before I…"

"Before you what, malen'kaya medsestra?"

The heat flamed into her face. "I thought you knew. You were so sweet to me. Must I say it first?"

"Tell me," he said gently.

"I love you."

She thanked God that he didn't laugh. That would have been unbearable.

"No." He gave her hand a squeeze. "You do not. You love that I am from far away and that I tell you of places you have *never seen and know nothing of. You love that you have cared for me and that I have needed you. You love that I am different from your Mr. Sheffield."*

"He's not my Mr. Sheffield," she said, determined not to sniff.

"He loves you."

"No," she said with a low laugh. "We've known each other forever, since we were babies."

"But he has come here to watch over you, to help you, to show you he is now more than the boy you grew up with."

"Because we're friends. That's all. Because he promised my father. Because he knew Papa wouldn't let me come without someone to look after me."

"Ah," Alexis said wisely. "He knew it was important to you."

"I don't want to talk about him. I want to talk about us."

"But there is no us, *malen'kaya medsestra*. I am sorry, but it takes time for true love to grow. And whatever happens with this surgery, I will soon be gone."

"No," she breathed.

"You are very young. Not only in years, but in experience. All this is new to you, very exciting, very grown-up, but it is only for a time. Soon you too will return home, and you will find that real love is in the day-to-day, in all those small moments that make up a lifetime. You must love someone as your Mr. Sheffield loves you, a love that grows slowly like the oak, and not something that blooms and is gone like the lily."

"He's not my Mr. Sheffield."

There was no more to say. Alexis didn't love her. He didn't even want to stay and see if he might one day care for her. He was going. One way or another, he would soon be gone.

He turned her face up with one gentle touch. "I have hurt you. I am sorry."

"You've been very kind, even when I've been so foolish."

"Oh no. Never think that. You are a dear, sweet young lady, and you have done me great honor. It takes courage to let another see into your heart, and courage is something I greatly admire. One day, the right man will be blessed by it and everything else you have to offer."

How could that be when she had never before felt this way about anyone and could never feel this way again?

He sighed deeply, and she immediately put one hand to his forehead.

"Oh, your fever is up, and here I've been talking all kinds of nonsense when you should be getting your rest."

"I am glad you told me," *he said. He took her hand once more and brought it tenderly to his lips.* "Might I ask one kindness of you?"

"Of course," *she said, forcing her voice to stay steady.*

"You will pray for me? While the doctor is working, you will pray for me?"

"I will. I've prayed for you all this time."

"I know." *He smiled.* "Sometimes I have heard you when you thought I slept. It was sweet comfort."

She smiled back at him.

"There is something I would like you to get for me," he said after a moment. "It is in the bag with my clothing."

The bag was an old pillowcase, too worn to be used. His clothing was what he had washed ashore in. She started going through it and felt something hard inside one of the pockets. Frowning, she pulled it out. It was a crystal egg on a jeweled, enameled pedestal. Inside the egg was the Savior rising from His tomb.

"Oh," she breathed. "It's beautiful." She brought it to him. "What is it?"

"It was a gift to my aunt from the czarina."

"The czar's wife?"

He nodded. "It was made for her by the House of Fabergé. The czarina gave it to my aunt in token of their friendship, and my aunt gave it to me to carry on my journeys from home. A reminder that I am in her prayers and that I must come back to her."

"It's beautiful," she said again.

He pressed the egg into her hands. "I want you to have it."

"Oh no, I couldn't possibly—"

"Please. Just to hold as you pray. To turn your eyes to the One who hears you."

She nodded and clutched the egg to her heart.

"And if it chances that this is my time to go to God," he added, "I ask that you do not grieve. My life and times are His, and I trust in Him to know what is best."

She couldn't hold back the tears anymore.

"Shh," he whispered. "Shh."

She stilled after a moment and blotted her eyes with the handkerchief from her skirt pocket. Then she stood up.

"Would you like some cold water from the icebox?"

He nodded, and she went to get it, hoping that she didn't meet anyone on her way to the kitchen and back. When she returned, he was fast asleep, and the pain lines that had been in his face were gone.

At the first light of dawn, she rose and washed from her face what was left of her tears. And then she wrote in her diary.

I have only a few more minutes of quiet. Everyone will be waking up. Doctors and nurses, orderlies and volunteers will be attending to their duties. Soon they will come and take Alexis to surgery. I must steel myself to let him go. I suppose I am a childish, sentimental thing after all, but he is a kind man, and I am truly thankful for that. I feel no less the fool for baring my heart to him, but I admire him all the more for his gentleness and delicacy.

His aunt gave him a beautiful crystal egg with a depiction of Jesus's resurrection inside as a remembrance of her. I will keep it with me, and I will pray for him and put him in God's hands. He knows the end from the beginning, whatever may come. I cannot let myself think on what might come of today's operation. I can only wait. And pray.

Chapter Twenty-One

THE NEXT MORNING, JULIA GOT an email from Rayna in response to her request for a copy of something that would give her a bigger sample of Willow Brenton's handwriting. The attachment was a photo of a letter on notepaper with a border of purple and yellow pansies and the name *Willow B. Sheffield* engraved at the top. It was dated May 5, 1895, and was evidently written to her husband while he was away on some matter of business. Julia couldn't help smiling at the girlish postscript: *Perishing until you are home again.*

The handwriting looked very similar to the letter the "little nurse" had written for Alexis to his brother. As soon as she got into the office, she asked Carmen to have a handwriting expert make a comparison and give an opinion on whether they could have been written by the same person. Then she got herself some coffee and went to catch up with Meredith.

"You look chipper this morning," Meredith said when Julia sat down in front of her desk. "Good news?"

"I'm pretty sure I've established that our client's ancestor did actually take care of the duke's relative after the hurricane. I'm having it confirmed, but I'm reasonably sure as it is."

"And?" Meredith pressed.

"And?"

"What about Bunny? What about Beau?"

Julia sighed. "Still no sign of Bunny. I'm trying to not give up on her, but it's getting harder and harder to believe we'll get her back."

"I've heard stories about pets that have been missing for years that eventually find their way home."

"I don't know if I could stand it," Julia said. "But at least Beau and I talked."

"He's not mad at you, is he?"

Julia chuckled. "He was afraid I was mad at him."

"What?"

"He put out the trash that night, and he was sure he was the one who let Bunny out. Now neither of us is sure what happened, but we agree that neither of us should feel guilty."

"Well, that's good," Meredith said. "I'm sorry she hasn't come home yet. I've been praying about it."

"It means a lot to know you're praying about it too."

"I know she's precious to both of you and can't be replaced. And I know this has been upsetting."

"Thanks. What would I do without you, Mere?"

"What would we do without each other?" Meredith asked.

"I don't even want to try to imagine. Hey, do you have any plans for lunch?"

"Just the tuna sandwich I put in the fridge. Why?"

"I was thinking about seeing if Maggie Lu came up with anything on this case, and then I thought how nice it would be to treat her to lunch. I know it's short notice, but I really want to thank her for being so willing to help out all the time. And I wanted to tell her that I talked to Beau about Bunny getting out. What do you think? Can the tuna wait?"

"The tuna can certainly wait," Meredith said. "I have something I have to do at three thirty, but as long as we're back before then, I'd love to have lunch with you and Maggie Lu. If she's available, of course."

"Great. Are you meeting with Mrs. Croft? I know she's worried about one of her employees cooking the books."

"Yes, but not until next week."

Julia looked at her expectantly, but Meredith didn't explain. Julia could have sworn that there was a sudden fresh pinkness in her cheeks.

"It's just an errand I have to take care of." Meredith busily rearranged the files on her desk. "I hope Maggie Lu can come to lunch."

Julia hadn't noticed earlier, but Meredith looked particularly nice today. Not that she wasn't always well dressed and well groomed, but today she seemed to glow. Julia couldn't help wondering if Quin was the reason, but then again, Meredith and Quin didn't habitually plan their dates for the middle of the afternoon. But maybe there was something in particular they *were* planning. Julia didn't dare ask about it.

"I'll give her a call," she said instead.

Meredith waited expectantly as Julia called Maggie Lu.

"Hey, Maggie Lu," Julia said. "How's it going?"

"You must have read my mind," Maggie Lu said, a laugh in her voice. "I was about to call you."

"Really?"

"I haven't found much yet. Granny Luv's things can be hard to search through, but I did find a couple of things that might interest you."

"That's great. Meredith and I were wondering if you could have lunch with us today, and we'd love to know what you found. I know it's the last minute, but we'd sure like to see you."

"I don't know," she said, "let me check my schedule. Hmm, my lunch with the mayor isn't till next week, and I think the yacht club luncheon was canceled, so I can just squeeze you in."

Julia snickered. "Whew. That was close."

"I'd love to have lunch with you. What time and where?"

"How about we pick you up at eleven thirty? Then you won't have to deal with the bus schedule."

"Perfect. I'll be ready."

"You know," Julia said, "if you wanted to tell me about what you found ahead of time..."

"Oh no," Maggie Lu said with another laugh. "You're stuck now. You'll have to wait until we're sitting at the table before you get to see."

"Fair enough. Is there any place in particular you'd like to go?"

"Surprise me."

"Okay. See you at eleven thirty."

They ended up at the Savannah Seafood Shack on Broughton. It was full of talk and laughter and the smell of spices and grilled and broiled dishes from the nearby ocean.

"I haven't been here in the longest time," Maggie Lu said once they were seated. "I don't know why, because the food is delicious. Good choice."

"It's been a while for me too," Meredith said. "I think we get in ruts sometimes and forget Savannah has great variety of restaurants to choose from."

Julia nodded. "Beau and I came here a couple of months ago, and I've been craving the Low Country Boil ever since."

They ended up agreeing to share the big bowl of shrimp, sausage, corn on the cob, onions, and potatoes in a spicy Louisiana seasoning with crab cakes on the side.

"This is a treat," Maggie Lu said while they were waiting for their order. "And here I thought I'd be finishing up the chicken casserole I made on Wednesday."

"It'll be good tomorrow too," Julia said. "We're glad you could come."

Meredith leaned closer to Maggie Lu. "Julia won't say it, but we're dying to know what you found out for the Clarke case."

Maggie Lu laughed low. "I could tell. Like I told her, it isn't much. I don't know if it will help you find what you're looking for, but it's interesting."

She took a folder out of her purse. "Do you want the good or the bad first?"

Julia glanced at Meredith. "I'd rather get the bad over with as soon as possible."

"Me too," Meredith said.

"Okay." Maggie Lu put a newspaper clipping on the table. "Some of Granny Luv's relations had farms out on the Sea Islands when the hurricane hit, and I'm assuming her mother was the one who kept some articles about it. This one was in a scrapbook. It's about how the rebuilding was going along and what all the

Red Cross was doing when it finally got there. But here on the back…"

She turned the clipping over to show an article titled "Body of Savannah Scion Found."

"Oh," Julia said as she picked it up and began to read.

The body of Oliver Lee Brownwell, son of shipping titan J. L. Brownwell, was found washed up near Fort Wentworth. It is believed that the 27-year-old went down with his yacht, The Dove, *when he was bringing her home following his visit to New York and was struck by the terrible hurricane that devastated the Sea Islands and the coast. He is survived by his widow, the former Miss Maylee Winslow, and their two children as well as his parents, Mr. and Mrs. J. L. Brownwell, and brothers and sisters…*

The rest of the article went on to list the names of his siblings, his achievements, and his political expectations. There was no mention of his Russian passenger.

"At least we know what happened to him," Julia said, passing the article over to Meredith.

"Another piece of the puzzle," Meredith said. "For what it's worth."

"The other one's a little bit happier," Maggie Lu assured them. "It's about missionary work. It references a meeting that was set to take place in 1899, so it was considerably later than the hurricane."

Julia was a little puzzled about what this had to do with the Clarke case, and she could tell Maggie Lu was enjoying her confusion.

"Just look at this." Maggie Lu gave her a faded pamphlet that was titled *Light of the World* and was published by the James and Eliza Rogers Missionary Society. "This was with some things that Granny Luv had from her parents' church, used to mark the page in one of the hymnals."

Julia looked through it for a moment. Inside were several short articles about the society's mission work, where they had traveled, and the help and hope they had brought to the needy around the world.

"Wow. They really accomplished a lot in just two years. They were all over the place: China, Greenland, Abyssinia, India, Persia, Alaska, and the Pacific Islands."

"I know," Maggie Lu said. "Considering how slow travel was back then, they couldn't have stayed long in any one place."

"It's amazing, but I'm not sure how this connects to our case."

"Look at the back of the pamphlet."

Julia turned it over. On the last page under the title "Our Story" was a grainy photograph of a tall, thin, middle-aged man with a walrus mustache. On his arm was a woman in wire-frame glasses. He was wearing a black frock coat and she wore a white, rather severely tailored dress. A shoulder-length lace veil was pinned into her gray hair, and she carried a bouquet of daisies.

"That's their wedding picture?" Julia asked.

"Yes," Maggie Lu said. "According to the pamphlet, they were married in 1897 before they began traveling the world preaching the gospel."

"They've got to be in their fifties."

"Nothing wrong with that. But that's not why I brought it to show you. Look at the bride's maiden name."

Julia scanned the short article. It talked about the couple feeling a strong call to help those in need and spread the gospel. Then it mentioned the revival meeting in Raleigh, North Carolina, where "James Rogers met a kindred spirit in Miss Eliza Cunningham, the Savannah spinster who longed, as he did, to reach out to the uttermost part of the earth with the good news of Jesus Christ."

Julia caught a startled breath and then started to laugh. "It's Miss Cunningham." She passed the pamphlet over to Meredith. "The spinster lady who took Willow Brenton to Beaufort to help with the hurricane relief."

Meredith glanced at the page too, smiling from ear to ear. "You're amazing, Maggie Lu. How in the world do you find these things?"

Maggie Lu shrugged. "Sometimes I don't find any of the things I'm looking for. Sometimes I don't really know what to look for. But sometimes it comes right to hand. I like to think it's a little bit of divine guidance when it's really needed."

"Well, you're definitely a godsend," Julia said, reaching over to squeeze the older woman's hand. "We can't thank you enough for all the help you give us."

"There's nothing better than knowing you can do somebody some good," Maggie Lu said.

Their lunch came then, and they spent the next little while eating and chatting about this and that. Julia told Maggie Lu about her confession to Beau.

"I'm glad you talked to him," Maggie Lu said, helping herself to a crab cake. "But nobody's called you about her? Not even for a reward?"

"Nothing yet. Beau had one false alarm, but that's all."

Maggie Lu gave her a sympathetic look. "You keep holding on. My group is still praying for you. I believe she'll come back just at the right time."

"I hope so," Julia said.

"It's Good Friday. That was the darkest day in the history of the whole world. But the next Sunday was the greatest. You just have to remember that Sunday's coming."

"Amen," Meredith said.

They focused on finishing their lunch after that, chatting about what was going on with Meredith's grandkids and with Maggie Lu's granddaughter and great-grandson. Then the conversation turned back to the Clarke case.

"I'm sorry I didn't discover something more specific that would help you find that egg," Maggie Lu said.

"But it does fill in some gaps," Julia said, as she put down her fork and pushed back her plate. "After that lunch, I don't think I have any gaps left."

"Mmm, it was delicious though," Meredith said. "I'm not going to want any dinner."

"Me neither, but I'm not leaving any of my crab cake behind." Maggie Lu ate the last bite. "I'm so glad we did this. If I had to eat that casserole one more day in a row, I think I'd have run crazy."

"We're glad you came," Meredith said.

The three of them hugged briefly, Julia settled the check, and then they drove Maggie Lu back home.

"It was nice of Maggie Lu to let me hang on to this article and to the pamphlet," Julia said when she and Meredith got back to the office. "Rayna will want to see them, even though they don't strictly apply to the case."

"We ought to have Carmen make copies for the file at any rate. Did you find out what the Russian signature said at the end of the letter Willow wrote for Alexis?"

"Oh yeah. It says 'Brother Alexis.' I thought it was going to be his name, but it's more affectionate than that. Something else Rayna will want to know about."

Meredith chuckled. "That's pretty cool about Miss Cunningham finally getting married and then traveling all over the world. Probably what she dreamed of all her life."

"A good lesson in never giving up," Julia said thoughtfully. "And about things happening in the fullness of time."

Chapter Twenty-Two

Willow spent the morning changing sheets. Today, while Alexis was having surgery in what used to be the library, Miss Cunningham had said it was an opportune time to do the beds.

"It will be a far more comfortable resting place for our patients while you change their sheets than putting them on the floor as we've been forced to do up until now," she said matter-of-factly. "I'll send one of the orderlies in to help you. You go get the linens you need from the laundry. And you may as well put fresh sheets on Alexis's bed too."

Willow knew she must have looked stricken at that, because Miss Cunningham gave her a gentle smile.

"No, I'm not saying he won't come back. We can't think that at this point. But any patient who has undergone surgery needs to have everything he comes in contact with as clean as possible. The doctor may want to keep him where he is for a time, but if he does come back here, we don't want the slightest chance of hospital fever setting in."

"No, ma'am," Willow said, and she hurried out to get five sets of clean sheets and pillowcases from the laundry.

When she returned to her room, she found Elliot there talking to Mr. James.

"Our friend was showing me the box he made," Elliot said, taking the load of clean linens from Willow's arms.

"I'm sorry, Mr. James," she said. "I've been meaning to ask you how you were doing on it."

"All done, Miss Willow," he said. "It's not a very big thing, but I think it turned out kind of pretty. Mr. Elliot said he could polish it up for me if he gets time this afternoon."

"There's some linseed oil in the toolshed," Elliot said. "I think that's all it'll need to make that wood shine."

"What do you think, Miss Willow?" Mr. James asked.

Willow took the box from him. It was the right size for a lady's trinket box, maybe a foot long and four inches high and eight inches deep. Somehow, he had taken the scraps Elliot had found for him and made something truly lovely from them.

"It's beautiful," she said to the old man, making his dark eyes light with pride.

"I couldn't do my best work, you know, lying here in bed most of the time," he said, ducking his head, though there was a pleased smile on his lips. "But I guess little by little finally does the trick. And Mr. Elliot was good enough to keep my knife sharp for me."

Elliot shrugged. "I figure a craftsman's got to have the right tools."

Willow put her hand around the crystal egg she was carrying in her pocket and gave him as much of a smile as she could manage. "Elliot, will you help Mr. James over to Al—to the other bed?"

"Are you ready, Mr. James?" he asked cheerfully. "Better hold on to that box."

He lifted the old man—box, blankets, and all—to the cot Alexis had occupied for the past month. By this time, Willow was well used to bed making, and she quickly stripped the now-empty cot and covered it again with fresh sheets complete with hospital corners that even Miss Cunningham could find no fault with. Once she had changed the pillowcase, Elliot put Mr. James back into his own bed.

Willow fluffed his pillow and made him as comfortable as possible. "Are you warm enough? I keep forgetting that it will be October tomorrow. I know we won't have much real cold for a while yet, but the nights have been getting cool."

"I'll be happy to make a fire in the fireplace if you'd like," Elliot said. "Silas and I have been cutting and stacking wood for when it gets cold."

"Maybe tonight," Willow said. "It's pleasant so far, don't you think?"

"Are you warm enough, Mr. James?" Elliot asked.

"My old bones seem always cold, sir," Mr. James said, "but once I get my blanket back, I think I'll be doing well until tonight."

"*I'll get your blanket for you,*" Willow told him, "*but you'll have to wait a few minutes to get all tucked in again. Once I get everyone's sheets changed, the orderlies will have to change everyone's nightgown.*"

That elicited a low grumble from the other three patients in the room.

"*We're all right, miss,*" *one of them said.*

"*You know how Miss Cunningham is about keeping clean,*" *she said to them.* "*We're to have no hospital fever here if we can help it.*"

"*You sound more like her every day,*" *Elliot said under his breath.*

She was momentarily mortified, but then she giggled at the touch of mischief in his eyes. It was so nice to have someone around from home.

She changed out the sheets for the other three men and then, with a heavy heart, she changed the sheets on Alexis's bed.

"*We mustn't lose hope,*" *Elliot said softly as he helped her bundle all the dirty sheets together.*

She managed a nod, but it didn't matter what she hoped. Alexis would be gone soon enough, one way or the other.

By the time she had taken the bundle to the laundry to be boiled and starched, Elliot and one of the orderlies had helped all four of her patients into clean nightshirts. All that was left for her to do was tuck them under their blankets and make them as comfortable as possible. She couldn't help noticing there was a neatly folded nightshirt at the foot of Alexis's bed too, and unbidden tears filled her eyes.

Elliot said something to the orderly who had helped him, and then he came up to Willow and took her arm.

"I think you've had a long morning. Will you walk with me a moment?"

"Walk? Where?"

"You've never been to see my little palace out in the gazebo. I thought you might like to see what I made of it."

"You know I can't leave. My patients—"

"Jones will look after them for a few minutes. We're not walking to Savannah or anything."

She looked toward the orderly, and he nodded.

"It's no problem, miss. I'll be here until you get back."

She walked with Elliot out onto the rear porch and then into the rose garden. The high winds had stripped most of the blooms and leaves from the bushes. But they were still green, and what flowers were left were colorful and fragrant.

"I know," he said quietly as they made their slow way toward the gazebo.

She looked up at him, not sure what he meant.

"I know you love him," he said. "I know you do, and I know this is hurting you right now. I'm sorry."

"Why do you think that?" she asked warily.

His smile was bittersweet. "Do you think I can have known you since we were both children and not know? You're not very good at hiding your feelings. And besides, he told me so."

The heat rushed into her face. "What?"

"He and I talk sometimes when I help with the patients."

"He did not tell you he loves me."

"No," Elliot said. "Just that you love him."

"Well, I don't," she snapped, walking faster. "I don't love him. I'm just smitten. I'm a stupid, flighty girl who doesn't know anything about real love or real life or anything."

He tugged her arm, slowing her again. "You know that's not true."

"I'm too flighty to be anyone's wife."

"You feel things deeply. You're passionate about what you want to do. There's nothing wrong with that. Besides," he said, "you won't always be twenty-two." His expression turned playful. "Someday you'll be twenty-three."

She tried to hide her smile. "I appreciate that you came here just because I wanted to come. I know Papa trusts you to look out for me."

"That's not why I came."

Before he could say anything more, Miss Cunningham waved at them from the back porch, the gesture grim and urgent.

"We'd better go back," Elliot said, hurrying Willow toward the house.

Miss Cunningham took them to the little room that Dr. LeClaire conducted private consultations in.

"Sit down," she said to Willow.

Willow's stomach tightened, and she slipped her hand around the egg in her pocket, her prayers echoing in her heart. "What is it?"

"*Sit down, please.*"

"*Please,*" Elliot murmured, and he guided her to a chair.

Willow complied and caught a hard breath, already knowing what Miss Cunningham was going to say.

"*I'm sorry,*" the older woman said gently. "*Mr. Voronin passed on a few minutes ago.*"

Elliot slid one arm around Willow's shoulders.

"*Thank you for telling me,*" she said with a calm she hadn't expected.

"*He felt no pain,*" Miss Cunningham assured her. "*The doctor did all he could to save him, but there was too much internal damage. Dr. LeClaire said—*"

"*No.*" Willow stopped her. "*I really don't want to know. He told me last night what I needed to hear. I'm all right.*"

"*He asked me to write to his family for him. If anything happened. He asked me to write a letter to you too. He told me he loved you very much, his little nurse, and didn't want you to grieve.*"

He said he loved her, not that he was in love with her. She would love him that way too. It was what he would have wanted and was nothing to be ashamed about.

"*I'll try not to,*" she said.

Miss Cunningham handed her a folded sheet of paper. "*This is to you. It was very important to him.*"

"*Thank you.*"

Willow clutched the letter for a moment, and then she unfolded it. It took only a minute to read, and somehow she didn't cry.

"Thank you," she said again when she folded it up and put it in her pocket with the crystal egg. "I'd better get back to my room now. We left an orderly in charge, and he'll be wondering where we've gone."

Elliot glanced at Miss Cunningham and then helped Willow to her feet. When they got to the room with her patients, Willow asked Elliot and the orderly to move the men out onto the breezy porch.

"You could all use some sunshine and fresh air," she said to them.

They all seemed to perk up at that, eager for even a brief change of scenery. Only Mr. James declined the offer, saying he was comfortable where he was.

"Are you all right?" Elliot asked Willow quietly.

She nodded, and he touched his lips to her forehead. Then he and the orderly took the men out to the porch.

"Miss Willow?" Mr. James said once all the other men were gone.

She went to him. "Is there something I can get for you?"

He nodded toward Alexis's bed. "He's gone, I think."

A hot tear slipped down her cheek in spite of herself.

"I'm sorry," he said. "He was a kind man, a good man, even if he wasn't from around here."

"Yes, I agree. I'm glad I met him, even if just for a time."

Mr. James picked up the box he had made and held it out to her. "I'd like you to have this, miss."

"Oh, I couldn't possibly take something as nice as this."

"Sure you can." There was something of pride and sorrow and wisdom in his expression. "I didn't know who it was for when I started it, but I realize now it's meant to be yours. There's part of it I haven't shown you yet."

He pressed on one end of the box, and she wasn't sure how it happened, but suddenly the end popped open, revealing a small hidden compartment.

"That's amazing," she breathed.

"I put that in because all young ladies have their secret treasures." He looked steadily at her. "And maybe what he gave you would fit nicely into it."

Her hand flew again to the object hidden in her pocket. "What?"

"I told you I don't always sleep the night through." He patted her arm. "I heard what he said, and I know he wanted you to have that. A way to remember him and to know how thankful he was for you. I heard him telling Miss Cunningham what to write in that letter to you. Maybe you're not ready for anybody to ask you why. And maybe your mama might not like her daughter having a gift like that from a man she didn't hardly know."

She started to protest at that, but she knew he was right. Mama and Papa were both very strict about what was appropriate for a young lady to receive from a young man not her fiancé.

Mr. James chuckled in the soft, warm way he had. "Maybe they wouldn't like you having something from a strange old man neither, but it's just a wood box made from scraps. That's not so much they'd think you'd be obliged."

"Are you sure? You've worked so hard on it."

"Go on ahead and see if it would fit right."

She took the egg from her pocket and settled it in the secret space. A perfect fit.

"Now, you get some cotton or suchlike, Miss Willow, and pack it around there so it won't rattle, and it'll stay there safe and sound till you're ready to tell your folks about it."

He shut up the box and handed it to her. She clutched it to herself, unable to say anything.

"Go on now," he told her kindly. "You go on outside awhile and have a cry. You're going to be all right."

She touched his arm in thanks and then stole out through the side door where she could at least for a few minutes have some time alone.

Miss Cunningham says the Red Cross will at last be here sometime tomorrow, *she wrote in her diary late that night.* It is too late for Alexis but not for the others. I have heard of how much these poor people have accomplished with very little help or supplies, but now they should be able to do much more. Miss C. asked us all to stay on here until the work is done and then join her in petitioning the church to allow single ladies, at least in small groups, to go abroad to the mission fields.

I have decided I will remain here in Beaufort a while longer, until things aren't so dire, but then I will go home.

I miss Mama and Papa and Savannah, and I need to decide what I am to make of my life. Perhaps I am only twenty-two, but as Elliot says, I will one day be twenty-three and, I pray, wiser than I am now. And perhaps eventually I will tell him, and my parents too, about Alexis and what he left me.

Chapter Twenty-Three

JULIA GROANED WHEN HER ALARM went off on Sunday morning. Sunday. Easter Sunday. She didn't feel much like celebrating. She and Beau had spent most of Saturday searching the neighborhood for Bunny again. They walked around calling and asking everyone they met if they had seen the cat. Folks were kind and sympathetic but not helpful.

She and Beau had put on brave faces, telling each other not to give up hope, but she wondered if he was feeling as discouraged as she was. Maggie Lu had told her that Sunday was on the way after a dark Good Friday, but now Sunday was here and things looked just as bleak.

Beau turned over and covered his head with the bedspread. "Five more minutes."

She managed a smile. "I'll take my shower first. We can't be late this morning, okay?"

"Yeah," he mumbled. "Yeah, sure."

"Help me feel thankful and not sad," she prayed as she got dressed. "Help me remember the miracles You've done, the great ones and the small ones. Help me to trust in You."

She and Beau had a quick breakfast and made it to church on time. She struggled at first to sing the songs of celebration and rejoicing, but she chose to sing them anyway. Soon her emotions matched the words, and then she was ready to hear what the pastor had to say about trusting God when things looked darkest. Whatever else happened around her, she had much more to be thankful for than to be sad about.

"I'm glad we came," Beau said as they got into their car afterward. "I needed that."

"We both did."

They headed to the Downhome Diner for lunch. Evidently they weren't the only ones with the idea.

"It's packed," Julia said as Beau tried to find a parking place. "Maybe we should have made a reservation."

"I guess places do get full on holidays. Do you want to see how long the wait is or just go ahead and join the crowd?"

Before she could answer, his phone rang.

"Get that for me, will you?" he said. "I can't stop here in the middle of the street."

She looked at his phone as it rang again. "Not a number I recognize. Probably a sales call."

"No, it could be about Bunny."

It would be pretty unlikely if, after almost a week, this was a call about Bunny, but she answered it anyway.

"Hello?"

There was a pause, and she was about to hang up, when she heard someone take a breath.

"Uh, yeah," a man said. "I, uh, I saw your flyer about your cat."

Julia's heart started pounding. "About Bunny? Did you find her?"

Beau's eyes widened, and he had to swerve a little to miss a car that was parked too far from the curb.

"I might have," the man said. "She fits the description I saw, but there are a lot of tabby cats out there."

"Is she okay?" Beau asked. "See if she's okay."

"Is the cat all right?" Julia asked the man.

"She seems to be. She was pretty hungry when I found her, but I gave her some tuna, and she ate it right down."

"That's good." Julia nodded vigorously at Beau. "I'm relieved she's all right."

"I'm glad I saw your sign," the man said. "I hate for anybody's pet to be lost. I hope this is the right one."

"Yes, we do too. Where can we meet you? Is she at your house?"

"Uh...we're at Forsyth Park right now. Could you come here? We can wait for you."

"Forsyth Park?" Julia repeated, and Beau immediately headed that way.

"Yeah," the man told her, "but I can meet you anywhere. I mean, if it's not too far. I'm on foot."

"Oh no, that's perfect," Julia told him. "We'll be there in about ten minutes. Don't leave. Please."

"We'll be here."

Julia started to hang up, and then she stopped herself. "Oh, wait. Please wait!"

"Yeah?" the man asked.

"I didn't get your name. How will we know where you are?"

"We're at the fountain, on the north side. My name's Gil, and I have on a Dallas Cowboys cap."

"Okay, good. We'll be right there. Don't move."

He chuckled. "See you soon."

Julia ended the call. "Oh, hurry," she told Beau. "I don't want him to leave."

"What did he say?" Beau asked, speeding up a little.

"He said she's fine and ate some tuna. How in the world did she get over to the park?"

Beau's laugh was breathless, relieved, and bewildered all at once. "Maybe that's where she used to live. Who knows what would make her go back there?"

"My question is how this man knew we were looking for her when all the notices were put up around our neighborhood."

"We'll have to ask him that," Beau said. "How did he sound?"

"Friendly enough. He was kind enough to feed her. The thing that puzzles me is that he said if we wanted to meet somewhere else, it would have to be somewhere close because he'd have to walk."

"Maybe he lives near the park and was out for a walk when he saw Bunny."

"Then how would he have known she was missing in the first place?"

"He could have walked from our neighborhood, I guess," Beau said.

"That's about six miles. Not too long a walk I guess, for him or Bunny. I suppose he'll tell us all about it once we see him. It's got to be her."

Please, Lord, she prayed silently, *let it be Bunny. Please let it be Bunny.*

They reached Forsyth Park in record time and parked as close to the fountain as they could.

"He told me he'd be wearing a Cowboys ball cap," Julia said, looking around as they walked.

Julia spotted the man sitting on a bench near the fountain reading a book. He had long, sun-bleached hair and a deep tan, and his jeans and army jacket were well worn. He looked as if he was in his fifties. As promised, he was wearing a Dallas Cowboys cap. There was a camouflage backpack on the ground at his feet, and sleeping on it was a curled-up tabby cat.

"Bunny!" Julia cried, and she and Beau hurried toward her.

Her head rose at the sound of her name, and Beau scooped her up and cuddled her close. She began kneading his chest and purring wildly.

"Where've you been, Jack?" Beau asked. "We've been looking all over."

Julia stroked her back and kissed the top of her head, and then she turned to the man who was still sitting there, smiling now.

"I guess she's yours," he said.

Julia held out her hand to him. "I'm so sorry. She's been gone since Monday, and we've been so worried. You must be Gil."

"That's right." He stood up and shook hands with her. "I'm glad I got the right cat."

"I'm Julia Foley, and this is my husband, Beau. You don't know how much we appreciate your getting in touch with us. We'd about given up, but it's Easter Sunday. What better day for miracles?"

He gave her a wistful smile. "Sure, if you can get them."

"Thanks for being part of ours," Beau said, shifting Bunny into one arm so he could shake hands with Gil too. "How'd you know about her?"

Gil reached into the back pocket of his jeans and unfolded a copy of their flyer with Bunny's picture on it. "I was walking through your neighborhood this morning, and I picked it up. You know, in case I saw your cat along the road. I stopped around lunchtime and opened up a can of tuna I had, and I saw her looking at me from behind a tree. She took off when I tried to get her, so I sat near her and put a piece of tuna next to me. She finally came and got it and then settled beside me. After that, we talked for a while and shared the tuna, and she fell asleep on my backpack, and that's when I called you."

"Where are you headed?" Julia asked him. "Back home?"

Gil gave her a wry smile. "Just heading up to Bluffton. My son lives there."

Julia remembered that he'd told her he would have to walk to wherever they agreed to meet. "That's in South Carolina, about twenty-five miles away. You're not planning to walk that far, are you?"

"It's okay. I walk a lot. I'll get there tonight or tomorrow. Whenever. I'm in no hurry."

"But—"

"Really, it's fine. I'm glad you got your cat back." He slung his backpack over his shoulder and then stroked one of Bunny's ears. "She's a good cat."

"Wait," Beau said. "You forgot your reward. We advertised a reward."

"Oh no," Gil said. "I don't need your money. I was glad to help. I know how it feels to be separated from somebody you love."

"But we want to keep our part of the bargain." Beau took his wallet from his pocket and pulled out some cash. "We want you to have this. It should be enough to get you where you're going and let you spend a couple of nights in a motel or something when you get there."

Gil tried to wave it off, but Julia took the money and pressed it into his hand.

"You take that," she said. "We don't want you to be separated from your loved one either."

Gil looked at the money. "I haven't seen my son in a long while. I thought this would be a good time to try to talk to him again. I've been too much of a drifter to be much of a father to him all his life, but yeah, I'd like to see how he's doing. Thanks."

"We can take you to the bus station, if you'd like," Beau said as Gil put the money into his pocket.

"Thanks, but I know where it is." Gil stroked the cat's furry cheek with the back of his fingers. "Bye, Bunny. Don't go wandering off anymore."

He waved and then jogged off in the direction of the bus station.

Beau shook his head, and then he looked at Bunny. "You picked a good one, Jack."

"I hope he and his son get to talk," Julia said.

"Me too." Beau put his arm around her, and they started back toward the car. "I'll have to stop at the ATM before I meet Quin, but I'm glad I had some cash on me. I almost never do."

Julia stopped and gave him a hug, squeezing Bunny between them.

"I'm so glad she's back."

Bunny made a purring mew and rubbed her cheek against Julia's.

"And don't scare us like that again," Julia added.

She cuddled the cat in her arms as Beau drove them home, and thanked God that Sunday had come.

Chapter Twenty-Four

JULIA WOKE UP THE NEXT morning with six pounds of cat standing on her chest. Bunny was giving her the usual accusatory "you haven't fed me yet" look.

"I missed you," Julia whispered.

She pulled the cat into a hug and kissed the top of her head. As soon as she released her, Bunny bounded off the bed and headed for the kitchen. Beau, who had evidently woken up in time to witness the exchange, laughed softly.

"The drama princess is ready to be served."

"She didn't do much of anything last night but eat," Julia reminded him.

"And how is that different from usual?"

Julia stayed there a few minutes longer, thankful to have her little family back together. It had been wonderful to call Maggie Lu and Meredith after she got home yesterday afternoon to tell them the news about Bunny's return and thank them again for their prayers. Now all she needed was to make some real progress on the Clarke case.

She had just gotten settled at her desk at the office when her phone rang. She put down the Clarke file and dug her it out of her purse.

"Rayna, hello," she said. "How are you? I was going to call you later this morning to let you know that we had an expert compare them, and the handwriting from the note you sent me matches the handwriting from the letter written on Alexis's behalf to his brother, Nikolai. So we can be sure that Willow met him at least at one point."

"That's great news," Rayna said, sounding almost breathless, "but I have something better. Can you come over to my grand-mother's house? Or can I come to you?"

"What is it? You didn't find the egg, did you?"

"Nothing like that, but it's something you need to see."

Julia checked her watch. It was still early and Meredith wasn't in yet. "Sure. I can come by your grandmother's. Do you want me to bring the information about the handwriting analysis?"

"That would be great."

"Okay, give me a few minutes to take care of a couple of things here, and then I'll head your way."

"See you soon," Rayna said, and she hung up.

Julia put her phone back into her purse and then checked her calendar for the day. She didn't have anything pressing until late afternoon. She drank down her still-hot cup of coffee and then went into the reception area.

"I'm going out to Jean Clarke's," she told Carmen.

"This early?"

"This early. Tell Meredith I'll be back when I'm back, and call me if anything urgent comes up, please."

"Okay."

Clutching the Clarke file, Julia headed out the door. It took only a few minutes to get to Jean's house. Rayna was there in the living room with her grandmother, but to Julia's surprise, Skip wasn't.

"Just us this morning?" she asked as the three of them sat down in the living room.

Jean put her finger to her lips. "Poor Skip was up late last night. I thought it would do him good to sleep in."

"As if he ever did anything else," Rayna said, but she smiled. "Anyway, I'd rather he didn't know about this until after you did, Julia. It might be very important to the case."

"I think you'd better give me the news straight out," Julia told her. "All this suspense is killing me."

The treasure box was sitting on the coffee table in front of her, but the lid was open. Something about it was different.

Julia nodded toward it. "Does it have something to do with that?"

Rayna picked it up, a gleam of excitement in her eyes. "I was looking at it last night, and I realized the mirror in it was cracked. It must have happened when Nanny dropped the box."

"I was wondering what was different about it. The mirror's gone."

"Right. I thought I'd put in a new one. I didn't want Nanny cutting herself."

"I wasn't going to cut myself," Jean said, frowning.

"Anyway," Rayna said, "when I took the mirror out of the frame, I found this behind it."

She handed Julia a piece of slightly yellowed paper that had obviously been folded several times. The handwriting on it, clearly a woman's, was hardly faded at all. She thought it looked familiar.

"Read it," Rayna said.

My dear little nurse,

Your Miss Cunningham is kind enough to write this to you for me while you are sleeping. I will soon have this operation Dr. LeClaire says I must have. He says I need not worry, but I can tell in his eyes that he worries himself. As I told you already, I do not fret for myself. My life and my times are in the hands of God, and He knows what is the best for me.

I wanted only to tell you again how much it has meant to me to have so lovely a lady to care for me while I am a stranger here. Please know that I treasure your prayers and your kindness. What I gave you last night to hold as you pray, to turn your eyes to Him in devotion, I wish for you to keep. If I cannot return it to the one who gave it to me, I would like you to have it. Perhaps you will remember too, as you look on it, that death is not the end.

I wish you all happiness and the love of a man worthy of having you, if there is any so worthy. He may be nearer than you think.

With all kind wishes,
Алексей

As in the letter from Alexis to his brother, Nikolai, the signature was made by a bolder, less steady hand. Julia flipped through her file and found the printout of the earlier letter. She knew Алексей was Russian for Alexis. Miss Cunningham had written this latest letter on his behalf before the surgery he didn't survive.

"This is Alexis's signature," Julia said. "Look."

Rayna and her grandmother both nodded eagerly.

"Then he gave the egg to her," Jean said. "Our family has the right to keep it."

"Do you think that's true, Julia?" Rayna asked anxiously.

"Mmm, I'm not sure." Julia scanned the letter again. "He doesn't specifically say in the letter what he gave her that night. I mean, I would think he was talking about the egg. That would explain a lot."

"Sure it does." Skip stumbled into the room in sweatpants and a T-shirt and with his hair sticking up all over his head. "Lemme see what that says."

"Skip, please—" his mother began, but he merely snatched the letter from Julia and read it over.

"This is great. It says right here that he wanted her to have it. He says he can't return it to the one who gave it to him. Isn't that his aunt or something? How much clearer could it be, for cryin' out loud?"

"If that's the case," Rayna asked, "why would she feel the need to hide the egg or the letter? She had what could be proof of Alexis's gift."

"Consider that she was very young at the time," Julia said. "And you have to remember that there were still fairly strict rules in those days about what gifts a young woman could accept from a man without seeming fast. If she took care of Alexis, she must have been very upset about his death. It's likely that her parents would have disapproved of her receiving a gift from a man, especially a foreigner and especially such an expensive gift."

"But wouldn't she have told her family about the egg eventually?" Jean asked.

"I would think so." Julia looked over the letter again. "She must have told her husband at some point, but maybe they thought it was safer to keep it hidden. She made sure her family knew the box was valuable. I expect she would have eventually told her daughter, but you've got to remember, she and her husband died when their daughter was still very young. They must not have had time to say anything about it, and then their daughter had no idea all her life that there was a genuine treasure in her possession."

"That leaves more for us, right?" Skip asked with a grin.

"I'd like to show this letter to Christian," Julia said. "It's not as specific as I wish it was, but maybe he'll read it and realize that it was a gift to someone in your family and withdraw his claim."

Rayna looked uncertain, but there was a touch of eagerness in her expression. "Do you think we could see him now?" she asked, smoothing her hair. "I don't want him to think I, uh, we have any hard feelings about the whole thing."

"Let me see." Julia got out her phone and called Christian. "I could give him a little more information about what we've found out at the same time. I trust you would have told me if the police contacted you about anything."

"They sure asked me a lot of questions," Skip grumbled.

Curious, Julia glanced at Rayna.

"It was just regarding the investigation," Rayna said. "They haven't come up with anything that they've told us about yet."

Julia nodded, waiting for Christian to pick up. "That's okay. While we're there, if we get to go, we can ask—Christian. Good morning."

"How are you, Julia?" Christian asked. "I was just wondering if you got any new information over the weekend."

"Actually, I have several things to tell you about. Rayna and I were hoping to come see you. Is now a possibility?"

Christian hesitated. "Uh, actually, that's a bit awkward at the moment. You can come by, of course, but everything's turned on its head here. My father had a spill in his car. He's going to be all right, but I'm afraid I need to get back home as soon as I can."

"Oh, I'm sorry to hear that."

"Yes. I'm thankful it's no worse than it was. But we'll have to finish up our haggling over the Resurrection Egg, if it's ever recovered, by telephone and email for the time being. I know Roy can handle things in my place if anything comes up."

"When are you leaving?" Julia asked. This emergency of his was sudden and very convenient.

All of the Clarkes looked startled and concerned at that point, and Julia held up one finger, urging patience.

"I have a flight booked for this afternoon," Christian said. "A quarter of four, I believe. So I'm not in a terrible rush, but I can't get tied up in anything either."

"Would it be possible for us to come by for just a few minutes? I promise I won't keep you, but Rayna's found something that might settle this whole matter between your family and hers and make it unnecessary for you to come back later."

"That sounds doable. Let me make sure I have my flight time properly in my mind before I positively agree. Would you hold a moment?"

"Sure."

"Thanks."

Christian must have put his hand over the phone, because whatever he was saying, and whatever response he got from Lumley, was very muffled.

"Julia," he said a moment later, "our breakfast things haven't been cleared away by housekeeping yet, and Lumley's still rushing about packing up everything, but if that doesn't bother you, by all means come by."

"Great. We'll head your way right now."

"See you soon."

Christian hung up, and Julia put her phone back into her purse. "We're on."

"Okay." Rayna looked flustered and eager all at once, and she smoothed her hair again. "I hadn't planned to go out. Do you think this is all right?"

She was wearing jeans and a cute floral top. She didn't look as if she had on any makeup besides the mascara that darkened her already-thick lashes.

"You look fine," Julia told her. "Christian's father was in an accident. He's going to be all right, but Christian is flying home this afternoon. He has time to see us, though, if we hurry."

"Let's go." Skip turned to the door.

Rayna turned on him, hands on hips. "We don't have time for a lot of discussion right now. We need to tell him about what we found and see if he'll consider dropping his claim. We don't need you making things worse, okay?"

"Worse?" Skip huffed. "Just because I'm not going to let him plow over Mom with his lawyers and his fancy titles and stuff. I want to—"

"Skip," Jean said, and her tone was as firm as Julia had ever heard it be. "We don't even know where the egg is at this point. Let Rayna handle it." She smiled at her granddaughter. "It's easier to catch flies with honey than vinegar."

Rayna's lips twitched, and her cheeks turned pink. "Nanny."

"Don't tell me you haven't noticed him too."

Julia kept her mouth shut, but she thought the older woman was right. Not that she expected Rayna to try to charm Christian into any kind of an agreement about the egg, but it wouldn't hurt to keep the animosity between the two families to a minimum, and that was never going to happen with Skip along.

"Mom," Skip whined.

"I'm really not feeling well," Jean said. "It would be better if you stay here with me in case I need something."

"Should we call your doctor?" Rayna asked immediately.

Jean shook her head. "No, honey. You go along with Julia now. If you can get this matter with the egg at least a little bit settled, I'm sure that'll make me feel a lot better. Skip, would you find my heating pad for me? I think it's under the sink in my bathroom."

Grumbling and dragging his feet, Skip left the room.

"You two had better go," Jean said once he was gone. "We'll be fine. He doesn't have a car." She lowered her voice a little more. "I hid the little bit of cash I had in my purse, so it's okay."

Rayna shook her head. "Nanny."

"Go on now. It's fine. Come back here when you're done and tell me how it went."

"We'll do that," Julia assured her.

"Mom!" Skip called from the back of the house. "Where'd you say it was?"

Julia managed not to smile. "Come on, Rayna, we'd better hurry."

She called Meredith once they got into the car, brought her up to speed on finding Alexis's letter, and arranged to pick her up on the way to Christian's.

***

Lumley opened the door of Christian's suite when Julia knocked.

"Good morning, Mrs. Foley," he said with a slight bow. "Mrs. Bellefontaine. Miss Clarke. Please come in. His Lordship is expecting you."

Christian was standing by the balcony door talking on the phone, but he smiled and gestured for them to make themselves comfortable on the couch. As he had mentioned, there was still a tray in the kitchen area with the remains of their breakfast on it. Evidently, Christian and Lumley had each had two soft-boiled eggs along with their grilled ham and toast. The eggcups were a dainty blue toile, and one of them still had a large uncracked egg in it. Three large suitcases and two carry-ons were near the fireplace.

"May I get coffee for you, ladies?" Lumley asked as the three women sat down.

"Yes, please," Julia said.

Meredith and Rayna nodded too.

Lumley waited a moment as Christian finished his call.

"Yes, about midnight, I'm afraid, and then we'll have to get from there to York and then out to Prescott Place. So don't wait up. Right. See you soon."

He hung up and then sat in the wingback chair nearest Julia and Rayna.

"Sorry about that. Just checking on my father."

"How is he?" Julia asked.

"Better than I thought, actually. He broke a bone in his right hand and has some cracked and bruised ribs, but the doctors are pleased that it's nothing worse. No internal damage, no punctures to the lungs."

"I'm glad," Rayna said.

He nodded. "Yes, so am I. But I'm sorry we aren't able to stay longer. Savannah is a charming city." He studied her face for a moment. "I would have liked to get to know it better."

A smile touched the corners of her lips. "Maybe you can come back sometime."

"I beg your pardon, sir," Lumley interrupted. "I thought I would go and get a fresh pot of coffee from the dining room."

"They won't bring it up?" Christian asked.

"I am certain they would, sir, but as time presses upon us this morning, I thought it would be more efficient to go myself."

"Ah, true. Very well. Don't be long."

"Of course not, sir."

Lumley bowed and slipped out of the room.

"Now, if you'll forgive me," Christian said, "I'd like to make our little talk as quick as possible." Again his eyes met Rayna's. "Plane to catch. I'm sure you understand."

"Of course," she said, and she looked at Julia. "Do you want to show him?"

Julia put the Clarke file on the coffee table and took out the letter Rayna had recently found.

"This was in the same box the egg was in," she said, handing the letter to Christian. "We're convinced it has bearing on the case."

His forehead puckered as he looked it over. "And you didn't know about it before?"

"It was behind the mirror inside the lid," Rayna explained.

"It doesn't specifically mention what this gift was."

"No," Julia said, "but it seems suggestive. You've read his aunt's letter to him, saying she wanted him to keep the egg to remind him she was praying for him and that he ought to come back to her. He says practically the same thing in this letter."

"Yes, I remember, but it's hard to say something this vague is proof positive. Is it possible for you to send me a copy of this? And one to Roy Keller?"

"Certainly. I can scan it and email it to you this afternoon."

Christian's phone rang, and he glanced at it. "I do beg your pardon," he said, standing, "but this is my father's private secretary. I really must speak to him."

"We understand," Meredith said.

He hurried into his bedroom, answering the call as he went.

As soon as he shut the door, Rayna looked over at the group of suitcases by the fireplace. "You know," she said, "if he did have something to do with stealing the egg, he'd have to get it out of the country somehow. And if he suddenly had to get back home, nobody would have much of a chance of finding it before he left."

Julia followed her gaze. "I've been thinking the same thing. I was about to ask him a few questions to see if his story holds up."

"And if he just happens to be a convincing liar?" Rayna got up and walked to the fireplace. "Maybe the egg is in one of his bags."

"Rayna," Julia said, careful to keep her voice low. "You don't have any evidence to show that's the case."

Rayna nudged aside one of the carry-on bags. "He wouldn't put it in anything that has to go through security, I'm sure. And I bet these two large suitcases are his."

She slid one of them away from the rest of the bags and turned it onto its side.

"Rayna," Julia said. "Don't do that. You can't—"

Evidently, she could. Rayna unzipped the case and started poking around in the neatly folded clothes inside. Everything was placed just so, the way Julia would have expected an English valet to pack them. If anything was disturbed, it would no doubt be obvious to Lumley.

Meredith looked at Julia and then warily toward the door.

"I'm not claiming positively that he's guilty," Rayna said under her breath. "In fact, I hope he's not."

"I thought you liked him," Julia said.

"I do. That's why I don't want him to leave until I'm sure he doesn't have the egg. If he's a jerk, I want to know now."

She lifted up several shirts and then some dark-colored slacks. Julia finally stood up, knowing they'd all be implicated if anyone caught them at this point.

"Rayna."

"You really ought to stop now," Meredith said sternly.

Rayna didn't stop. "I'm not letting him leave the country with our egg. I don't care whose son he is."

"I see."

All three women turned to see Christian standing in the doorway of his bedroom, his expression stiff and his dark eyes flashing.

"I'm so sorry," Julia began.

"I'm not," Rayna said, defiant fire in her own eyes. "Okay, yes, I shouldn't have touched your property, and no, I don't know that you've done anything wrong, but I had to check."

"You might have asked."

"I might have. I don't have proof you took the egg. If you didn't, I'll apologize, but it was a pretty odd coincidence that now that the egg is missing, you suddenly have to leave the country."

Christian merely stared at her, his face as hard and unchanging as granite.

Rayna crossed her arms over her chest. "Your father's so-called accident sure was convenient, don't you think? Just at the perfect time."

"The egg was stolen five days ago," he said with venomous calm. "If I were going to arrange for a 'so-called accident,' wouldn't I have done it nearer the time of the theft?"

"Maybe you didn't want to be that obvious."

"Rayna, please," Julia murmured, trying to defuse the situation, but she might as well have been downstairs helping Lumley get the coffee.

"We all need to sit down and settle this calmly," Meredith said.

Christian kept his eyes fixed on Rayna. "Is that what you think of me?"

She lifted her chin as if she wanted to fire back something wounding, but she wavered a little.

"Fine," he said, taking three long strides over to the suitcase. "Allow me to help you."

He dropped to one knee and started flinging shirts and slacks onto the floor.

"Wait," Rayna urged.

"No, I want you to see what's in here." He gave her a tight smile as he started pulling out more and more of his things, tossing them at her feet. "It wouldn't do for you to have your police stop me at the airport, would it? Personally, I'd rather have it out with you here and now."

"You don't need to—"

"I'm not seeing anything untoward in this one," he said when the first case was empty. "But I might have it in the other one. Shall we see?"

He opened the second suitcase and started clearing it out. Ties and socks and underwear joined the jumbled pile. There was what looked like a shaving kit in one of the pockets, and he thrust it into Rayna's arms.

"Best check that. I might have concealed the egg in the shaving soap."

Rayna bit her lip, just holding on to the bag, and Christian continued unloading the second case.

"This really isn't necessary," Julia said. She couldn't condone their childish behavior, but she couldn't say she wasn't pleased to have a good look at what was in those suitcases.

Meredith merely watched, one eyebrow speculatively raised.

"No, let's do it up right." Christian grabbed up a lumpy canvas bag. "In for a penny, in for a pound, eh? What better place to hide the loot than in the dirty laundry?"

He untied the bag and dumped it out with everything else. A wadded-up T-shirt hit the floor with a muffled thud, and the three of them froze. Christian frowned, Rayna's lips were pursed, Meredith's eyebrows went up, and Julia knelt down and spread out the shirt.

Nestled inside it was the Resurrection Egg.

Chapter Twenty-Five

CHRISTIAN SWALLOWED HARD AS HE stared at the crystal egg in Julia's hand. "I…don't know what to say."

"You had it all along," Rayna accused, her eyes narrowing.

"Rayna—"

"Don't even deny what you've done. And you're supposed to be a nobleman. I don't care how much the egg is worth—you've got millions more. My grandmother doesn't have much at all, and you think you have to steal from her? I can't even think of a name bad enough to call you."

"Rayna—"

Tears sprang into her eyes. "I was hoping I could trust you."

"That's a laugh. You were just searching my luggage, and you want me to believe you trusted me?"

"I needed to," she said, angrily dashing the tears away. "I couldn't let you leave before I at least looked. Now I'm glad I did."

"I didn't steal that egg, and if I had, it would be complete insanity for me to empty that suitcase as I did so you could find it there. I don't even touch the cases as a rule. That's Lumley's job."

"There's no reason you couldn't have put it in there after he packed everything," Rayna said.

"But the police searched everything here after the egg was sto-len," Christian told her. "Including the suitcases. So I don't know how it got here now."

Rayna's mouth tightened.

"Besides, I had no need to steal the egg, even if I were dis-posed to that sort of thing. It belongs to my family in the first place."

"Maybe not," she retorted. "Maybe you knew all along that Alexis gave the egg to Willow Brenton, and it didn't belong to your family anymore."

"Both of you, please," Julia said finally. "This isn't getting us anywhere."

Christian drew a slow breath. "You're absolutely right. Miss Clarke, I assure you that I did not know the egg was in my suitcase. You may believe that or not, just as pleases you."

Rayna glared at him.

"You said Mr. Lumley packed your bags," Meredith said, "and that you never touched them."

"That is part of his job," Christian told her.

"Then couldn't he have put it there? He packs and unpacks for you. He might have thought it wouldn't be found until you were both safely back in England."

Christian huffed. "Ridiculous. I know the man and trust him, and he couldn't have been the woman in the bank's video. But you can ask him whatever you want to when he comes back. For now, I think it would be a good idea to have a security company take charge of the egg until its proper owner is determined."

"All right, fine," Rayna said. "But I want Julia and Meredith to choose the security company, and I'm not letting the egg out of my sight until they take it away."

"We know a good company," Meredith said. "We can have them come get it. They can set up an agreement in which nobody will have access to the egg unless Rayna is present."

"Actually, it should be my grandmother, not me," Rayna said. "Don't you think so?"

"If we do it this way," Julia told her, "your uncle Skip will have a lot less chance of trying anything."

Rayna frowned. "That's true."

"We'll check with your grandmother to make sure she doesn't object, but I don't think she will. And this would only be temporary. Only until we get everything settled."

"Okay."

"That sounds fair," Christian said. "And, Julia, I would like you to find out how that blasted thing got into my suitcase in the first place."

"Oh no," Rayna said. "Julia is working for my family, and *I* want her to find out how it got there."

"All right, as long as we find out, I don't mind." He raked his fingers through his hair. "And I apologize, Miss Clarke, for my boorish behavior. Whatever else you think of me, I generally try to act like a gentleman."

"I provoked you," she admitted. "And I didn't exactly act like a lady. I'm sorry." She smiled. "But I'm taking that back if Julia finds out you stole the egg after all."

He chuckled. "Fair enough."

"Okay, you two," Julia said, putting the egg into her purse for the time being, "I'm going to get hotel security to send someone to guard the door. Meredith, will you please call the security company?"

"All right," Meredith said. "Christian, do you mind if I step into the other room to make the call?"

"Certainly not," Christian said. "Make yourself comfortable."

Meredith went into the room and shut the door.

"Rayna," Julia said, "if you would, please call your grandmother and tell her what's just happened and make sure she doesn't object to having the egg locked up where only you can get to it."

"Sure," Rayna said, getting her phone from her purse.

"I hope the security people come as soon as possible," Christian said. "I still need to catch my flight. I have to admit I feel a lot better about going back home than I did before the egg was found, even if finding it raises more questions than it answers."

Jean was amazed to hear that the egg had reappeared and was happy to give her permission to have it locked up for the time being. The security company Meredith called was one Magnolia Investigations used regularly, and they promised to send someone over right away to take custody of the egg. She had just told Rayna, Christian, and Julia what they said when Lumley came into the room.

"Good heavens, sir," he breathed, his eyes going immediately to the chaotic pile of clothes on the floor. "Was there an explosion?"

"No," Christian said, "but the Resurrection Egg turned up inside my dirty laundry."

"What?" Lumley gaped at him. "That is good news, sir, but how did it get there? It wasn't in anything I packed, I'm sure of it. In your laundry, did you say, sir?"

"In my laundry. But that's been piling up for the week, hasn't it?"

"It has, yes."

"I doubt you went through it before you packed it away."

"No, of course not. I merely added what you had from this morning."

"Then it could have been there earlier," Meredith said thoughtfully.

"How do we know you didn't put it there?" Rayna asked Lumley bluntly.

Lumley blinked at her. "Me, miss? Where would I have got it from? Whoever took the egg from Mrs. Clarke's bank was clearly a female."

"That's true," Rayna said reluctantly.

"It seems rather an obvious hiding place as well." Lumley started gathering up Christian's clothes and folding them again. "I'd think so anyway."

"Sometimes it's easiest to hide things in plain sight," Julia observed.

"What about the egg, Your Lordship?" Lumley asked, stopping what he was doing.

"Mrs. Foley has it for now," Christian said. "She's sort of neutral ground, as it were. A security company is coming to take it to one of their vaults for safekeeping."

"Ah, excellent idea, sir. Shall I check to see if housekeeping has a small box it could be placed in to protect it from getting damaged in the meantime?"

"Good idea. See to that if you would, please."

Lumley made a slight bow and excused himself.

"I feel like I ought to at least fold the clothes again," Rayna said, picking up a disheveled shirt.

"Nonsense." Christian took it from her. "You'll never get them exactly the way Lumley likes them, and then he'd just have to fold them all over again. Trust me, I know."

Lumley came in a moment later with a little box that would fit the egg just right.

"Pardon me, sir, but there is a gentleman outside who would like to speak to you."

"A gentleman?" Christian asked.

"From hotel security."

"Ah. Send him in."

"I'll go talk to him," Meredith said, and she went into the hallway.

"If I may, Mrs. Foley," Lumley said, "I'll pack up the egg right now."

"Of course."

Julia gave him the egg and watched him pack it. He fumbled for a moment with the piece of string he used to secure the box, but once it was tied, he handed the box to Christian under Rayna's watchful eye. Then he busied himself repacking the suitcases.

Meredith came back into the room a moment later. "I told the security guard that he needed to make sure nobody went into or out of the suite without our permission."

"Did the security company say when someone would be here?" Rayna asked her.

"It should only be a few minutes. Their offices are not far from here, and the manager said he had someone available now."

"Good." Rayna glanced at her watch. "I hope it's soon. I hate waiting."

There was a knock on the door, and they heard the guard's voice. "It's housekeeping," he said. "All right?"

Lumley opened the door, and Gwenda came into the room.

"Yes, it's all right," Meredith assured the guard, and he shut the door again.

"About time," Lumley said as he followed Gwenda to the cart with the breakfast trays still on it. "His Lordship has guests, and leaving this shocking mess on full display all morning says nothing positive about the service in this hotel."

Christian winced. "I'm afraid Lumley has very exacting expectations of staff wherever we go," he said to Rayna and Julia, and then he spoke louder. "It's quite all right, Gwenda. We realize things can get rather hectic at times. Please don't worry yourself. It seems we've all had rather a busy day."

"I'm very sorry, sir," she said in perfect English, as she pushed the cart toward the door. "Thank you for understanding."

Again, Lumley was right behind her, his face pinched with disapproval, but they both were stopped by the guard outside the door.

"All right for her to go?" he asked Julia.

Julia gave him a stern nod. "Check everything first."

She and Meredith examined the trays. There was nothing but dirty plates, empty eggshells, and crusts from the toast. Apart from the one egg that had been left uneaten, there was almost nothing left. The silverware was dirty and so were the coffee cups and juice glasses. The guard looked too, and shook out the crumpled napkins just to make sure.

"Clean as a whistle," he said.

"Thanks," Julia told him. "And thank you, Gwenda. You can go ahead now."

Gwenda gave her an uncertain nod and pushed the cart out of the room.

"I'd really like to see it one more time," Rayna said, leaning forward a little on the couch. "I probably won't be able to for a while once they lock it up."

"All right," Christian said. He started to undo the knot that secured the twine around the little box.

"Sir," Lumley said, reaching tentatively toward it. "If you'll allow me—"

"I've got it."

Christian fiddled with the knot for a moment more and then finally undid the string. Then he opened the box, and iridescent excelsior settled lightly on the carpet.

"Sorry, Lumley," he said.

Lumley flinched as Christian felt through the packing and brought out the object inside.

"What?" Rayna said, staring at him and then at Julia. "What's that?"

It was a small, black-marble ball flattened on one side.

"A paperweight, I'd guess," Julia said, taking it from Christian. "About the same weight as the egg."

Christian stood up, towering over his valet. "What is this, Lumley? Where's the Resurrection Egg?"

"Sir, I—I—"

"You were the last to have it," Rayna accused. "What did you do with it?"

"You saw me pack it away. Everyone here did." Lumley drew himself up, the picture of wounded dignity. "I would be happy to be searched, miss, if that would satisfy you."

"It would be a start," she said, and she opened the suite door and got the security guard. "We want you to search this man."

Eyebrows raised, the guard looked at Meredith.

"If you would, please," she told him.

"All right, sir," the guard said, turning Lumley to face him. "Please turn out your pockets."

Head high and lips pursed, Lumley did as he was asked. He submitted to being patted down, then Meredith had him search the luggage Lumley had just repacked.

"Nothing here," the guard said with a shrug.

"Thank you," Julia said. "Please wait outside."

The guard did as he was asked, and Lumley looked expectantly at the others.

"Sorry, Lumley," Christian began. "You being the last to handle the thing and all—"

"He could have hidden the egg somewhere in the room," Rayna said.

"But if he did, now he has to retrieve it, and we're watching his every move," Julia reasoned.

"He and Christian are going to be leaving the country shortly," Meredith said. "Then he won't be able to get it at all."

"I've no need to come back here," Lumley said disdainfully. "Ever."

Julia studied him for a moment. She knew the look. He thought he was safe. He thought he'd gotten away with the Resurrection Egg and no one could touch him. He had packed up the box and somehow made them think the egg was in it. The egg wasn't in the box when it was opened, but it wasn't in the room either. It wasn't on him. It had to have been smuggled out of the suite somehow. It had—

"The egg." Julia's heart suddenly raced. "It was the egg."

Meredith's eyes met hers. "Of course."

"What do you mean?" Christian asked. "We know the egg is what he took, but where is it now?"

"The egg in the egg cup. If the Resurrection Egg fit into one of those plastic Easter eggs at the hunt, why couldn't it be hidden the same way again?" Julia turned to Lumley. "What better way to get an egg out of a room than on a breakfast tray?"

Christian's mouth dropped open. "Good heavens."

Meredith threw open the suite door, startling the guard.

"Go inside and stay with that man there." She pointed at Lumley. "Under no circumstances let him leave the suite. And call the police."

Lumley sank into one of the chairs as the glaring guard came to stand next to him.

"I'm going to catch Gwenda," Julia said.

Meredith nodded. "I'm right with you."

They hurried out the door with Rayna and Christian on their heels.

"I'm sorry," Julia said to Christian, knowing the betrayal must be particularly painful.

"His family have been loyal to mine for over two hundred years," Christian said as they got on the elevator. "But that issue will have to wait. For now, I want to know how he did it. It's not as if he had a plastic egg in his room all this while."

Julia pushed the button for the lobby. "No, but I'm guessing Gwenda was in on this all along. She's the one who dressed up as Rayna's grandmother and got the egg from the bank."

Meredith nodded. "I was wondering why our pictures of the thief from the bank security cameras looked fuzzier to me after Lumley made copies of them for everyone. He must have deliberately given us copies of the copies so they wouldn't be very clear."

"Good heavens," Christian said again.

"Gwenda was in the kitchen," Julia said. "So when Lumley went to get a box for the egg, he got an eggshell from her too. I happen to know that this hotel gives out treats to their guests on Easter. I bet there are tons of plastic Easter eggs in the hotel pantry. All he had to do was distract us while tying up the box. He probably slipped the crystal egg into his sleeve when he switched it for the paperweight. He must have had the plastic egg on him and put the crystal egg into it when he was repacking the suitcases."

"When nobody was paying much attention to him," Christian said grimly.

"I see. And when Gwenda came up to get the breakfast trays, Lumley used another bit of sleight of hand to switch the eggs. And that's why he was over there scolding her. He must have shifted the soft-boiled one into her pocket or something."

Rayna nodded eagerly. "And when he was downstairs getting the box, he must have told Gwenda that she needed to come up and get the trays right away. Before the security company came."

"Exactly," Julia said as the elevator doors opened and they got out.

The four of them looked around the lobby, trying to spot Gwenda.

"There she is," Meredith murmured. "She must have gotten held up."

Gwenda was standing with her cart not far from the hotel restaurant, near a long hallway that Julia assumed led to the kitchen. An older man in a suit that happened to be the exact burgundy color of the hotel logo was evidently giving her instructions of some kind. The egg was still sitting placidly in its eggcup.

"Just walk normally," Christian advised, his voice low. "Don't scare her."

Gwenda spotted them when they were about thirty feet away and bolted down the hallway, pushing the rattling cart.

"What's going on?" the man in the suit asked as Julia, Meredith, Christian, and Rayna rushed past him. "Here now. I'm the manager. Guests aren't allowed down there. Hold on!"

They were all still about twenty feet away when Gwenda and her cart disappeared through the kitchen's stainless-steel doors. Julia and the others charged right after her.

"What is this?" the manager asked, huffing and puffing behind them. "I'm going to have to call security!"

"The police are on their way," Meredith said. "There's been a theft."

"Wait! What?"

"We've got to hurry!" Julia shoved open the kitchen doors. "Gwenda!"

The woman froze where she was, trapped between her cart and the enormous refrigerator as the others closed in. "What do you want?"

"What you stole."

"I don't know what you mean."

"Then why did you run?" Rayna asked.

"I saw the four of you bearing down on me, and you frightened me." Gwenda's eyes filled with tears. "Mr. Boswell, I don't know what they're after. I haven't taken anything. Go on and search me. All I did was pick up the breakfast trays from Mr. Kirkland-Wright's suite and bring them down to the kitchen. Is that a crime?"

"Come, come, Gwenda," the manager said, seeming to only now recognize his noble guest. "I'm sure this must be a simple misunderstanding." He turned to Christian. "I'm sure we can make it right, Your Lordship, whatever it is, if we simply talk it over."

"The only way to make it right," Christian said, "is for us to get back what she took."

"I don't know what he means," Gwenda insisted. "Search me. I've got nothing."

"What about that?" He nodded toward the egg still in the eggcup. "I suppose you have no objection to my taking this then?"

"No, sir." Gwenda looked at her manager as if Christian had lost his mind. "I don't know what he's on about."

"Oh, really?" Christian said. "Let's just see about that."

He grabbed the egg, and it immediately cracked in his hand, yolk, white, and shell squirting between his fingers.

Rayna covered her mouth to keep from laughing.

"Ugh." Christian grabbed a nearby dish towel and wiped his hand.

"Would someone like to tell me what's going on?" the manager asked.

Julia stared at the remnants of the egg on the plate. "Wait a minute." She fixed her eyes on Gwenda and saw her trying to edge her way around the cart and out of the corner she was in. "Keep her right there, Christian."

"My pleasure," Christian said grimly.

Julia threw open the door to the enormous refrigerator and immediately found what she was looking for.

"Here we are," she said, putting it on the counter.

"A bowl of eggs?" Rayna asked.

The manager shook his head. "Guests aren't allowed to handle food in the kitchen," he said. "The health department—"

"We're leaving in just a minute," Julia assured him. "As soon as I find the right one."

She felt several of the eggs until she finally found the one she wanted. The only one that wasn't cold. The only one that was plastic. She took it out of the bowl and with a firm twist opened it into two halves.

There lay the Resurrection Egg.

Chapter Twenty-Six

HALF AN HOUR LATER, THE security company had taken charge of the Resurrection Egg and the police were leading Lumley and Gwenda—protesting and squabbling all the way in thick Yorkshire accents—away in handcuffs.

Christian shook his head as they went through the hotel's delivery entrance and could no longer be seen.

"I'm sorry," Rayna said to him.

He gave her an uncertain smile. "I suppose anyone can be tempted if the lure is bright enough."

"Still, I know that must hurt. And... I regret more than that."

He looked at her expectantly.

"I'm sorry for acting the way I did," she admitted. "I guess being around Uncle Skip all my life, I tend to look at everybody with a little bit of skepticism."

"I don't blame you." He glanced at Julia. "I expect they'll be taking in Skip as well."

"Do you think so?" Rayna asked. "Poor Nanny is going to be heartbroken."

"I'm sure he'll be questioned," Meredith said. "Someone got your grandmother's ID and safe-deposit box key to Gwenda so she could steal the egg."

"But Nanny had hers at the time. And Skip and I were with her all that day."

"But Skip took them to try to get into the box himself," Julia reminded her. "I'm thinking that while he had them, he must have had duplicates made so he could try again later."

Christian gave her a grim nod. "Somehow he and Lumley got together."

"Right," Julia said. "And I'm pretty sure we'll find out that Lumley and Gwenda knew each other at some point back in Yorkshire. That is a Yorkshire accent she has, isn't it?"

"Yes. I thought Lumley was just trying to sound posh. I'd no idea he was trying to cover up any kind of connection between the two of them."

"The police will question all of them, I suppose." Julia sighed. "And we need to tell them our version of what happened too."

Christian checked his watch. "Quickly, if that's at all possible. I still ought to try to catch my plane."

***

Due to Julia and Meredith's connections with the Savannah Police Department, they were able to submit their statements quickly. Christian let the officer in charge know that he would be willing to return to testify in the case if and when it should come to trial, but he was told that both Lumley and Gwenda seemed likely to plead guilty in order to receive lighter sentences.

"And my uncle?" Rayna asked. "Skip, uh, Dalton Clarke?"

"He's waiting for a lawyer to be appointed to his case before he's questioned."

"Could we see him?" Julia asked. "Just for a moment?"

After a brief wait, they were taken to see Skip. He was sitting at a table in an interview room talking to one of the detectives. Julia spoke with the officer, and he let them have a minute alone, though he assured her he'd be right outside the door in case of any trouble. Skip looked as if he didn't have the heart to make trouble for the time being.

"I didn't think I'd see any of you here," he said dismally as Rayna, Meredith, and Julia took the three available chairs and Christian remained standing. "You're going to have to go home pretty quick, Raynie. Mom's going to need you."

"I know," Rayna said. "Oh, Uncle Skip, why'd you have to do this? How could you hurt Nanny? She would do anything in the world for you, and you treat her this way? Really?"

She looked sad and angry and hurt all at once. She also looked as if she pitied him.

He shrugged. "You know me. I always try to take the easy way out."

"And it never ends up being easy. Haven't you learned anything your whole life?"

He shrugged again. "I'm just an old dog who doesn't like learning new tricks."

"How'd you get into this?" Julia asked him.

"Yes, I'd like to know," Christian said, clutching the back of Rayna's chair. "How did you and Lumley fall in together? And where does Gwenda fit in?"

"He called me up that first night," Skip said, keeping his eyes on the empty table. "I didn't know who it was, and he wouldn't say, though I was pretty sure from the accent that it was your valet. He asked me if I could meet him somewhere, and said that if I did, he'd tell me how I could get a lot of money without getting myself into trouble. I told him no and hung up. I mean, why should I have to split the money when I could have it all myself? But after I couldn't get the egg out of Mom's safe-deposit box, I called him back. I told him I was ready to listen."

"And?" Meredith asked.

"He told me to meet him in this little bar off the highway. I was right about it being Lumley, but he was sharper than he looked. He asked me if I could get Mom's safe-deposit box key and her ID without her knowing it."

"But Rayna has her key."

Skip shook his head woefully. "I had a copy made when I took it the first time. Just in case, you know?"

Julia gave him a stern look. "Isn't that illegal?"

"Illegal doesn't mean impossible. I know a guy."

Julia shook her head. Skip was the kind who always knew a guy.

"And Mom never paid a lot of attention to her ID card. She doesn't have much she uses it for, so I figured I could borrow it and put it back without her ever knowing it was gone. I knew a guy who could make a passable copy of that too."

"And the signature was easy enough to forge from the card."

"I didn't see how it could go bad," Skip moaned, dropping his face into his hands. "I was with Mom when the egg was taken. There's no way anybody could have suspected me."

"Is that what Lumley told you?"

Skip nodded, not looking up. "Mom cut me out of her will years ago. Everything is going to Rayna. Once I gave Lumley what he needed from Mom, all I had to do was stick close to her the next day, and nobody could accuse me of anything. And besides, they might decide the egg belongs to that duke or something, and then none of us get anything. This way I had a chance to at least get part of it."

"Now you're likely to get part of a jail cell," Meredith said.

Skip lifted his chin. "Not just me. Lumley and that lady friend of his—if I go, they go."

"They're going," Julia assured him. "And your testimony will help make sure of that."

Skip cracked a smile. "I don't know why I'm here anyway. Sure, I took Mom's things, but that's all I did, and she won't press charges."

"True," Christian said. "I mean, besides the charge of conspiring to steal the egg, you're in the clear, right?"

Skip's expression fell.

"What about Gwenda?" Julia pressed. "Did she come over from England when Lumley did?"

"No," Skip said. "She'd already been here a few months. Lumley knew her from England, and when he heard about the egg turning up and about Mr. Kirkland-Wright coming to claim it, he remembered she lived here in Savannah and called her up. He had her get a job at the hotel."

"And since he's always been in charge of making my travel arrangements," Christian said, "it must have been easy for him to book us at the same hotel."

Skip nodded glumly.

"But the woman who took the egg from the bank had an American accent. A Georgia accent."

Skip shrugged. "Gwenda could put on a convincing accent when she wanted to."

The detective opened the door and announced the arrival of Skip's court-appointed lawyer.

"That's our exit cue," Julia said, and Meredith, Christian, and Rayna followed her out to her car.

Christian glanced at his watch again. "By some miracle, I think I still have plenty of time to get my things and take a taxi to the airport."

He opened the front door on the passenger side of Julia's car so Rayna could get in.

"If you don't mind," Rayna said, opening the rear door, "we really ought to talk for a minute about everything. And it would be a lot easier if I don't have to crane my head around to do it."

"All right," Christian said, ignoring the knowing grins Julia and Meredith exchanged.

He shut the door once Rayna was seated and walked around to the other side of the car. Julia got in and buckled herself in behind the wheel.

"Thanks to you both, Julia and Meredith," Christian said once they were underway, "for figuring all of this out for us. I suppose even though we've found the egg again and it's in safe hands, we still haven't settled who it actually belongs to."

"That might take a while," Rayna said, "but I don't think Nanny's in any real hurry. All she wants is for the egg to go to the rightful owner."

"Then we agree on that. At least we have a lot of evidence about how the egg got here and how it ended up in your grandmother's box. You know…" A smile touched the corners of Christian's mouth. "I'd have to talk to my father about all this of course, but I'm actually quite satisfied that Alexis meant for Willow to have that egg. I'm sure Father will agree, but I know he would still like to have the Resurrection Egg to go with the Renaissance Egg. They do belong together after all, but that doesn't mean we couldn't perhaps arrange to buy it from your grandmother. What do you think?"

"I don't think Nanny feels very comfortable having something so valuable around the house," Rayna said. "And I'll feel better if she has a nice nest egg to keep her comfortable for the rest of her life. It's up to her in the end, but I think she might like that idea very much. Would you like to come talk to her? Do you have time?"

Christian glanced at his watch.

"If you keep it short," Julia offered, "you could have a quick chat with Mrs. Clarke, at least give her something to think about. Then we could pick up your bags, and I could get you to the airport on time. How about you, Mere? Do you have a few minutes to go to Jean's and see what she thinks of Christian's idea? I can drop you back at the office afterward."

"I wouldn't miss it," Meredith said.

Christian beamed at them. "That would be great. I believe we can just manage it."

"Believe it or not," Rayna said, "I've enjoyed meeting you. And, despite our occasional differences, I hope we can stay in touch, no matter who ends up with the egg."

"I'd like that. No matter what."

Christian took out his business card, and before he gave it to Rayna, Julia saw him write something on it. Perhaps his personal cell number?

Meredith gave Julia a subtle wink, and Julia smiled. Then she turned the corner and headed to Jean's house. Once they had a chance to talk to Jean, she would drive Christian to the airport, drop Meredith at the office, and then go home herself, home to Beau and Bunny. Her own family had been reunited, but now she wondered if Rayna and Christian might not end up creating something lasting together too.

It was far too early to even speculate on that, but as they chatted together in the back seat, she smiled to herself at the thought. Easter was over, but today, like every day, was still a time of miracles and new beginnings. She was going to enjoy keeping up with them both and with the final disposition of the elusive Resurrection Egg.

What was lost had been found.

Dear Reader,

I hope you'll forgive me for fudging a few dates in order to make this story work. The Sea Islands Hurricane hit on August 27, 1893. Fabergé's Renaissance and Resurrection Eggs weren't actually made until 1894. As far as I can tell, neither of them was ever mentioned as being missing, though seven of the famous bejeweled eggs are at this time believed lost. Until 2014, an eighth egg was also thought to be lost. A scrap metal dealer bought what he believed to be a gold ornament and planned to melt it down, but then he found out it was the Third Imperial Easter Egg, worth over thirty million dollars!

Though, as I say in the story, the eggs were made at the request of Czar Alexander III as gifts for his wife, Maria Feodorovna, she did not, of course, make a gift of the Resurrection Egg to my fictional Russian countess. It is true that many experts believe the Resurrection Egg is the surprise that was created to be inside the Renaissance Egg. They certainly look beautiful together.

It was a lot of fun to write this book. Trying to figure out how to tie a famous Russian Fabergé egg to a hurricane that hit the

Georgia/South Carolina coast in 1893 was an interesting challenge. Add in an Easter egg hunt, a dodgy uncle, and a missing cat, and there were a lot of plates to keep spinning. Still, they all lived happily ever after....

Love,

DeAnna

About the Author

THE AUTHOR OF TWENTY-NINE TRADITIONALLY published books and with more to come, DeAnna Julie Dodson has always been an avid reader and a lover of storytelling, whether on the page, the screen, or the stage. This, along with her keen interest in history and her Christian faith, shows in her tales of love, forgiveness, and triumph over adversity. A fifth-generation Texan, she makes her home north of Dallas with three spoiled cats and, when not writing, spends her free time quilting, cross-stitching, and watching NHL hockey. Her first novels were a trilogy of medieval romances for Crossway Books, and she has since written a number of contemporary mysteries for Annie's Fiction and for Guideposts and has more in the works. Also, as Julianna Deering, she writes the Drew Farthering mysteries set in 1930s England for Bethany House. She is represented by Wendy Lawton of the Books & Such Literary Agency.

The Truth Behind the Fiction

SEA ISLAND HURRICANE

ON AUGUST 27, 1893, THE Sea Islands Hurricane, the fourth deadliest in US history, struck near Savannah. Called "That West Indian Monster" in the newspaper headlines, the hurricane and the heavy storm surge that followed it killed at least two thousand people and left twenty thousand or more homeless.

The Sea Islands of Beaufort, near the border between Georgia and South Carolina, were mostly populated by formerly enslaved people and their descendants. "The inhabitants of the islands are nearly all colored people," said Sheriff Reed, a Black man who traveled to Columbia to testify about the devastation the hurricane had left behind. "They farm on ten- or twenty-acre farms. Since the war, many of them had accumulated much, and in recent years have become pretty well-to-do. Now they lose everything in a single night and are as poor as they were at the end of the war."

At least seventy thousand people were affected by the hurricane and its aftermath. Many lost everything they had, and the crops in their fields were either washed away or poisoned by salt water. Christian charities and philanthropists donated thousands to relief in the face of the lack of funds from the state legislature, though real recovery didn't begin until, over a month after the storm, Clara Barton and the Red Cross finally arrived.

Private donations were turned over to the organization and brought relief to the many whose livelihoods had been destroyed by the hurricane. In her autobiography, Barton wrote, "The submerged lands were drained, three hundred miles of ditches made, a million feet of lumber purchased and homes built, fields and gardens planted with the best seed in the United States, and the work all done by the people themselves."

After ten months, thanks to a robust relief campaign, the refugees were living on their own property and once more producing their own food. Today, the descendants of some of those people still farm on the Sea Islands (though they are now neighbored by exclusive resorts and golf courses), a tribute to the strength and resiliency of their ancestors.

SOMETHING DELICIOUS FROM A
Downhome Southern Kitchen

LOW COUNTRY BOIL

This super easy feast is popular in the Low Country of Georgia and South Carolina, especially at outdoor events.
Yields 15 servings.

Ingredients:

1 tablespoon seafood
seasoning such as
Old Bay
5 pounds small new potatoes

3 (16-ounce) packages of
cooked kielbasa sausage
8 ears fresh corn
5 pounds whole crab
4 pounds fresh shrimp

Directions:

Cut sausage into one-inch pieces. Husk corn and remove silk, then break each cob in half. Break crab into pieces. Peel and devein shrimp.

Heat a very large pot of water. Add Old Bay Seasoning (or whichever seasoning you enjoy) and bring to a boil.

Add potatoes and sausage and cook for about 10 minutes.

Add corn and crab and cook 5 minutes more.

Add the shrimp and cook for another 3 or 4 minutes. The shrimp should be pink and the crab should be opaque and flaky.

When everything is done, drain off the water and serve. For cookouts, it's traditional for the food to be dumped onto a newspaper-covered picnic table and eaten off paper plates.

Enjoy!

*Read on for a sneak peek of another exciting book
in the Savannah Secrets series!*

Forever and a Day
By Marlene Chase

"'ALL THE DARLING BUDS OF May.' What do you think made the famous bard use such an expression?" Meredith Bellefontaine shifted into park and silenced the engine. She and Julia had arrived at the office after a Monday morning breakfast at their favorite coffee spot.

"Buds can be darling, I suppose," Julia Foley said, cocking her head in contemplation. "But Shakespeare sure didn't know Georgia. The buds have long since burst into full flower, and it's going to be nothing short of hot by noon." She winked. "I hope Beau gets my car into the shop early before it gets too warm, because he plans to walk home. Thanks for picking me up, by the way."

"My pleasure," Meredith said, leaning back against the headrest. "Besides…" She smiled at her longtime friend and business partner. "You treated to blueberry scones, so debt paid in full." She made no move to get out, feeling the kind of euphoria that spring in any climate can evoke.

She was in a celebratory mood anyway. May was the month blocked out for mothers—at least one day of it—and she sensed a keen anticipation. This year's observance would be a special one.

"On second thought, the buds *are* darling," Julia intoned with emphasis. "Beau brought me some late tulips Saturday in the most perfect color. Today they're still tight as little purple fists and make me happy even on a Monday morning." Julia adjusted the lavender paisley scarf at her neck and smoothed her silver hair.

They'd been partners at Magnolia Investigations since Meredith had reopened her husband's business. She never could have done it without her old college friend, never could have recovered from Ron's unexpected death and moved ahead with life. Julia had been a gift direct from God.

"And judging from your mood this morning," Julia added, "I'd say your weekend was good too." Meredith knew Julia was waiting for a recap.

The weekend had been delightful. She'd spent yesterday with her older son, Carter, Sherri Lynn, and the children. After church they had picnicked on the deck of the beautiful Italianate home she and Ron had lovingly shared. They'd enjoyed fried chicken, potato salad, and all the trimmings. Kinsley and Kaden had occupied themselves in the little yard below the deck.

Saturday had been special too. She and Quin had spent it at the Savannah Botanical Gardens. They'd walked the nature trails in companionable wonder and visited the Reinhard House, a unique survivor of Savannah's nineteenth-century architectural history. Quin had been remarkably relaxed. It had taken time, but Meredith had come to terms with Ron's passing and allowed herself to love again. And she did love Quin.

They had walked hand in hand through the long afternoon as flowers bloomed around them. The look in his bicolored eyes had brought warmth to her cheeks. Who would have thought when she met the silver-haired lawyer on a prickly case that they would have become so special to one another? Particularly when she had held him at arm's length for so long.

"Hey!" Julia's voice broke into Meredith's reverie. "How come there's no sign of the Chihuahua?"

Meredith frowned. Julia was right. Carmen's little Ford Focus with the bobblehead dog in the rear window wasn't parked in its usual spot. Carmen was usually the first one to the office. Julia had mentored their slightly sassy but dependable assistant, who had escaped a somewhat checkered past. Judge Julia had been on the juvenile bench and seen something promising in the young woman who came before her court. Now Meredith couldn't imagine Magnolia Investigations without Carmen.

"I'm sure she'll be along with a good explanation for the boss ladies," Meredith said with a shrug. "Boss ladies" was Carmen's name for them. Though she was decades younger than Meredith and Julia, she looked after them like a mother hen.

"Ha! I can hear it now. *¡Culpa mia!*' Well, no mocha latte for her!" Julia said with a laugh. "On to the grindstone." She eased herself out of the car.

They entered the building through the back door and walked past their offices and into the reception area, where Carmen was usually preparing for the day's activity. It startled Meredith to feel the emptiness of the room. Julia went into her office, and Meredith heard the clunk of her purse falling on the desk.

Meredith lowered herself into her chair and gazed through the floor-to-ceiling windows that revealed a spectacular view of Forsyth Park. She never tired of this view. It was always fun to anticipate each new day's adventure.

She sighed, feeling nostalgic as she often did in spring with Mother's Day approaching. At this time of the year, she missed her mother most. What she wouldn't give to be with her for the upcoming Mother's Day celebration at Wesley Chapel.

A rustling brought her back to the moment. She looked up to see Julia standing in front of her, a paper gripped in her hand. Her brow was furrowed and her lips moved, but she made no sound.

Meredith searched her partner's face. "What?"

Julia glanced up then down at the paper and laid it in front of Meredith.

Boss Ladies, I have to go away for a few days. I know it comes as a surprise and probably ticks you off that I didn't warn you, but— here the fluid lines sloped slightly downward—*there's something I've got to do. I've arranged for a temp to take my place until I get back. Might not take that long, but I've paid her for a whole week anyway. Thanks for understanding. I'll be in touch.*

Meredith read and reread the lines penned in Carmen's bold strokes as Julia stood silently with her arms folded. This was not like their intrepid assistant, and Meredith certainly did not understand. She studied her partner's face.

"Well," Julia said. "What's so important that she couldn't tell us?" She sounded hurt. "And hiring a temp on her own…"

"And paid for it in advance," Meredith said, peering out the window as though she would find an explanation written there.

Carmen was careful with her money and rarely had any extra cash. She hadn't even been able to afford air-conditioning in her old car, which was why they had it installed as a gift.

Julia snatched up the note again and scrutinized it with a fixed frown. "You'd think she would have given us some warning, not just gone off like this."

Tossed from one inadequate foster home to the next, Carmen had practically raised herself. Despite being used by people who should have befriended her, she'd survived. Later, Julia had arranged for her to work at Magnolia Investigations. She learned fast and worked hard. Her "boss ladies" came to appreciate her—more than that, to care a great deal for her. The relationship was even closer for Meredith since her son Chase had begun to date Carmen.

"It must have been important," Meredith soothed. "And she did say she'd be in touch. Don't worry—"

"Who said I was worried?" Julia folded the note. "Carmen knows her way around better than anyone I know. She can take care of herself." But a flash of concern in her gray eyes belied her words.

The front door suddenly slammed, bringing them both to attention. They left Meredith's office and were met with a flustered stranger with windblown blond hair. She rushed in on high heels and sported a huge purse with kittens frolicking on the vinyl surface. Over her red dress, she wore a little black shrug.

"Oh, I am so sorry!" she exclaimed. "I can't believe I'm late on my first day! I promise it won't happen again. Carmen said you were great bosses, but I wouldn't blame you if you just told me to get on out. I know I would be mad if—"

No telling how long she would have gone on, but Julia broke into her breathless opening gambit. "Excuse me," she said, taking a step back as though to get a better perspective on their surprise visitor. "I'm Julia Foley, and this is Meredith Bellefontaine. We're the owners of Magnolia Investigations. Are you—?"

"Cindy Jeffrey." The flashy blue bag slipped from her thin shoulder. "I know Jeffrey sounds like a boy but that's really my last name. Now, anyway." She nodded vigorously. "I suppose my real name is Cynthia, but everyone calls me Cindy. You know, just Cindy. Cynthia sounds so smug, don't you think?" She stretched out her hand in greeting, but Julia seemed frozen.

Meredith took the warm, sweaty hand, sympathetic to the young woman's nervousness. "Cindy," she repeated. "I assume you're the replacement Carmen arranged for?"

"Ain't she the sweetest thing?" Cindy effused.

Carmen was many things. "Sweet" wasn't how most people characterized her. Sassy, smart, resourceful, but "sweet"? Meredith and Julia knew Carmen to be warm and sensitive on the inside, but she greeted the world with a bold exterior.

Cindy raced on, filling any potential gap with words. "She knew I was looking for a job—something that wasn't waiting tables. I tried the waitressing thing, you know, but I was terrible at it. Just could never get the orders right. And Carmen, well, she thought I'd be a good fit here, you know?" She seemed to run out of breath and then to virtually deflate. Her chin dropped. "And now on the very first day I'm half an hour late."

"Cindy," Julia said, touching her arm. "It's all right. We know things happen." She indicated Carmen's desk near the front door.

"You can put your things in one of the desk drawers. The bathroom is around the corner." She nodded, indicating the way. "We'll give you a few minutes to settle in." She gave Meredith a meaningful glance before smiling at Cindy. "There's coffee down the hall—"

"Oh no, I'll get right to work." Cindy pushed her bag under the desk. "I've wasted too much time already." She wiggled as she settled into Carmen's chair, steadying her hands on the padded arms. She glanced around the room as though to take everything in, all the while still talking. "I'm usually more considerate of people's time. I know everyone's busy—and you guys more than anybody. Thank you so much—and I'll work hard. I don't want to disappoint you. Oh, this is a really great computer."

As she reached a hand to touch a key, the bolero shrug slipped off her shoulder. Cindy quickly pulled the garment back in place but not before Meredith saw a dark bruise.

"I think a good computer makes such a difference, don't you?" Cindy continued. "And this phone is cool. I only use a cell myself, but I—" She lifted the receiver, cleared her throat, and spoke into the phone that hadn't rung. "Magnolia Investigations. How may I help you?" She looked up like an expectant child. "There, how was that?"

"You settle in," Meredith said quietly, wondering about the bruise and the young woman's over-the-top entrance. "Carmen keeps a manual of office procedure in her front drawer. Familiarize yourself with it and meet us in the conference room in fifteen minutes."

"Sure," Cindy chirped, pulling out the drawer. "And thanks. Again, I'm really sorry for being late. Like I said, it won't happen again."

Meredith left her to pore over the manual. If Meredith had to guess, she'd say Carmen was trying to help this young woman who appeared to have never worked in a business office.

Meredith stopped to fill her mug at the coffee machine and went into Julia's office. She dropped down in one of the Louis XV chairs with their unique needlepoint cushions and released a sigh. "It could be an interesting week."

"With any luck, just a day or two," Julia said, frowning. She paused a few seconds and added, "I just don't get it. Carmen has been a little preoccupied lately but..."

She was right. Carmen *had* been rather quiet, not necessarily secretive, though Meredith recalled another time when she seemed to shut them out. They had later learned that she and Chase had been keeping their growing relationship quiet.

"What could be so important that she wouldn't let us in on it?" Julia wondered aloud. When her cell phone suddenly pinged, indicating a text, Julia grabbed it.

"Carmen?" Meredith asked, but she knew from her friend's expression that the message hadn't come from their assistant.

Julia grimaced and, after a brief conversation, put the phone down. "Why did I ever give that woman my cell number? She's going to drive me batty yet."

"Not Eulalie Collins again."

Julia let out an exasperated breath. "There's only one. How she got to be president of the League of Women Voters in this county, I'll never know. I wish we'd never taken her case—"

"Or that it had turned out better," Meredith said, commiserating. Eulalie had hired them several months earlier to investigate a break-in at her private office. An important file went missing, and she was sure a fellow board member who had her eye on her job had stolen it. When Julia did a thorough search, she found the file jammed in the back of Eulalie's desk.

The woman, however, had continued to assert that someone had hidden it there. She was not happy when Magnolia Investigations suggested no further exploration into the incident. She had begun to drop in unexpectedly or call to demand that they complete the job for which they were hired.

"I think she's lost a few eggs from her basket, if you ask me," Julia said.

"You can't help feeling sorry for her," Meredith said. "She's difficult all right, especially phoning and ranting on and on, but Carmen doesn't take any of her nonsense." She gave Julia a wistful look as both contemplated their assistant's absence.

"Maybe we'd better warn the temp about Ms. Collins," Julia said.

"Did you notice her arm?"

Julia pursed her lips. "I thought it might be part of a tattoo at first, but it could be a bruise."

"With definite finger marks—like someone squeezed her a bit too tightly."

Julia held Meredith's gaze for a moment. It wasn't exactly something they could question Cindy about in their imminent orientation in the conference room. Why Carmen had chosen to go away for a few days was unknown, but the temporary help she had arranged for might turn out to need help herself.